CURSED BY MIDNIGHT AND MORNING

Harlow Ann Leroux

The Wretched Raven

CONTENTS

HARLOW ANN LEROUX

CURSED BY
MIDNIGHT
AND
MORNING

Chapter One

She hurled another jagged shell into the darkening ocean, watching it disappear beneath the foamy waves. The beach stretched empty in both directions, just how she liked it at dusk, when her body finally decided to wake up and function like a normal person.

"Stupid sun," she muttered, kicking at a clump of seaweed. Her limbs felt alive now, energized by the fading light, but where was this energy eight hours ago when she needed to transplant the seedlings into the garden to take advantage of the full sun during the day?

She bent down to collect another handful of broken shells, their edges sharp against her palm. The tide pulled back, revealing glistening wet sand that reflected the purpling sky. This time of day always felt like it was hers. When others retreated indoors, she felt like herself.

She thought of the earlier argument as she launched another shell toward the horizon. "I'm just asking for some basic bloodwork, Mom. It's not normal to barely function during daylight hours."

Her mom had been chopping carrots for dinner, as root vegetables were one of the few things besides raw meat and fish that Cassie's stomach could handle, and her knife had stilled mid-slice.

"Cassie, we've been through this. Doctors ask questions we can't answer."

"So I'm supposed to live my entire life gardening by artificial lights? I have a degree I can barely use because I can't stand in the sun without feeling like I'm going to pass out!" she said.

"Our family has always lived differently. Your grandmother..."

"I don't care about Grandma's remedies! They don't work!" She cut her mom off.

Her mom's eyes had flashed then, that dangerous look that meant she'd pushed too far. "You think modern medicine has answers for what runs in your blood? They'd put you in a lab, Cassie. They'd take samples. They'd notice things. Things you can't explain, and things they'd never let go without researching."

"Notice what? That I'm anemic or have some vitamin deficiency? That's exactly what I want them to notice!" Cassie's frustration slipped out as her voice got higher.

Her mom set down the knife, her voice dropping to that eerie calm that always made the hair on her arms stand up. "There are things about yourself you don't understand yet. Things I've protected you from."

"Then tell me!" Cassie demanded.

But her mom didn't. She stood there, not talking. Cassie didn't want another stony silence that lasted until she apologized. She stormed out to the shore for refuge.

She found a perfectly intact sand dollar and sent it skipping across the water's surface. It went a total of four bounces before it sank. The ocean breeze picked up, carrying the scent of salt and seaweed. Her frustration curdled into something heavier. What was so wrong with wanting answers? Her younger sister Claire never seemed to have these problems. She slept through the day and thrived in the night hours, seemingly unaware of the daytime activities that passed without her notice. Her mom always said she was just like her father, who was a banished night witch, but always stopped short of explaining how she was like her father.

She would only say night witches were taboo, and to speak of them called forth dangerous, negative elements.

Cassie dug her toes into the cool sand. She watched the last remnants of sunlight dance across the horizon, and she felt herself start to waken more. The energy flowed into her limbs, her mind sharpened, and her senses heightened, all making her feel more awake, more vibrant, and alive. Even the colors around her seemed more vivid.

"Why?" she whispered to the empty beach.

The waves offered no answer, just their endless rhythm against the shore.

She pulled her phone from the back pocket of her jeans, the screen illuminating her face. She had the number for the medical clinic saved. One call, one appointment. Her mom didn't need to know. Whatever secret she was keeping, whatever she thought might be discovered, couldn't be worse than living half a life.

Could it?

Cassie put her phone back into her back pocket for now and watched the last sliver of sunlight slip beneath the horizon, painting the sky in hues of orange and purple. The beach felt like a refuge, but it was also a cage. She kicked at a clump of sand, sending grains scattering into the cool evening air. The waves rolled in rhythmically, but all she could think about was how much she wanted to step into the world outside her mom's protective embrace.

"Mom's just scared," she muttered to the waves, kicking again as if she could kick away her mom's fears. "But I can't live like this forever."

The wind whipped through her auburn hair, sending strands tumbling across her face. The sea's salty scent mingled with the faint smell of jasmine from the garden behind her house, reminding her of home, but also binding her to it in ways she resented. Even though her house was at least half a mile away, her senses were sharp, and she picked up the smallest hint of a scent.

She remembered late-night talks with her younger sister Claire under the glow of their shared lamp, dreams of travel and adventure that felt so far away. Claire's laughter echoed in her mind as they daydreamed about visiting Paris or hiking in Yosemite. But every time Cassie broached the subject of getting out during daylight, Claire's eyes would cloud with worry. Even though there were only three years between them, Cassie sometimes felt like Claire was older than her 21 years suggested. She was cautious and preferred to be buried inside a book.

"Remember what Mom said?" Claire would murmur. "Humans aren't safe."

But what did that even mean? What had happened before she was born that made them so wary? Why had their father been banished?

Cassie reached out her hand and swirled it in a circular pattern, her fingers dancing through the air with practiced precision. Grains of sand lifted from the beach beneath her, rising and twisting into a miniature vortex that sparkled in the moonlight. The tiny particles obeyed her will, spinning faster as she concentrated, feeling the familiar tingle of magic coursing through her veins. Cassie knew her mom wanted to protect her and had always wanted to shield both her daughters from the outside world, but her mom had methodically taught both her and Claire how to protect themselves since they were old enough to understand the power that flowed in their blood.

They descended from a line of powerful witches stretching back generations, their abilities passed down like precious heirlooms from mother to daughter. Cassie and her sister had paid rapt attention to all the lessons their mother and grandmother had imparted, spending countless evenings practicing incantations by candlelight, memoriz-ing protection spells, and learning to harness the elements. The sand tornado now hovering above her palm was just one of the simplest manifestations of abilities that ran deep through her. Abilities that sometimes frightened her with their intensity when she was alone with her thoughts.

Her silver-blue eyes reflected the swirling sand as she contemplat-ed the contradictions of her upbringing: taught to be powerful yet hidden away, given knowledge but denied the freedom to explore the world where she might need to use it. The root vegetables and raw fish diet that kept her healthy was just another reminder of how different she was, how separate from the humans her mom warned against.

A chill swept through the air as night settled in around her. Cassie shivered and wrapped her arms around herself. She turned back to-ward home, feeling more restless than ever. Their small shop on Main Street awaited her return, its warm lights flickering like fireflies against the night sky. Midnight Mochas, Books, Vines, and Wines was their mom's creation, centered around their family. They served an assort-ment of coffee, tea, pastries, and local wines in between cozy tables nestled among foliage and bookshelves. When she and her sister were young children, their mom had started out with only a tea and coffee shop and a few baked goods, then added the local wines, and as Cassie and Claire grew, their passions for books and plants expanded the store into something more.

The bell above the door chimed softly as Cassie stepped inside. The scent of earth and greenery enveloped her first; plants filled every corner between and around the bookshelves and tables. Hanging ferns swayed gently overhead while vibrant flowers beckoned from their pots on rustic racks. Ivy crept down the sides of the bookshelves and around the ledges of the windows.

Her mom stood behind the counter, sorting through some herbs and labeling jars with neat cursive strokes. She used many of the herbs and some flowers Cassie grew for baking sweet and savory pastries, cookies, and cakes for the shop.

"Did you enjoy your walk?" her mom, Catherine, asked without looking up.

Cassie forced a smile as she shrugged off her jacket and hung it by the door.

"Yeah, I just wanted some air," she replied, moving closer to examine a new batch of scones lined up on the counter. "These look great."

Her mom looked up, eyes narrowing slightly as they met Cassie's gaze. "Make sure you keep an eye on those during your shift this evening. They need extra care, or Mr. Davenport will take a few too many with his purchase. Then, Mrs. Davenport will show up, blaming us for his high blood sugar."

"I will," Cassie promised, though part of her wished to take charge and run things during daylight hours instead of being confined to nighttime shifts. Mr. Davenport came to read his mystery novels on Wednesday nights, a respite from Mrs. Davenport.

"Have you thought about my suggestion?" her mom asked suddenly, lifting an eyebrow.

Cassie clenched her jaw at the reminder of their earlier conversation about another night class on herbal remedies.

"I'd rather take something more... practical," Cassie replied cautiously.

"Practical?" her mom echoed with a hint of disbelief. "What does that even mean?"

"I mean... I want to learn about how to interact with people outside our little world." Her voice grew firmer as she continued. "I want to grow and sell plants during daylight and meet customers who exist during the day. Not these insomniacs who treat our shop like it's an extension of their home."

Her mom set down a jar filled with dried lavender and crossed her arms over her chest. "Cassie, those regular customers keep a roof over our heads. We get new people coming through all the time who enjoy the late evening hours we are open."

Cassie stepped back from the counter, frustration boiling inside her like a dormant volcano ready to erupt. Her mom constantly downplayed her desire to experience more of the day, and it frustrated her.

"What happened before I was born? Why won't you tell me? Why won't you tell me about my dad?" The words rushed out of her. She leaned forward slightly, daring to confront her mom head-on for once.

Her mom's face hardened. Tension crackled between them like static electricity.

"Some things are better left unknown," her mom said sharply before turning back to her work.

"But I'm not a child anymore!" Cassie protested, feeling heat rise to her cheeks. "I need answers!"

Silence stretched out between them like an endless chasm. Cassie's heart raced as desperation surged within her, a longing for understanding mixed with an unquenchable thirst for freedom from fear's tight grip.

Claire appeared at the door just then, looking fresh and wide awake. She always woke up just after the sun dipped down, refreshed and happy. Cassie set an alarm to wake up before sunset and was never fully rested.

"Hey! Are you two fighting again?" Claire grinned playfully before sensing the tension in the room and shifting gears quickly.

Cassie's glare lingered on their mom before breaking away toward Claire's warmth instead, a much-needed reprieve from their mom's coldness.

"No fights here," Cassie said flatly as Claire stepped closer, offering support without needing words.

"Well then!" Claire smiled brightly despite sensing both women still simmering beneath thin layers of civility with unspoken thoughts hanging heavy in the air like morning fog that wouldn't lift any time soon.

"We're just talking about scones and the Davenports."

"Just one scone. Or else we'll hear all about how we sold him too many and practically forced him to eat them at once." Claire's smile widened even more as she drifted into the next room.

Her mom sighed but offered no further rebuttal; a temporary ceasefire between mother and daughter lingered over a shop filled with green life yearning for sunlight beyond its four walls while night cloaked everything outside until dawn broke anew once more. But it would break without Cassie, because she grew drowsy with the approaching dawn, and everything in her would rebel at the morning light.

After a long silence, her mom's shoulders slumped as she set down the jar she'd been labeling. The shop felt suddenly too small, too cramped with unspoken words hanging between them.

"Cassie," she said, her voice softer now, "I didn't know how to explain what happened before you were born." She glanced at Claire, who hovered uncertainly by the door. "I've tried to find the right words for years."

Cassie crossed her arms, the familiar irritation bubbling just beneath her skin. "You could start with anything. Literally anything would be better than this... this wall between us."

Her mom moved around the counter, dried lavender still clinging to her fingertips. The scent wafted through the air as she approached.

"I will tell you everything. One day." Her mom reached for Cassie's hand, her touch hesitant. "But now isn't the right time."

"When will it be the right time?" Cassie pulled her hand away. "When I'm thirty? Sixty? When I've spent my entire life living half in shadows?"

Claire stepped between them, her presence a buffer against the rising tension. "Maybe we should all just take a breath."

"It's dangerous, Cassie." Her mom's voice dropped to barely above a whisper. "Delving into the past brings attention we can't afford. Until I can resolve certain... complications, the past needs to stay in the past."

"Complications?" Cassie's voice cracked. "That's all I get? More vague warnings?"

In her mom's eyes, a startling green that was different from Cassie's silver-blue, flashed with something ancient and afraid. "There are people who would hurt you if they knew what you are. What we are."

Devoid of customers, the shop fell silent except for the soft ticking of the antique clock on the wall. Outside, the moon hung full and bright, bathing the world in silver light that called to something deep within Cassie's blood.

"I'm just trying to protect you," her mom whispered.

"By keeping me in the dark? By making me feel like a freak?" Cassie's voice trembled. "I can't live like this anymore."

Her mom reached out again, this time grasping Cassie's wrist with surprising strength. "Promise me you won't seek answers on your own. Promise me you'll wait until I can tell you properly."

The intensity in her mom's eyes made Cassie hesitate. Whatever secret lay buried in their family's past clearly terrified her mom.

"Fine," Cassie said, the word tasting bitter on her tongue. "But don't make me wait forever."

Chapter Two

A hundred miles off the Central Coast of California, Alexander Ross stood in the cockpit of the Galeon yacht, moonlight glinting off the sleek black tactical gear that hugged his muscular frame. The gentle rocking of the vessel beneath his feet did nothing to disturb his perfect balance, a perk of being over two centuries old. The Pacific stretched dark and endless around them, their position carefully calculated to remain undetected by both human radar and witch-sensing spells.

Sam Starke checked his equipment beside him, methodically inspecting each piece with the precision of someone who had survived multiple wars. His smaller yacht, one built more for speed than comfort, was docked near the one they currently stood upon. The third vampire, Nikolai, monitored their surveillance equipment, his fingers dancing across digital screens displaying thermal images of the coastal town.

"The King's orders were explicit," Sam said, his voice low despite being miles from any listening ears. "Capture and contain. No casualties unless absolutely necessary."

Alexander nodded, eyes fixed on the distant shoreline. "Casualties would violate the treaty. The witches would retaliate."

"And yet here we are, about to conduct an operation on witch territory." Sam's lips curled into a humorless smile. "Technically, we're already violating the treaty."

"Which is why we get in and out before dawn." Alexander tapped the reinforced case containing the sedative vials. "These hybrids are an anomaly the King needs to understand."

Nikolai glanced up from his station. "Feed's clear. Coastal patrol passed twenty minutes ago. Next sweep in forty-five minutes."

Alexander unfolded a detailed map across the navigation console. "Our targets are here and here. Two separate locations, but close enough that we can coordinate the extraction simultaneously."

The map showed a small coastal town with two buildings circled in red, one near the shore and another further inland. Surveillance photos were pinned beside each location, showing two women who appeared normal to human eyes, but whose thermal signatures revealed the impossible dual nature that had brought Alexander's team into forbidden territory. They had first come to investigate reports of a vampire inside the territory of the witches, but upon observation of the young woman on the beach last night, what seemed to be a vampire report turned into something much more.

Sam studied the images. "They appear unaware of what they are. The younger one especially."

"Makes our job easier," Nikolai commented.

Alexander's jaw tightened. "It makes our job necessary. If they don't understand their nature, they're unstable. Dangerous."

He'd been tracking these anomalies for weeks, gathering intelligence that pointed to something unprecedented: individuals who somehow carried both vampire and witch bloodlines. The very possibility challenged everything the supernatural communities had established since the Treaty of 1783. The older one showed signs of deliberate concealment; the younger seemed genuinely unaware of her dual nature.

"The boats are ready," Sam said, nodding toward the two smaller crafts, designed for silent approach, secured alongside the yacht. "Once we have them, we separate immediately. You take the older target north. I'll head northwest with the secondary. Different routes back to Vancouver."

Alexander checked his watch. "Almost midnight. That's our window, before the next patrol."

He secured the case containing the sedative to his tactical belt, feeling the weight of the forbidden substance and the mission. The sedative was powerful enough to neutralize both aspects of the hybrids' nature, vampire strength and witch magic, but it required precise dosing. Too much could kill; too little would leave them conscious enough to fight back or, worse, alert others.

"Remember," Alexander said as they prepared to board the smaller vessel, "these aren't just anomalies. They're people who likely have no idea what they are. We do this cleanly."

Sam's expression remained impassive. "The King didn't send me for my bedside manner, Ross."

"The King sent you because you follow orders," Alexander countered. "And our orders include bringing them back unharmed."

The night air carried the faint scent of saltwater as they slipped into the smaller craft. Alexander took the helm, guiding them toward shore with minimal wake. The coastal town grew larger in the distance, lights twinkling innocently, unaware of the supernatural drama about to unfold.

Nikolai's voice came through their earpieces. "Thermal signatures confirm both targets are at their expected locations. The primary target appears to be in some kind of shop. The secondary target is moving between rooms in the residence."

Alexander felt a strange tightness in his chest as they approached. Two centuries of serving the vampire kingdom had taken him on countless missions, but something about this one felt different. The photographs of the primary target, a woman with silver-blue eyes that held secrets beyond her apparent years, had lingered in his thoughts more than professional interest should allow.

"Five minutes to shore," he announced, pushing those thoughts aside. "Final equipment check."

They verified their communications, weapons, and, most importantly, the sedative doses. Each carried precisely measured syringes calibrated to the estimated body weight of their targets. They also had separate sedatives formulated for any witches they might encounter.

"Remember," Alexander said as the shoreline loomed closer, "we're in witch territory. Their wards might not detect vampires specifically, but they'll sense any magic we use. Stay physical, stay fast."

Sam nodded, his expression hardening into the cold efficiency that had made him the King's preferred enforcer. "Forty minutes from extraction to open waters. Then we're in the clear."

The boat slowed as they approached a secluded stretch of beach, engines nearly silent thanks to vampire engineering. Alexander felt the familiar pre-mission focus settling over him, senses sharpening, unnecessary thoughts fading away.

Yet as they prepared to disembark, that strange feeling returned. Something about this mission, about these targets, felt personal in a way he couldn't explain. The woman with the startling eyes seemed to call to him across the distance, like a melody half-remembered from another lifetime.

"Let's move," he said, pushing the thought away once more. "We have hybrids to catch."

The beach sand crunched beneath Alexander's boots as he moved with inhuman speed across the shoreline. He kept to the shadows, a darker shape within darkness, his movements too swift for human eyes to track. Behind him, Sam veered inland toward the secondary target while Alexander continued toward the small shop nestled between two larger buildings near the harbor, its weathered exterior almost invisible against the night sky.

The air filled his lungs, an unnecessary breath, but one that helped him process the scents around him. Humans, primarily. The lingering exhaust of fishing boats. The sweet decay of seaweed at low tide. And something else, something that made the predator within him stir with interest. It was faint but unmistakable, the distinctive magical signature of a hybrid, like electricity crackling beneath the surface of ordinary reality.

"In position," Sam's voice came through his earpiece, slightly distorted by the coastal interference. "Secondary target is alone. Proceeding with extraction."

Alexander approached the back of the shop, noting the hand-painted sign swinging gently above the door: "Midnight Mochas, Books, Vines, and Wines." His primary target was still inside despite the late hour. Through the window, he caught glimpses of movement, a solitary figure moving between shelves. He moved to the rear entrance, testing the handle. It was unlocked and open. Slowly, he tested the door. It swung open silently on well-oiled hinges, as if inviting him in.

"I'm in," he whispered, his voice barely disturbing the air around him.

The shop's interior was a maze of shelves filled with an eclectic collection of items. Plants of all shapes and sizes filled every space that leather-bound and new print edition books did not, creating a lush, literary jungle. Hanging ferns brushed against his shoulders as he navigated through the narrow passages. Bottled herbs and rocks that would appear merely decorative to human eyes, but which Alexander recognized as possessing genuine magical properties, imbued and magnified by witches, lined several shelves. Crystal prisms hung in the windows, ready to catch the morning light that was still hours away.

The smell of coffee and fresh-baked goods flooded his senses, merging with the smell of leather and soil from the plants. Cinnamon, chocolate, and the earthy aroma of freshly ground coffee beans lingered in the air, evidence of the day's business. The scent caused him to pause and take in more before moving. In his line of work, it was an aroma that he didn't encounter often. It promised warm nights and gentle moments. As head of vampire security, those weren't frequent experiences for him. Usually, his world smelled of blood, fear, and the sterile environments where he was given his assignments.

Sounds of someone moving around emanated from a back room, separated from the main shop by a soft butter yellow, hand-sewn curtain with delicate embroidery along its edges. Alexander moved toward it, his footsteps making no sound on the wooden floor that creaked slightly under his weight, though not enough for human ears to notice. Through the curtain, he caught glimpses of a woman working at a table, her back to him, dark auburn hair falling in waves past her shoulders, catching the light with copper highlights.

She hummed softly, a melody that struck Alexander as hauntingly familiar, though he couldn't place it. Something old, perhaps centuries old, stirred memories he couldn't quite grasp. The sound resonated in his chest, creating an unexpected sensation of almost recognition. It pulled at something deep within him, like a forgotten promise from another time.

He prepared the syringe, removing it from its protective case with practiced precision. The glass gleamed in the dim light, the clear liquid inside ready to do its work. One quick movement, and she would be unconscious before she could raise an alarm. Simple. Efficient. The mission parameters were clear. He'd done this dozens of times before without a second thought.

Yet he hesitated, his hand frozen in mid-air.

The woman turned slightly, her profile illuminated by the soft light from her work table, where she appeared to be trimming plants and potting the clippings into new, smaller pots. Her fingers moved with practiced skill, gentle yet confident, and her features were delicate yet strong. She had high cheekbones and a determined set to her jaw. When she blinked, he caught a flash of her striking eyes from the surveillance photos. They seemed to glow with an inner light, not quite human, not quite other. In person, they were even more striking than in the photographs, as if he were looking into a deep mountain lake that reflected the light of a full moon, shining brightly in a dark winter sky.

Chapter Three

Cassie felt a presence behind her. Part of her sensed a threat, but the part that didn't was what caused the most apprehension. She felt like she was going to meet someone she knew, someone she missed, someone who was like her and whom she'd been searching for. She kept humming to keep them attuned to her and to avoid tipping them off that she was aware of them.

The melody flowed from Cassie's lips without conscious thought, an old lullaby her mother used to sing, though she couldn't remember learning it. Her fingers continued their work, separating mint cuttings and nestling them into fresh soil. The scent of earth mingled with the plant's sharp, sweet fragrance as she pressed the soil around tender stems.

Behind her, the presence remained motionless. Not breathing. Not shifting weight. Impossibly still in a way no human could manage.

Cassie's skin prickled with awareness. She'd never felt anything quite like this before, this strange doubling of fear and familiarity. The shop's back room suddenly felt both too small and infinitely vast, as if the space between her and the stranger contained worlds.

She reached for another pot, deliberately keeping her movements unhurried. Her heart hammered against her ribs, but she refused to let her hands shake. Whatever, whoever, stood behind her was dangerous.

She knew this with bone-deep certainty. Yet something else whispered that the danger wasn't meant for her.

The mint cutting slipped from her fingers. She bent to retrieve it, using the motion to shift her position slightly, angling her body toward the curtained doorway without being obvious. From the corner of her eye, she caught a glimpse of dark clothing, a tall figure half-hidden in shadow.

"You can come in properly," she said, surprising herself with the steadiness of her voice. "Lurking behind curtains isn't very polite."

Silence stretched between them. The humming died in her throat as she straightened, finally turning to face the intruder.

He stepped through the curtain with fluid grace. Tall, broad-shouldered, dressed in black from head to toe. His face might have been carved from marble, all sharp angles and perfect symmetry. But it was his eyes that froze the breath in her lungs, dark as midnight, ancient with knowledge, and fixed on her with an intensity that made her feel simultaneously exposed and recognized.

"How did you know I was there?" His voice was deep, touched with an accent she couldn't place.

Cassie set down her garden shears, buying time while her mind raced. "Although the shop has been open for most of the evening, we don't get many customers this late."

A lie. She'd sensed him. Felt him like a change in atmospheric pressure.

"You're not surprised." Not a question but an observation, his head tilting slightly as he studied her.

"Should I be?" Cassie leaned against the worktable, her fingers curling around its edge. "People find their way here at strange hours sometimes."

Something flickered across his face, confusion, perhaps, or recalculation. He took another step forward, and Cassie noticed he moved with predatory precision, each motion controlled and deliberate.

"My name is Alexander Ross." He offered the information like a peace treaty.

"I didn't ask." The words slipped out before she could stop them, sharper than intended.

His lips curved slightly, not quite a smile. "No, you didn't."

They regarded each other across the small room, locked in silent assessment. Cassie felt something stir inside her, an awareness that had slumbered her entire life suddenly awakening. It rushed through her veins like electricity, making her fingers tingle.

"Cassie Marlow," she offered finally, surprised by her own willingness to give him her name.

Alexander moved through the space with unnatural fluidity, examining the shelves of herbs and tinctures with apparent fascination. His fingertips hovered above a sprig of dried wolfsbane without touching it.

"You're not from Harmony," Cassie said. It wasn't a question. She would have remembered him, would have felt him before now.

"Vancouver." He turned to face her. "Though I've traveled extensively."

The word hung between them, weighted with unspoken centuries. Cassie's stomach tightened with hunger, a different kind than she was accustomed to. Not the raw, primal need for bloody meat or raw fish, but something more complex.

"What brings you to a small coastal town in California?" She reached for a cutting tool, her fingers wrapping around the wooden handle. Not that it would help if he meant her harm. What would help her was what she was already drawing upon. The well of power inside her, the words of the witches whispered through generations from parent to child, the words of power that helped them to survive and teach them again.

Alexander's gaze dropped to her hand, a knowing smile touching his lips. "The same thing that keeps you indoors during daylight hours, I imagine."

The implication stole her breath. No one had ever noticed. Not even her mother or sister.

"I don't know what you mean," she lied, her heart hammering against her ribs.

"Don't you?" Alexander's eyes held hers. "I think you do."

The air between them charged with unspoken understanding. Cassie's fingers loosened around the cutting tool, letting it clatter back onto the worktable. Her mind raced with possibilities, questions she'd harbored her entire life suddenly pressing against her lips, demanding release.

"What am I?" The words escaped in a whisper, surprising her with their vulnerability.

Alexander stepped closer, his movement causing no disturbance in the air, no creak of floorboards beneath his weight. Impossible stillness wrapped around him like a second skin.

"You're like me," he said simply. "Or partly so. A hybrid, I suspect."

Cassie's breath caught. The room seemed to tilt slightly, decades of feeling different, of raw meat cravings and sunlight sensitivity suddenly crystallizing into potential meaning. But that was impossible.

"My mother is a witch," she offered, the words feeling both inadequate and monumental. "A powerful witch."

Alexander's eyebrows lifted slightly. "And your father?"

The question hung between them, heavy with implication. Cassie swallowed hard, feeling the pieces of her fractured identity shifting, realigning.

"I never knew him. My mother refuses to speak much of him. He was a night witch."

"Perhaps he was more than a night witch," Alexander said, his voice gentling, "and there was a reason for her silence."

"No." Cassie shook her head, denying his words. But inside, she was rolling on waves of nausea she struggled to keep back as understanding rocked her world.

"I need to take you back with me to determine who your father is," Alexander told her.

"Take me back?" Cassie took a step backward, her hand instinctively reaching for the silver pendant hidden beneath her shirt. "I'm not going anywhere with you."

Alexander remained perfectly still, watching her with those ancient eyes. "You've lived your whole life with questions. I'm offering answers."

"By kidnapping me?" Her voice rose, indignation momentarily overwhelming fear.

"By introducing you to others like yourself." His tone remained measured and reasonable. "There's a community in Vancouver. People who understand what you are and what you need."

The pendant warmed against Cassie's skin, a familiar comfort. Her mother's magic, woven into silver and stone. Protection. Warning.

"My family is here," she said, though the words felt hollow. Her mother had kept secrets.

For her, they felt like massive, life-altering secrets.

Alexander's expression softened almost imperceptibly. "Your mother has hidden half of who you are. Don't you want to know why?"

The question struck like a physical blow. Yes, she wanted to know. She had always wanted to know why she craved raw meat, why sunlight caused her to feel exhausted and lethargic, and why she felt so different from her mother.

"If I wanted to force you," Alexander said quietly, "we wouldn't be having this conversation."

Cassie knew, with bone-deep certainty, that he was right. But it didn't matter. He could try to force her all he wanted. She would fight him. She wasn't without her own power to protect herself. She had been raised on self-defense spells taught to her by her mother, and it appeared, for this very reason. Cassie pulled herself to her full height and centered her body weight, preparing to defend herself.

"The conversation is now over." Cassie's voice hardened with warning.

Cassie's fingers tingled with unfamiliar energy as she faced Alexander across the small back room. The air between them crackled with tension, heavy with unspoken threats.

"You should leave," she said, her voice steadier than she felt. "Now."

Alexander remained perfectly still, his dark eyes assessing her with clinical detachment. "I understand your reluctance. But this isn't a request."

The words hung in the air for a heartbeat before Cassie felt something shift inside her. A dam breaking. Power surged through pathways she hadn't known existed within her body. It bubbled up from some deep, primal place, not the careful, measured magic her mother had taught her, but something wilder, darker, hungrier.

"I said no." The words came out distorted, her voice dropping to a register she'd never heard from her own throat.

Alexander's eyes widened fractionally, the first genuine surprise she'd seen on his face. He moved toward her with inhuman speed, a blur of motion that should have been impossible to track.

But Cassie saw him. She saw the trajectory of his approach with perfect clarity, as if time itself had slowed around her.

She raised her hand instinctively, not knowing what she intended, only that she needed to keep him away. Energy exploded from her palm, a blast of pure force that sent shelves of carefully arranged herbs and tinctures crashing to the floor. Alexander flew backward, smashing into the wall with enough force to crack the plaster.

Cassie stared at her hand in shock. This wasn't witch magic. Not the careful spells and rituals her mother had taught her, built on intention and preparation. This was raw, untamed power flowing directly from her core.

Alexander recovered quickly, straightening with fluid grace despite the impact that should have broken bones. His expression had shifted from confident to wary.

"Impressive," he said, brushing plaster dust from his shoulder. "But uncontrolled. You're dangerous to yourself and others until you learn to harness what you are."

"Stay back." Cassie raised both hands now, feeling that strange energy coiling inside her, ready to strike again.

He circled to her left, moving with predatory grace. "Your father must have been someone of significance. No ordinary vampire could produce such powerful offspring, especially with a witch."

The word hit Cassie like a physical blow. Vampire. It was impossible. Vampires were the mortal enemies of witches. They had almost wiped each other out before a truce was signed at the end of the American Revolution.

Vampires were immortal, but they weren't immune to the magic of the witches and could be disarmed and killed. While the witches weren't immortal, their lifespans were approximately three times that of a normal human, but they had very few children in their lifetimes, leading to smaller populations. Vampire children weren't born; they were made.

Yet what he said stunned her, made her question all she knew. She recognized a kernel of truth she'd somehow known yet refused to acknowledge, crystallized in that single word: vampire. Again, she thought of her food choices and her nocturnal schedule. The heightened senses she'd always attributed to her witch heritage and her father being a night witch. Yet was a night witch simply a vampire? There was no way her mom would have been with a vampire. Her grandmother was a respected coven leader. Neither of them would have ever violated the sacred laws of the witches.

"You're lying," she whispered, even as something deep inside recognized the shocking truth.

Alexander lunged again, this time feinting right before coming at her from the left. Without thinking, she reacted. Her body moved with a speed and precision she'd never possessed before. She caught his wrist in midair, her fingers closing around it with crushing strength.

The contact sent a jolt through her system, as if something dormant in her blood had awakened at the touch of another vampire. Her vision sharpened further, the world suddenly rendered in painful clarity. She could see the individual fibers in Alexander's black shirt and could hear the absence of a heartbeat in his chest.

"Let go," he warned, his voice dropping to a dangerous register.

"Make me," Cassie snarled, shocking herself with the feral quality of her own voice.

His free hand shot out, aiming for her throat, but Cassie was already moving. She twisted, using his momentum against him, and hurled him across the room. Glass shattered as he crashed into the display cabinet containing her rarest botanical specimens.

The sound of destruction cut through her battle haze. The shop. Her livelihood. Her sanctuary.

Alexander rose from the wreckage, glass fragments falling from his clothing. A thin line of blood traced his cheekbone where a shard had caught him. The scent hit Cassie like a physical force, rich and intoxicating. Her gums ached suddenly, a sharp pain that made her gasp.

"Your fangs are coming in," Alexander observed, his tone almost clinical despite their battle. "It appears to be triggered by blood and combat. Usually, it happens in anticipation of your first feeding, but you're different."

Cassie's tongue found the sharp points descending from her canines. Horror and fascination warred within her as her body transformed, responding to stimuli she'd never encountered before.

"What's happening to me?" she demanded, her words slightly slurred around the new dental arrangement.

"You're becoming what you truly are. Interesting." Alexander wiped the blood from his cheek, studying the red smear on his fingertips. "Half witch, half vampire. A creature with access to both bloodlines' power. That's going to rattle a few cages."

The shop's main room bell jingled, signaling the front door opening. Cassie froze, suddenly aware of the destruction surrounding them, of her altered appearance. No customer would understand what they were seeing.

"Cassie?" Her mother's voice, tight and high with worry, called from the front of the shop. "Claire isn't at home, and the house has been ransacked."

Cold dread washed over Cassie. Claire. Her little sister. The gentlest soul she knew must have met with another one of his kind.

Alexander's expression shifted subtly. Recognition. Knowledge. Satisfaction.

"What have you done?" Cassie whispered, connecting the dots with horrifying clarity.

"Not me," he said quietly. "Sam. My king sent us both, me for you, him for your sister."

Rage unlike anything Cassie had ever experienced erupted through her system. The lights in the shop flickered wildly as power surged from her in waves. Plants in their pots withered and blackened. The remaining intact glass in the room cracked in spiderweb patterns.

"Where is she?" Cassie advanced on Alexander, her newfound strength making the floorboards creak beneath her feet.

"Safe," he said, raising his hands in a placating gesture. "For now. Sam would never harm her without orders."

"Cassie?" Her mother's panicked voice came closer, followed by the sound of footsteps approaching the back room.

Alexander's eyes flicked to the doorway, then back to Cassie. "Your mother kept secrets that put both her daughters in danger. Ask her about your father. Ask her why the vampire king of the Pacific Northwest wants her children."

The curtain separating the back room from the shop proper was shoved aside as Catherine Marlow burst into the room. Her bright red hair was disheveled, her eyes wild with worry. Those eyes widened as she took in the destruction, Alexander's presence, and finally, Cassie's transformed appearance. She vibrated with a glowing, charged red aura.

"Where's Claire?" Catherine demanded, eyes blazing, and lifted her arm towards Alexander.

"Mom, they took her," Cassie let out a guttural wail.

Alexander used the distraction to move toward Catherine like a wraith, his supernatural speed carrying him there before a shaken Cassie or surprised Catherine could stop him.

Catherine's arm lifted, and he slammed into it as she unleashed a powerful burst of energy. The syringe in his hand moved at the same moment the blast hit him and flung him backward. He slammed into a workbench, the plants toppling off, the dirt from the containers spilling over him.

Cassie wasn't paying attention to him. She watched in horror as her mom collapsed, crumpling to the ground in a heap. Her energy was gone. She didn't move.

Cassie screamed, and the store raged with her. The walls and foundation shook.

Chapter Four

All around her, the shop exploded in a multitude of sounds. The sounds of shattering, groaning, and ripping reached her ears as her magic surged out from her in wild, chaotic waves. Splinters from the shattered shelves pelted her and her mom, and the floor quivered beneath her.

She screamed. Plants tore through the air and slammed into the walls around her. Alexander scrambled to his feet, holding his chest, where he had been hit with a powerful energy charge from Catherine.

"Cassie," he hollered at her through the flurry of destruction she was pulling around them.

She didn't respond to him as her magic tore loose from her control, hurling plants and shelves in every direction. The room roared as they burst into flames, wildly pitching mid-air. One of the shelf boards dipped low and cracked against her mom's temple.

"*Stop!*" Her voice was high-pitched, and she didn't know whether she was yelling at the vampire or at herself. Ash and flaming embers swirled as more boards and other materials picked up speed and ignited in response to her fury.

Alexander took a quick step backward, then another, putting distance between them. "Stop! You're going to hurt yourself and everything around you." He shouted back at her.

"You drugged my mother," Cassie screamed, her ire making the floor split beneath her feet, jagged fractures racing outward.

"She would have destroyed me before the truth came out." He raised his palm towards her, as if to calm a spooked animal, and lowered his voice to a gentle, soft tone. "You'll find out the truth soon."

"You believe I'm still coming with you? Are you out of your mind?"

"You're coming with me," his voice was still gentle but firm, "because you and your sister are the truth."

Her magic pulsed, wild and draining. The shop howled and reflected her rage.

He took a small step back towards her, his palm still up. "Cassie, you need to stop. You are tearing everything around you apart. You're hurting your mom."

She didn't want to listen to him, but she was. The walls were charred, and the air was electrified, and things were slamming into her mom. Her magic continued to pulse around her, uncontained, uncontrolled, draining her and making her feel guilty for the damage it inflicted.

"Tell me where my sister is!" Cassie tried to pull back her magic, but it felt out of control. It lashed out again, hot and without direction.

"She's being transported to Vancouver, just as you will be." His voice remained maddeningly calm. "The King needs to understand what you are, both of you. Vampires in the land of the witches threaten the truce."

Cassie had no idea what she was doing, operating purely on instinct and fury. Her hands thrust forward, and another pulse of energy sent Alexander crashing into the wall. More plaster cracked, and dust filled the already electrified air.

A wave of dizziness swept over Cassie. The room tilted alarmingly, and her knees threatened to buckle. The surge of strength that had filled her moments before ebbed away, leaving her hollow and shaking.

Alexander didn't hesitate and moved with blinding speed, closing the distance between them before Cassie could react. His hand clamped around her wrist, his grip like iron.

"Your body doesn't know how to manage the vampire strength yet," he said, his voice almost gentle despite the circumstances. "It's consuming your energy too rapidly, and is too wild."

Cassie struggled against his hold, but her newfound strength was fading fast. Her vision blurred at the edges, and her breathing came in ragged gasps.

"Let me go," she panted, trying to summon another blast of power. Nothing happened. The well inside her had run dry.

"This isn't what I intended. I'm sorry for that." Alexander's grip remained firm but not painful. "But I can't let you do any more damage."

Cassie's gaze fell to her mother's still form on the floor. Catherine looked small and vulnerable, nothing like the formidable witch who had raised her. Tears stung Cassie's eyes. Ash, splinters, and dirt covered her mom, and she could see blood welling at her mom's temple, where a board had slammed into her head.

"What did I do?" she whispered, her voice breaking. She'd only wanted to protect herself and her mom, but her magic burned out of control. Guilt and shame at the destruction and harm she'd inflicted wrapped around her chest and squeezed, momentarily robbing her of breath.

Without further hesitation, Alexander produced another syringe. She felt the needle prick and tried to jerk back, but he held her firm.

"Let me go," Cassie mumbled, but the fight left her as more shame filled her. Encroaching darkness blurred the edges of her vision. Her limbs felt leaden, refusing to obey.

"I've got you," Alexander's gentle voice seemed to come from far away.

Cassie collapsed as her mother had moments before. One of the last images she saw was her mother, lying too still and motionless on the ground in front of her, and her own hands, blackened with the ash of her destruction.

Cassie reached out, feeling for her mother's aura to soothe the pain she had caused, but there was no response. Her energy recoiled back into her, as if it was afraid of the harm it had caused.

With her last ounce of energy, she looked up at the vampire that held her. She tried to summon her energy to burn him, to repel him, but her magic flinched away, as if it feared what she might do.

Alexander's eyes found hers, and there was something sad in them, or maybe it was weariness. "This is mercy." He drove the needle in, picked her up, and carried her out the door. Cassie tried to fight the drug coursing through her system, but it was already shutting her down.

As Alexander carried her onto the waiting skiff, Cassie caught sight of another figure standing in the waves, holding the raft-like boat. Tall, lean, with sharp features and calculating eyes. He was a vampire, like Alexander.

"You took longer than expected," the other man's accent thicker than Alexander's.

"There were complications, Nikolai." Alexander's grip on Cassie remained firm as she attempted one last weak struggle. "She's stronger than we anticipated. Let's hope she learns fast. The King doesn't have patience for wild things."

The man studied her with clinical interest. "If we are able to make it back without alerting the witches, the King will be pleased. Sam has already left with the other target."

Claire. They were talking about Claire. Anger flared again in Cassie's chest, but her body was too depleted to respond.

"My sister," she managed to whisper. "If she's hurt, I will destroy you."

Alexander set her carefully on a padded bench, then climbed in after her.

Cassie wanted to scream, to fight, to unleash that power again. But darkness was closing in, her consciousness slipping away despite her desperate attempts to hold on.

The last thing she saw was Alexander's face above her, his dark eyes holding something that might have been regret.

Then darkness claimed her.

Chapter Five

Consciousness returned to Cassie in fragments. First came the gentle rocking motion beneath her, then the distant hum of powerful engines. The soft texture of expensive bedding registered next, followed by the scent of cedar and salt air. Her eyelids were impossibly heavy, but she forced them open, blinking against the dim light of an unfamiliar room.

She was lying in a bed in a luxurious yacht cabin. Polished mahogany paneling gleamed softly in the ambient lighting. A small porthole revealed nothing but darkness beyond. This was no fishing boat.

"Claire," she whispered, the memory of her sister's abduction flooding back with brutal clarity.

Cassie tried to sit up, but her body refused to cooperate. Whatever sedative Alexander had used left her limbs feeling leaden, her movements sluggish and uncoordinated. She managed to prop herself up on her elbows, fighting against the wave of dizziness that threatened to pull her back under.

The cabin door opened, and Alexander stepped inside. He'd changed from his tactical gear into more casual clothing, dark jeans and a fitted black sweater that did nothing to diminish his dangerous aura.

"You're awake sooner than expected," he said, studying her with those ancient eyes. "The sedative should have kept you unconscious for at least another hour."

"Where's my sister?" Cassie demanded, her voice raw. "Where's Claire?"

Alexander moved to a small built-in cabinet and poured water from a crystal decanter into a glass. "She's safe." His expression revealed nothing.

"That's not an answer." Cassie struggled to sit up fully, her anger providing strength her body lacked. "Where is she?"

"On another vessel." Alexander approached the bed and offered the water. When Cassie made no move to take it, he set it on the nightstand beside her. "For security reasons, we're traveling separate routes to Vancouver."

Cold fear washed through her. "She must be terrified."

"Your sister is unharmed and well, according to my last update." Alexander's tone remained neutral, professional, though he avoided eye contact. "She's been sedated less heavily than you. Your powers required a stronger dose."

Cassie glared at him. "You mean you drugged me more because I fought back."

"Because you demonstrated abilities we weren't prepared for," he corrected. "Abilities that could have harmed yourself and others if left unchecked."

The memory of that strange power surging through her returned, the raw energy that had exploded from her core, the inhuman strength that had allowed her to throw Alexander across the room. It was both foreign and familiar, like discovering a limb she hadn't known she possessed.

"What am I?" The question escaped her lips before she could stop it.

Alexander sat on the edge of a built-in desk across from her. "That's what the King wants to determine. You and your sister appear to be hybrids, half witch, half vampire." He paused for a moment, considering. "Something that shouldn't be possible. Yet here you are."

Cassie's hand went to her mouth, remembering the sharp points that had descended from her gums during the fight. "My mother would never..."

"Your mother has been keeping secrets her entire life," Alexander interrupted. "Including who and what your father is."

The yacht pitched slightly as it cut through the waves, racing north through the darkness. Cassie clutched the edge of the berth, fighting both physical and emotional vertigo.

"How long have I been unconscious?"

"Just over two hours. We're making good time." Alexander nodded toward the porthole. "Dawn is still a few hours away."

Cassie's gaze darted around the cabin, assessing potential escape routes. The porthole was too small. The door behind Alexander was the only way out, and in her weakened state, she had no chance of getting past him.

"Don't," he said. "Even if you could overpower me, which you can't right now, we're miles from shore. The water temperature would exhaust you before you could swim half the distance."

"You don't know what I'm capable of," Cassie said, though she knew he was right. Her body felt drained, her newfound powers inaccessible.

"Actually, I have a better idea than you do." Something like sympathy flickered across his features. "You've lived your entire life with half your nature suppressed and untrained. What you did back at the shop was pure instinct, fueled by adrenaline and fear. Without proper guidance, those abilities will remain dangerous and unpredictable."

Cassie looked away, unwilling to acknowledge the truth in his words. "And I suppose your King is offering this guidance out of the goodness of his heart?"

"The King has his reasons," Alexander replied carefully. "But yes, understanding what you are is in everyone's best interest, including yours."

"What about my mother?" Cassie asked, her voice catching.

"The sedative will wear off. She'll be disoriented, and hopefully unharmed." Alexander's expression hardened slightly. "She's fortunate that's all that happened. Harboring vampire offspring on witch territory violates the treaty. Under other circumstances, the consequences would be severe."

Cassie's fingers curled into the expensive sheets, guilt choking her. She swallowed once before responding. "She was protecting us."

"From what?" Alexander challenged. "From knowing who you truly are? From developing the skills to control your dual nature?"

"From people like you who would kidnap us in the middle of the night!" Cassie snapped.

A tense silence fell between them. The yacht's engines hummed steadily beneath them, carrying her farther from everything she'd ever known.

"Sleep," Alexander said finally, rising to his feet. "Tomorrow will be a long day."

Alexander froze. His posture shifted from casual to alert in an instant, muscles tensing beneath his casual clothing.

Cassie was about to question him when she heard it too, the distant but unmistakable sound of another vessel's engines approaching their yacht. The sound registered with startling clarity, as if her ears had suddenly become fine-tuned instruments capable of detecting nuances that should have been impossible from this distance.

She scrambled off the bed, ignoring the lingering dizziness from the sedative. "Is that Claire? Is that the other boat?"

Hope surged through her veins, giving her strength. If Claire was nearby, maybe there was a chance they could escape together. Her feet hit the polished floor as she moved toward the porthole, straining to see through the darkness.

Alexander was at the door in a flash, his movement so swift it barely registered. "Stay here," he commanded, his voice dropping to a dangerous register. "We're not in Canadian waters yet."

"I don't care about waters," Cassie pressed her face against the glass, trying to catch a glimpse of the approaching vessel. "If my sister..."

"It's not your sister's boat," Alexander cut her off. "It's likely a witch patrol."

The words stopped her cold. "Witch patrol? They could help us!"

Alexander turned back, his expression grave. "Think, Cassie. What would a witch patrol do if they found you, a hybrid, on a vampire vessel?"

The implication hit her like a physical blow. She'd spent her entire life in witch territory, raised with stories of the ancient enmity between the two supernatural races. The treaty that had ended centuries of bloodshed was fragile at best, maintained through strict territorial boundaries and minimal contact.

"They'd see me as a violation of the treaty," she whispered, the realization dawning. "An abomination."

The word made her stomach twist. She hadn't said it aloud before, and hearing it was sharp, visceral. She'd read the word before in an old coven book of her grandmother's, scribbled on the margin near the vague reference to a night witch. Back then, it hadn't applied to her. Now it felt personal and isolating.

"At best, they'd separate you from your sister permanently," Alexander confirmed, his voice softening slightly. "At worst..." He left the thought unfinished, but Cassie could fill in the blanks.

The sound of the other boat's engine grew louder, and Alexander moved to the cabin door. "Stay here. Stay quiet. If they board us, hide in the bathroom. Don't come out until I come for you."

"Why are you protecting me?" Cassie demanded, confusion warring with fear. "You're the one who kidnapped me."

A shadow of something passed across Alexander's face, regret, perhaps, or something more complex. "My orders were to bring you to Vancouver safely. That's what I intend to do."

Before she could respond, he slipped through the door, closing it firmly behind him. Cassie heard the distinct click of a lock engaging.

She pressed her ear against the door, surprised to find she could hear Alexander's footsteps as he moved along the corridor, the soft murmur of voices as he reached the deck. Her enhanced senses seemed to be working better now than they had at the shop, perhaps because she was away from the protective wards her mother had placed around their home and business.

The approaching vessel was closer now, its engines throttling down as it neared their yacht. Cassie could hear the slap of waves against its hull, the creak of metal and fiberglass as it rocked on the water.

A voice called out across the water, amplified by what sounded like a megaphone. "Attention vessel! This is the Northern California Coastal Patrol. Prepare to be boarded for inspection!"

Cassie's heart hammered against her ribs. They didn't announce themselves as the Northern California Coastal Witch Patrol, but she knew who they were. Alexander was right, though; the witch patrol couldn't help her. They would see her as evidence of a treaty violation. Still, they might be her only chance to escape Alexander and find Claire.

She moved to the porthole again, pressing her face against the cool glass. In the darkness, she could make out the silhouette of a sleek patrol boat, its running lights cutting through the night. Figures moved on its deck, their outlines blurred by distance and darkness.

Alexander's voice carried back to her, somehow audible despite the distance and closed door. "We're a private yacht heading north to Vancouver."

"You're not authorized to be in these waters, vampire," the patrol officer responded, a sneer in his voice. "Treaty regulations require us to investigate."

Footsteps sounded overhead as Alexander moved across the deck. The yacht's engines had been cut, leaving only the gentle rocking of the vessel on the waves.

"I assure you, there's been a misunderstanding," Alexander said, his voice smooth and persuasive. "We're simply passing through on our way to Canadian waters."

There was a pause, then the sound of something heavy hitting the deck of their yacht. They were boarding.

Panic surged through Cassie. If they found her, what would happen? Would they return her to her mother, or would they see her as something to be studied, perhaps even dissected and destroyed?

She moved quickly to the small bathroom attached to the cabin, following Alexander's instructions despite her misgivings. As she closed the door behind her, she caught her reflection in the mirror and froze.

Her eyes had changed. The silver-blue irises were now ringed with an eerie luminescence that seemed to glow in the dim light.

Her skin was paler than usual, almost translucent, and when she parted her lips in shock, she saw the tips of fangs extending from her gums.

"What am I becoming?" she whispered to her reflection.

Above her, footsteps and voices moved across the deck. The witch patrol was searching the yacht, and it was only a matter of time before they found her. Should she let them? She was a witch too, even though the events of the past few hours revealed her to be something more. Deciding to take her chances with her own people, the ones who had raised and cared for her, she opened the bathroom door and walked to the bedroom door.

Cassie's fingers trembled as they closed around the doorknob. She paused, listening to the muffled voices above. These were her people, witches who had protected her community for generations. Surely they would help her.

Yet Alexander's warning echoed in her mind: an abomination, a treaty violation.

Cassie twisted the doorknob, ignoring the warning voice in her head that sounded suspiciously like Alexander's. The lock clicked open with surprising ease. Either Alexander had forgotten to secure it properly, or her newfound strength had made short work of it. A more remote possibility was that he trusted her. She shook her head to clear it. He shouldn't trust her. Then she slipped into the narrow corridor, her heightened senses immediately overwhelmed by the sounds and smells of conflict above.

The yacht pitched violently beneath her feet as she made her way toward a steep staircase leading to the deck. Thunder rumbled overhead, not natural thunder, but the unmistakable resonance of weather manipulation magic. The witches were creating a storm to aid their assault. Weather manipulation wasn't simple, and it took a powerful witch or multiple witches to modify the weather.

Cassie gripped the polished wooden railing as another wave slammed against the hull. Through the small portholes lining the corridor, she caught glimpses of churning water and flashes of unnatural lightning. Her stomach lurched with each roll of the vessel, but determination drove her forward.

The sounds of combat grew louder as she climbed the stairs. Grunts of exertion, the distinctive crackle of offensive spells, and the dull thud of bodies colliding. When she reached the top, rain immediately lashed her face, driven by magically enhanced winds that seemed to target the yacht with unnatural precision.

Through the downpour, Cassie made out the chaos unfolding across the deck. Alexander and another vampire, Nikolai, she remembered him from their earlier conversation, were engaged in combat with four male witches. The patrol officers wore the distinctive dark green uniforms of the Northern California Witch Guard, their hands glowing with various magical energies as they attacked.

Alexander moved with inhuman speed, evading spells that left scorch marks on the deck where he'd stood moments before. He was fighting defensively, she realized, trying not to harm his attackers. Nikolai showed less restraint, his movements brutal and efficient as he grappled with two witches simultaneously.

A massive wave crashed over the starboard side, sending gallons of seawater washing across the deck. Cassie staggered, her feet sliding on the slick surface. She grabbed a nearby railing to steady herself, the metal cold and slippery under her fingers.

One of the witches noticed her emergence from below deck. He broke away from the fight, turning toward her with recognition dawning in his eyes, not recognition of Cassie personally, but recognition of what she was.

"Vampire!" he recoiled, lips curling as he hissed over the howling wind, raising his hands as crackling energy gathered between his palms.

"No, wait!" Cassie called out, raising her hands in a placating gesture. She needed him to believe her. "I'm not what you think, I'm from Harmony. My mother is Catherine Marlow! Please, you have to believe me."

The witch hesitated for a fraction of a second, his brow furrowing in confusion. Then his expression hardened once more.

"Liar!" he spat, hurling a binding spell toward her, a complex weave of energy designed to immobilize supernatural creatures.

The spell hit Cassie square in the chest, and she braced for the paralyzing effect she'd seen such spells produce. But instead of freezing her in place, the magic seemed to wash over her like water, briefly illuminating her skin before dissipating harmlessly.

The witch's eyes widened in shock. "What the hell?"

Cassie was as surprised as he looked. The spell should have worked. She'd seen her mother use similar bindings on humans and other creatures before. But something about her dual nature had rendered it ineffective.

Her stomach dropped. There would be no convincing him now. He'd just proven to them both that she wasn't one of them.

The yacht lurched again as another magically enhanced wave struck the hull. Both Cassie and the witch struggled to maintain their footing. In the brief moment of distraction, Alexander glanced toward her, his expression darkening when he saw her on deck.

"Please," Cassie tried again, taking a tentative step toward the witch. "I'm not your enemy. I was kidnapped from Harmony. These vampires took my sister too."

The witch studied her face, uncertainty flickering in his eyes. He was younger than she'd initially thought, probably not much older than herself. His hands remained raised, ready to cast another spell.

"If you're from witch territory, then submit to a truth spell," he challenged, beginning to trace the complex pattern in the air that would compel her to speak only truth.

Before he could complete the casting, the yacht pitched violently to port. The witch stumbled, his concentration broken. Cassie slid across the wet deck, unable to find purchase on the slick surface. She collided with the witch, sending both of them careening toward the railing.

The witch grabbed her arm, his fingers digging into her flesh as he tried to steady himself. The contact triggered something primal within Cassie, a surge of that strange new power she'd experienced in the shop. Her vision sharpened, colors becoming more vivid despite the darkness and rain. Strength flowing into her limbs, her muscles coiling with energy that demanded release.

"Let go of me," she growled, her voice dropping to a low pitch.

The witch's eyes widened as he stared at her face. Cassie knew what he was seeing, the luminescent glow of her irises, the inhuman pallor of her skin, perhaps even the sharp points of fangs extending from her gums.

"Abomination," he whispered, horror and disgust replacing the uncertainty in his expression. His grip on her arm tightened painfully as his free hand began tracing a different pattern, not a binding spell this time, but something more destructive.

Fear and anger surged through Cassie in equal measure. She was tired of being told what she was without having any say in the matter. With a snarl that surprised even herself, she grabbed the witch's wrist, halting his spell-casting.

"I said, let go."

She twisted, using that strange new strength to break his grip. The witch stumbled backward, his spell disrupted. Cassie advanced on him, no longer seeking to reason but driven by an instinct to defend herself. The witch recovered quickly, his hands again weaving complex patterns as he muttered an incantation under his breath.

A bolt of pure magical energy shot toward Cassie. She dodged with newfound reflexes, the spell missing her by inches and blasting a hole in the yacht's railing. The witch cast again, this time sending multiple energy projectiles hurtling toward her.

Cassie moved with inhuman speed, evading the attacks as she closed the distance between them. The witch's eyes widened in alarm as she suddenly appeared before him, her movement too quick for witch perception. She grabbed the front of his uniform, lifting him off his feet with strength that should have been impossible for her slender frame.

"I'm not your enemy," she hissed, her face inches from his. "But I'm not helpless either."

The witch struggled in her grip, fear and revulsion plain on his face. "What are you?" he demanded, his voice shaking.

Before Cassie could respond, another massive wave struck the yacht. The deck tilted sharply, and both Cassie and the witch lost their balance. They tumbled across the slick surface, a tangle of limbs and desperation. The railing slammed into her back, the metal bending slightly from the impact.

The witch scrambled to his feet, again raising his hands to cast another spell. Cassie reacted instinctively, lashing out with a kick that connected with his chest. She'd meant only to push him back, to create distance, but her enhanced strength sent him flying across the deck.

Horror bloomed in her chest as she watched the witch crash through the damaged railing, his body arcing out over the churning water. A scream tore from his throat, cut short as he plunged into the storm-tossed sea.

"No!" Cassie lunged for the broken railing, peering desperately into the darkness below. The waves frothed and churned, black as ink in the night, with no sign of the witch.

Behind her, the battle continued. Alexander and Nikolai had gained the upper hand, subduing the remaining witches with brutal efficiency. Cassie watched, frozen in horror, as Alexander pinned one of the patrol officers to the deck, producing a syringe similar to the one he'd used on her mother.

"Stop fighting," Alexander commanded as he administered the sedative. "We have no desire to harm you."

The witch's struggles weakened as the drug took effect, his eyelids fluttering before closing completely. Alexander moved to assist Nikolai, who had the remaining two witches cornered near the bow.

Cassie turned back to the churning water, her enhanced vision scanning desperately for any sign of the witch she'd sent overboard. The storm was beginning to abate, the magically conjured weather losing its potency as the witches who had summoned it succumbed to the vampires' attack.

"He's there!" she called out, spotting a dark shape being tossed by the waves about twenty yards from the yacht. "Help him!"

Nikolai appeared beside her, moving with uncanny vampire speed. He shed his jacket in one fluid motion, then dove over the railing into the turbulent sea. Cassie watched, her heart racing, as he cut through the water with powerful strokes, swiftly reaching the struggling witch.

Alexander approached, his clothing torn and wet from the fight. "I told you to stay below," he said, his voice tight with controlled anger.

"They're my people," Cassie replied, not taking her eyes off Nikolai as he swam back toward the yacht, towing the unconscious witch. "I thought they would help me."

"And now you see why I warned you." Alexander's tone softened slightly. "Neither world will accept you easily, Cassie. Not until they understand what you are."

Nikolai reached the yacht, hauling the witch's limp form up to Alexander, who lifted him onto the deck with effortless strength. The witch coughed weakly, expelling seawater from his lungs. He was alive, at least, though his skin had taken on a bluish tinge from the cold.

"He needs warmth," Cassie said, moving toward him.

Alexander placed a restraining hand on her arm. "He's fine. The sedative will keep him unconscious, but his vital signs are stable."

Cassie pulled away from his touch, her emotions a storm as chaotic as the one that had just passed. "I didn't mean to hurt him. I just wanted him to stop attacking me."

"You're stronger than you realize," Alexander said, studying her with those ancient eyes. "Another reason you need training."

Across the deck, Nikolai was administering additional sedatives to the male witches. Their bodies went limp one by one, all fight draining from them as the drugs took deeper effect.

"What are you going to do with them?" Cassie asked, watching as Alexander wrapped a thermal blanket around the half-drowned witch.

"Leave them on their patrol boat with enough fuel to drift back to shore," he replied. "They'll wake in a few hours with hazy memories of what happened. By then, we'll be in Canadian waters."

Alexander straightened, surveying the damage to the yacht. The deck was scorched in places from magical attacks, and the broken railing gaped like a missing tooth along the starboard side. The storm had subsided completely now, leaving only gentle swells that rocked the vessel in a deceptively peaceful rhythm.

"Help me move them," he said, nodding toward the unconscious witches.

Cassie hesitated, then moved to assist. Together, they carried the patrol officers back to their own vessel, which was tethered alongside the yacht. Nikolai had already started the patrol boat's engines, setting them to idle.

As they laid the last witch on the deck of the patrol boat, a profound sense of isolation washed over her. These were her people. She'd grown up among witches, learned their ways, and believed herself to be one of them. Yet they had attacked her without hesitation, seeing her as an abomination to be destroyed.

She stepped back onto the yacht, watching as Alexander untied the lines connecting the two vessels. The patrol boat began to drift away, carrying its unconscious crew back toward the California coast.

"They would have killed me," she said quietly, the realization settling like a stone in her stomach.

Alexander paused in his work, turning to face her. His expression held no smugness or superiority, only a somber understanding. "Yes, they would have. Not out of cruelty," he hesitated, "but fear. Fear of what they don't understand."

Cassie wrapped her arms around herself, suddenly cold despite the mild night air. The enormity of her situation crashed down upon her, rejected by the witches, kidnapped by vampires, her sister taken to an unknown fate, her mother left behind. She had no place, no truth, no home.

"What happens now?" she asked, her voice small against the vastness of the ocean surrounding them.

"Now we continue to Vancouver," Alexander replied, moving to restart the yacht's engines. "The King is waiting."

Cassie remained at the railing, watching the patrol boat's lights grow smaller in the distance. She had never felt so utterly alone, caught between two worlds that each seemed determined to either control or destroy her. The wind dried the tears on her cheeks before they could fall, leaving only the salt of the sea spray on her skin.

Behind her, the yacht's powerful engines rumbled to life, propelling them northward through the darkness toward a future as uncertain as the depths beneath them.

Chapter Six

The yacht cut through the dark waters, each wave sending a shiver of spray over the bow. Cassie stood transfixed at the railing, watching the last pinpricks of light from the patrol boat disappear into the distance. The adrenaline that had sustained her through the fight was draining away, leaving her trembling in its wake.

A violent shiver ran through her body. The cold seeped into her bones, made worse by her damp clothes and the night wind whipping across the deck. She wrapped her arms tighter around herself, but it did little to stop the trembling. As she no longer had to move to remain safe, her body grew cold. She had sent a witch overboard, another of her own kind whom she had harmed. Maybe the vampire was right. She wasn't safe, and she didn't belong with the witches. She shivered again, feeling the bitter coldness go deeper, and from more than just the temperature.

"You're freezing." Alexander's voice came from behind her.

Cassie didn't turn. "I'm fine."

"Your lips are turning blue, and you're shaking like a leaf." His footsteps approached, and then something warm and heavy settled around her shoulders. A thick blanket, smelling faintly of cedar.

She clutched it reflexively, drawing it close. The immediate warmth was a relief she couldn't deny. The action was one of kindness, but she wasn't sure she deserved kindness. She didn't know what she was, or the danger she posed. She wanted to accept the vampire's kindness without thought, but he was also the one who had kidnapped her and shattered her world with the reality she now faced.

"Come below deck," Alexander said, his tone unexpectedly gentle. "It's warmer down there."

"I don't take orders from kidnappers," Cassie replied, but her teeth chattered as she spoke, undermining her defiance. A twinge of guilt tickled her throat, but she ignored it. Snapping at him was easier than thinking about how she had hurt her mom and the witch on the boat.

Alexander sighed. "It wasn't a request, but it wasn't an order either. It was a suggestion based on the fact that you're suffering from shock and exposure."

Cassie turned to face him. His expression was unreadable in the dim light, but his posture lacked the threatening edge it had held earlier.

"Fine," she conceded, too exhausted to argue further.

She followed him down the narrow stairs to the cabin below. She was struck again by how surprisingly luxurious the space was: polished wood paneling, recessed lighting, and plush seating. A small kitchenette occupied one corner, and a door presumably led to sleeping quarters.

Cassie sank onto one of the cushioned benches, still clutching the blanket around her shoulders.

"I'm exhausted," she admitted, "but I don't think I could sleep if I tried."

Alexander moved to a cabinet and pulled out a thick, fuzzy bathrobe in a deep navy blue. "You should get out of those wet clothes. The other bathroom is through there." He nodded toward a door opposite the sleeping quarters.

Cassie took the robe without argument. The prospect of dry clothing was too tempting to refuse on principle. She made her way to the bathroom, a compact but well-appointed space with a small shower stall and gleaming fixtures.

She peeled off her damp clothes, wincing as the fabric clung to her skin. The bathrobe was impossibly soft against her chilled flesh, the sleeves falling past her fingertips. She belted it tightly, gathering the excess material around her smaller frame. Alexander was considerably larger than she, and the robe engulfed her completely. It reminded her of how small she felt.

Cassie hated that the robe felt good. She didn't like that her body welcomed the comfort, and her pride wanted to reject it.

After hanging her wet clothes over the shower rod, Cassie paused with her hand on the doorknob. A thought struck her.

She emerged from the bathroom to find Alexander waiting, leaning against the kitchenette counter with his arms crossed.

"Earlier, you didn't lock the door," she said.

A small chuckle escaped him, the first genuine amusement she'd seen from him. "Would it have stopped you?"

Cassie blinked. "What?"

"The lock," he clarified, his eyes crinkling slightly at the corners. "With your strength, you could have ripped the door off its hinges if you wanted to."

The realization struck her like a physical blow. He was right. Earlier, when she'd fought him in the shop, she'd displayed a strength she never knew she possessed. The memory of the witch flying backward from her push flashed through her mind. She'd sent a grown man airborne.

"I... I didn't think about that," she admitted, pulling the robe tighter around herself, as if it could shield her from this new reality.

"You're still learning what you're capable of," Alexander said. "It's why you need guidance."

"Your guidance, you mean." The bitterness crept back into her voice. "Taking me to your king like some sort of prize." She didn't want guidance. She wanted her world back, the one she had before he entered it.

Alexander pushed away from the counter, his expression sobering. "Not a prize. A puzzle. A miracle, perhaps."

"I'm not a thing to be studied," Cassie snapped.

"No," he agreed, surprising her. "You're not. But you are something unprecedented, Cassie. Someone that shouldn't exist, yet here you stand."

Cassie sank back onto the bench, exhausted. The robe pooled around her, its weight comforting despite its source. He was calm, and she wanted to clash, but didn't have the energy. She felt raw and wanted him to respond to her, to give her a reason to ignore her emotional turmoil.

"What happens when we reach Vancouver?" she asked, unable to keep the fear from her voice.

Alexander took a seat across from her, maintaining a respectful distance. "The King will want to meet you. Beyond that, I can't say for certain."

"And Claire? My sister?"

"She'll be there too. The King gave explicit instructions that both of you were to be brought unharmed."

Cassie closed her eyes briefly. At least Claire would be there. Whatever faced them in Vancouver, they would face it together.

"Now, try to sleep if you can," Alexander said softly. "You have a long journey ahead, and the boat ride will be brief in comparison."

"I won't be able to sleep," Cassie said, staring at the polished wood ceiling of the cabin. "Even with everything that's happened, I'm wide awake."

Alexander raised an eyebrow. "It's night."

"Yeah. I'm always awake at night," she said. "During the day is when I struggle. I'll probably want to crash when the sun comes up."

A look of understanding crossed Alexander's face. "Your vampire nature."

Cassie flinched at the word. Vampire. It still felt foreign, impossible yet undeniable after what she'd experienced tonight.

"The sun doesn't kill us, contrary to human fiction," Alexander explained, his tone shifting to something almost professorial. "But it does make us more sluggish, slower. Sleep becomes nearly irresistible for younger vampires."

"Like a natural sedative," Cassie murmured.

"Precisely." Alexander leaned back against the wall. "The older you are and the more powerful your bloodline, inherited from your sire, the more you can withstand the effects."

Cassie considered this. "So when I was little..."

"You must have a powerful sire to be able to move about at all during daylight, especially for how young you are." Alexander's eyes narrowed thoughtfully. "I witnessed you at the shore as the sun was going down. You were already moving with more energy than most young vampires could manage at that hour."

The implications made Cassie's head spin. Her father wasn't just any vampire. He must be someone significant. She remembered her mother's evasiveness whenever she asked about him, the fear in her eyes.

"You said 'sire,' not 'father.'" Cassie looked up at him. "Is there a difference?"

"Sometimes. A sire is the vampire who turns a human. But in your case..." Alexander hesitated. "You weren't turned. You were born. Something we thought impossible. It's common knowledge that vampires cannot have children."

The yacht rocked gently beneath them as they cut through the dark water. Outside the porthole, stars glittered across the black canvas of night. Cassie watched them, finding comfort in their constancy while everything else in her life had been upended.

"How did you become a vampire?" she asked suddenly, turning back to Alexander. "How were you turned?"

Surprise flickered across his features, quickly masked by his usual composure. "That's not relevant to our situation."

"It is to me." Cassie met his gaze steadily. "You know everything about me, what I am, where I live, even things about myself I didn't know. I know nothing about you except your name and that you kidnapped me."

Alexander remained silent, his dark eyes unreadable. For a moment, Cassie thought he would refuse to answer.

"I was turned in 1415," he said finally. "During the Battle of Agincourt."

Cassie blinked. "You're that old?"

Alexander smiled briefly. "I am."

"I'm sorry, I don't know that battle. I know so little of history. My sister is the history nut. I'm into things that bloom and grow." Cassie returned his smile with a sleepy one of her own. "What happened?"

He moved to the small porthole, staring out at the night sea. The memory seemed to transport him somewhere far away.

"I was a man-at-arms, fighting for Henry. The French outnumbered us five to one. The mud was everywhere. The blood, the screams of dying men, it was everywhere." His fingers flexed, as if still gripping a sword. "I took an arrow to the thigh, then a mace to the ribs. Left for dead, barely able to move in the thick, suffocating mud. It was a terrible place for a battle."

Cassie found herself leaning forward, drawn into his story despite herself, the bathrobe slipping slightly off one shoulder.

"Callimachus found me still clinging to life," Alexander continued. "He'd been watching the battle, amused by our human folly. But something in me, stubbornness maybe, made him pause." A bitter smirk twisted his lips. "He offered me a choice: die in the muck or rise as something more."

Cassie's breath hitched. "You said yes."

"Not immediately." His gaze sharpened. "I told him to go to hell where he belonged. Then the pain got worse." A dry chuckle escaped him. "When I changed my tune, he was amused, said I had fire."

The yacht creaked around them, the engine a distant hum.

"And then?" Cassie whispered.

Alexander turned to face her. "I chose life, in the only form it was offered."

"Do you regret it?" The question slipped out before she could stop it. If what she was experiencing was choosing life, she wasn't sure she wanted it, and that terrified her.

A wry smile touched his lips. "I've had many centuries to ponder that question. The answer is no, I don't."

Part of her wished he'd said yes. Then she could reject her future with the vampires more easily. His answer only meant more uncertainty.

Cassie studied him with new eyes. The rigid vampire who had crashed into her life hours ago now had a history, a beginning. It humanized him in a way that made her uncomfortable. It drew her to him. She hadn't wanted to get to know him in this type of intimate manner, and now it sat between them, pulling her closer when she needed distance.

"Was it hard to become a vampire?" Cassie asked.

"Hard is a matter of perspective," he mused. His gaze drifted momentarily into the shadows of memory. "I was a soldier one day, and then I became something else entirely. The transition granted me time to contemplate my new existence. My sire transformed another from that same bloody, muddy field, and together we navigated the darkness, bound by circumstance rather than birth, brothers forged in death's shadow rather than life's beginning."

"This King," she ventured. "Is he... cruel?"

"He is practical," Alexander replied carefully. "And very, very old. Age brings perspective that can seem cold to younger eyes."

"That's not an answer."

"It's the only one I can give you." Alexander's expression softened slightly. "You and your sister represent a mystery he will want to solve, not destroy."

Cassie nodded slowly, processing this. "And my father? Will I meet him in Vancouver?"

"That depends on who he is." Alexander leaned forward, his elbows resting on his knees.

The yacht's engines hummed steadily beneath them, a constant reminder of their northward journey. Cassie's thoughts turned to Claire, alone and frightened on another vessel.

"My sister," she said. "Will she be okay? She's always been gentler than me. More sheltered."

"Sam is less patient than I am," Alexander admitted, "but he won't harm her. The King's orders were explicit."

Cassie closed her eyes, exhaustion finally beginning to creep through her defiance. The night's events, discovering her true nature, fighting Alexander, confronting the witch patrol, had drained her more than she wanted to admit.

"You should try to rest," Alexander said, noticing her fatigue. "We'll reach Canadian waters soon enough."

"I told you, I won't be able to sleep."

"Then just close your eyes." His voice had lost its edge, becoming almost gentle. "You've had quite a night, Cassie Marlow."

She leaned back against the cushions, the soft robe enveloping her like a cocoon. Despite her protests, her eyelids felt heavier with each passing minute. The rhythmic motion of the yacht through the water was unexpectedly soothing.

"Alexander?" she murmured, hovering on the edge of consciousness.

"Yes?"

"If I'm half vampire... does that mean I'll live forever?"

Through the gathering fog of near-sleep, she heard his quiet answer.

"That's one of many questions we're going to find out, Cassie."

Her chest ached at the thought of outliving everyone she loved. As she drifted off, Cassie thought she felt a blanket being gently tucked around her, but she couldn't be sure if it was real or just the beginning of a dream.

Chapter Seven

Cassie woke with a start, momentarily disoriented by the unfamiliar surroundings. The gentle rocking beneath her triggered memories of the previous night, the fight at her shop, her mother drugged, the confrontation with the witch patrol. Though exhausted, she bolted upright, the blanket someone had draped over her sliding to the floor.

Her gaze darted to the porthole, and she froze. Beyond the small circular window lay a vista that stole her breath. The dark waters of the harbor stretched before her, but beyond them rose a sprawling cityscape unlike anything she'd seen before. Gleaming skyscrapers reflected the morning light, their glass facades shimmering like jewels against a backdrop of snow-capped mountains. The city seemed to rise organically from the water's edge, modern architecture blending with lush greenery in a way that appeared both deliberate and natural.

"Vancouver," she whispered, pressing her fingertips to the cool glass. Her eyes wanted to close as they always did in the sunlight, but she kept them wide open to take in the view. She withdrew her hand from the glass. Even though she wasn't betraying anyone by admiring the view, it didn't feel right.

The contrast between the peaceful harbor waters and the vibrant urban landscape created a strange juxtaposition that mirrored the conflict within her. Despite everything and the pressing exhaustion, the kidnapping, the revelations about her nature, the separation from her mother, Cassie felt an unexpected thrill of excitement. She'd never left California before, never seen a major city outside of San Francisco.

"You're awake." Alexander's voice came from the doorway. "I expected you to still be sleeping."

Cassie turned to find him watching her, his expression unreadable. He'd changed into fresh clothes, dark jeans and a charcoal gray button-down that somehow made him look both casual and intimidating.

"Is that really Vancouver?" She ignored his observation and gestured toward the porthole, unable to keep the wonder from her voice. She wasn't going to let him see her weakness. She was determined to be as awake and alert as possible.

"It is." He stepped further into the cabin. "We arrived about twenty minutes ago."

Cassie turned back to the window, drawn to the unfamiliar skyline. "It's beautiful."

"It's home," Alexander replied simply.

A complicated mix of emotions churned inside her, anxiety about meeting the vampire security crew milling about outside and their king warred with a spark of curiosity about this new world. The realization that she was genuinely excited to see Vancouver felt like a betrayal of her situation, yet she couldn't deny the feeling.

"What happens now?" she asked, still gazing at the city.

"We dock, and then my team escorts us to meet the King."

Cassie wrapped the oversized robe tighter around herself. "My clothes are still damp."

"There are fresh clothes in the wardrobe," Alexander nodded toward a built-in cabinet she hadn't noticed before. "They should fit well enough for now."

As she moved toward the wardrobe, questions bubbled up faster than she could process them. "Are there witches in Vancouver too? Is the whole city full of vampires? Do humans know about you? How old is the King? What's the city like? Do you have special vampire buildings, or do you just live among everyone else?"

Alexander blinked, seemingly taken aback by the rapid-fire interrogation. "One question at a time."

"Are there witches here?" Cassie pulled out a simple black T-shirt and jeans from the wardrobe. She felt the tiredness in her limbs and straightened upright, making a concentrated effort to force more strength into her spine, pushing through the desire to curl back up on the bed and sleep until sundown.

"No. Vancouver is vampire territory. The witches have Portland and Seattle."

"The whole city is vampires?" She grabbed a pair of soft gray socks. She wanted to meet whoever stocked the clothing in her room to find out where they sourced these items. They were nicer than many of her finer clothes back home.

"No, it's primarily human. We maintain a parallel society, as we do everywhere."

Cassie paused, another question forming. "So humans don't know about vampires?"

"Some suspect, a few know, and most choose not to see." Alexander checked his watch. "You should get dressed. We're expected."

"But what about the government? Is it run by..."

"Cassie." His tone was firm but not unkind. "There will be time for all your questions later."

She clutched the clothes to her chest, nodding reluctantly. "Fine. I'll change."

In the small bathroom, Cassie quickly changed into the borrowed clothes. They fit better than she'd expected, though the jeans were a bit loose around the waist. She caught her reflection in the mirror and barely recognized herself. Her skin was pale, her silver-blue eyes seemed more luminous than before, and her hair was tangled from sleep and sea spray. She looked both more and less like herself, tired but as if some essential quality she hadn't known she'd possessed had been enhanced.

When she emerged, Alexander wasn't alone. Nikolai stood by the cabin door, his lean frame tense with readiness. He nodded to her, his expression neutral.

"Good morning," he said, his accent thicker than Alexander's. "Sleep well?"

"As well as one can after being kidnapped," Cassie replied dryly.

A small smile touched Nikolai's lips. "She has spirit, this one."

"Too much for someone so young and in the morning hours," Alexander muttered.

Cassie ignored him and moved back to the porthole, drawn once more to the view of Vancouver. "Is that the tallest building in the city?" She pointed to a distinctive skyscraper.

"That's Vancouver Lookout," Alexander answered, his tone softening slightly. "And no, it's not the tallest anymore, but it offers the best views of the city."

"And those mountains?"

"The North Shore Mountains. Grouse, Seymour, and Cypress."

"Do vampires hike?"

Nikolai let out a short laugh. "Some do. Not me."

"What about in winter? Do you ski? I've never seen snow."

Alexander checked his watch again. "We need to go."

But Cassie couldn't stop herself. "Is the ocean always that color? It's different from California. And those islands, are those..."

"Perhaps we should let her ask these questions while we walk to the car," Nikolai suggested, amusement dancing in his eyes. "Otherwise, we might be here until sunset."

Alexander shot him a look that might have been annoyance, but Cassie caught the faintest twitch at the corner of his mouth. "Fine. Questions while walking. But we need to move now."

As they left the cabin and climbed the stairs to the deck, Cassie continued her barrage. "How old is the city? Do vampires live longer here than other places? Is it always this beautiful? What's that building with the sails?"

"That's Canada Place," Alexander answered as they stepped onto the deck. "And Vancouver is relatively young for a major city, established in the 1860s."

The morning air was crisp and cool, carrying the scent of salt water and something distinctly urban, a mix of concrete, coffee, and distant greenery. Cassie inhaled deeply, cataloging the new smells with her enhanced senses.

"Are there special vampire neighborhoods? Do you have, like, secret vampire bars?"

Alexander guided her toward the gangplank, where three men in dark suits waited on the dock. "We live throughout the city, and yes, there are establishments that cater specifically to our kind."

"What about blood? Do you hunt humans, or is there some kind of vampire blood bank?"

Nikolai snorted behind her. "She's certainly curious."

"She's stalling," Alexander replied, though there was no heat in his words.

Cassie frowned. "I'm not stalling. I'm gathering information about my kidnapper's home."

Nikolai laughed while Alexander snorted.

Nikolai surprised Cassie. She had stereotyped him as a vampire-type bodyguard, but he had a personality that she didn't expect. She suspected she would enjoy his company more if she had met him in different circumstances.

As they reached the dock, the three waiting men straightened to attention. They were clearly vampires. Cassie could sense it now, a subtle difference in their energy that her newly awakened senses detected.

"Sir," the tallest of them addressed Alexander with a respectful nod. "The cars are ready."

"Thank you, Davis." Alexander placed a gentle but firm hand on Cassie's lower back, guiding her forward. "This is Cassie Marlow. She's to be treated with all the courtesy and respect you would extend to a guest of our King."

The men regarded her with undisguised curiosity, their eyes lingering on her face. Dread pooled in Cassie's stomach. She wasn't a new specimen for them to examine. She lifted her chin, refusing to feel intimidated.

Alexander appeared more at ease on his home grounds. She felt more disoriented now that they were here in Vancouver, and didn't want these vampires to sense her growing nervousness.

"Is my sister here yet?" she demanded, glancing around the marina. Her earlier curiosity had given her a few moments' respite from worry about her sister. Without the distraction, her fear for her sister snapped back into place.

"Cassie," Alexander said, putting his hand at the small of her back. "We'll talk as we drive." His voice had a sharper edge.

Trepidation flooded through Cassie. Claire wasn't here.

Two sleek black SUVs with tinted windows waited at the end of the dock. As they approached, Cassie continued her questioning, nervous energy and worry flooding her.

"What's the residence? Is that where your King lives? Is it like a castle or something?"

Alexander sighed as he opened the rear door of the first SUV. "It's the seat of government for the vampires of Western Canada. And no, it's not a castle."

"Disappointing," Cassie muttered as she climbed into the vehicle.

The interior was luxurious, with soft leather seats, dark wood trim, and what looked like bulletproof glass separating the front and rear compartments. Alexander slid in beside her while Nikolai took the passenger seat up front.

As the SUV pulled away from the marina, Cassie pressed her face to the window to keep from putting her head back against the headrest and closing her eyes. She took in the city with eyes forced wide. The streets were busy with morning commuters, and the sidewalks were filled with people going about their day, unaware of the supernatural politics unfolding around them.

"They all look so normal," she said softly.

"What were you expecting?" Alexander asked.

"I don't know. Something... different." She watched as they passed a coffee shop where people sat at outdoor tables, sipping from paper cups and scrolling through phones. "It's just like any other city. At least it seems to be."

"That's the point. We exist alongside humans, not apart from them."

They drove through downtown, passing gleaming office towers and busy intersections. Cassie couldn't help but notice how at ease

Alexander seemed here, his posture relaxing subtly as they moved deeper into the city.

"How long have you lived here?" she asked, turning away from the window to study him.

"Since about 1863," he replied. "I helped establish the vampire presence when the city was still young."

"That's... a long time."

A small smile touched his lips. "Not by vampire standards."

"We witches live a long time, too," Cassie muttered and turned back toward the window.

The SUV turned onto a tree-lined street that wound upward, away from the bustling downtown core. The buildings became more residential, elegant homes set back from the road behind manicured gardens. Finally, they pulled up to a massive iron gate flanked by stone pillars.

Davis lowered his window and spoke into an intercom. The gates swung open silently, revealing a long driveway that curved toward what could only be described as a mansion. The structure was imposing yet beautiful, a blend of modern and classical architecture that somehow complemented both the surrounding forest and the distant city skyline visible from its elevated position.

"This is where your King lives?" Cassie couldn't keep the awe from her voice.

"This is where the business of vampire governance happens," Alexander corrected. "The King has his own residence elsewhere."

"Alexander, where is my sister?" Cassie couldn't hold the question in any longer. With each mile, her nervous chatter had worsened as she tried to swallow the worry of where her sister had been taken. She'd thought that when she arrived, her sister would be here.

As they pulled up to the entrance, Cassie grew more apprehensive. The reality of her situation came crashing back. She was about to meet the vampire king who had ordered her kidnapping, who might hold the key to her mysterious parentage, and who controlled the fate of both her and her sister. He might be able to tell her where her sister was.

The SUV stopped at the foot of wide stone steps leading to massive double doors. Nikolai exited first, scanning the surroundings with practiced vigilance before opening Cassie's door.

"Welcome to Vancouver, Miss Marlow," he said with a slight bow that might have been mocking or genuine. She couldn't tell.

"Thank you for the escort, Mr. Bodysnatcher Nikolai," Cassie retorted in a sing-song voice. Nikolai let out a short laugh as he straightened back up.

Alexander emerged behind her, his hand coming to rest lightly on her shoulder. "Remember," he said quietly, "you're not a prisoner here. You're a guest of significance."

Cassie looked up at the imposing building, then back at Alexander's face. She tilted her head and scowled at him. "A guest who was kidnapped and drugged."

"Details," Nikolai murmured with a hint of a smile. Alexander let out a sigh and gestured for Cassie to step forward. *A guest who had the pleasure of armed guards.*

The second SUV pulled up behind them, and more security personnel emerged. They formed a loose perimeter around Cassie and Alexander as they ascended the steps. Cassie wondered if they'd understand if she decided to curl up and take a nap on the pristine steps. She lifted her eyes to Alexander.

"Is all this security for me?" Cassie asked, eyeing the stoic faces of the vampire guards. "Am I that dangerous?"

"The security is standard," he replied. "But yes, you are potentially quite dangerous, as you demonstrated on the yacht."

The massive doors swung open as they approached, revealing a soaring entry hall with marble floors and a sweeping staircase. Cassie hesitated at the threshold, a final moment of resistance before stepping into this new world.

"It's okay, Cassie. I won't let anything happen to you," Alexander spoke softly to her, lowering his voice so that it was barely perceptible enough for her to hear.

Cassie took a deep breath, squared her shoulders, and stepped through the doorway. Whatever awaited her in this vampire stronghold, she would face it with the same determination that had carried her through the chaos of the past twenty-four hours.

The doors closed behind them with a sound of finality, sealing Cassie Marlow into a world she never knew existed. A world that, according to Alexander Ross, was now partly hers.

Chapter Eight

Cassie stepped through a large set of double doors into a grand hall. The heavy oak panels swung silently on well-oiled hinges, revealing an expansive space that stretched before her like an indoor cathedral. Ornate chandeliers hung from the vaulted ceiling, their crystal pendants catching the morning light streaming through tall windows and scattering rainbow fragments across the polished marble floor.

The air inside carried a distinct smell: old books, beeswax polish, and something else she couldn't quite identify, something ancient and slightly mysterious. It reminded her of the rare botanical specimens she nurtured in her greenhouse back home in Harmony, those that only revealed their fragrance under specific conditions and for a very brief time.

Cassie paused at the threshold, her eyes widening as they swept across the magnificent space, drinking in every intricate detail of the breathtaking grandeur while her slender fingers absently tucked a wayward strand of deep auburn hair behind her ear. The vastness of the hall made her feel small and out of place, like a greenhouse succulent suddenly transplanted into an ancient forest. A flutter of anxiety rose in her chest, her usual confidence momentarily deserting her as she stood frozen between two worlds, the familiar one behind and this imposing new realm ahead. She was suddenly, overwhelmingly nervous. Even more so than she had been on the ride here. But now, she didn't feel like talking.

Alexander's hand brushed the small of her back with unexpected gentleness, the warmth of his touch seeping through the thin fabric of her dress as he guided her forward. The gesture felt oddly protective rather than controlling, as if he sensed her hesitation and sought to reassure rather than direct. His presence beside her was steady and grounding, a counterbalance to the intimidating splendor surrounding them, and despite her independent nature, Cassie found herself grateful for the subtle support as she took her first tentative steps into the hall.

Cassie stepped further into the grand hall, fighting against the drowsiness that threatened to overtake her. The morning sunlight streaming through the glass windows made her eyelids heavy, the kaleidoscope of colors dancing across the marble floor only intensifying her fatigue. Each beam felt like a physical weight pressing down on her shoulders, a reminder of her body's unnatural response to daylight. She blinked rapidly, forcing her eyes to remain open despite the burning sensation. She needed to see Claire, to know her sister was safe, that singular thought alone kept her upright and moving forward.

"When do I meet with the king?" she asked, struggling to keep her voice steady despite her exhaustion. The words felt thick in her mouth, her tongue heavy as she fought against the biological imperative to seek darkness and rest.

Alexander guided her toward an ornate seating area at the far end of the hall, his hand returning to the small of her back with that same unexpected gentleness. The carved mahogany chairs were upholstered in deep crimson velvet that reminded Cassie of freshly spilled blood, an unsettling association she quickly pushed aside.

"Soon. He's expecting us," Alexander replied, his deep voice reverberating through the cavernous space. His eyes constantly scanned their surroundings, ever vigilant despite the apparent security of their location.

Cassie's gaze darted around the magnificent hall, past the towering columns and gilded fixtures, searching for any sign of her sister's familiar face or the sound of her laughter. Part of her brain cataloged potential exits and hiding places even as anxiety gnawed at her insides. She watched as Nikolai and the other men exited, then turned back to Alexander.

"Where's Claire? You said she'd be here."

A flicker of something, concern, perhaps crossed Alexander's face, momentarily disrupting his composed expression.

His dark eyebrows drew together, creating a small furrow that Cassie hadn't noticed before. "Sam should have arrived with her by now."

The subtle shift in his demeanor sent a chill through Cassie's body, momentarily chasing away her fatigue like a splash of ice water. Her horticultural training had taught her to notice minute changes. The slight drooping of leaves before wilting became visible, the barely perceptible discoloration that preceded disease, and she recognized the same warning signs in Alexander's carefully controlled features.

"What do you mean 'should have'? Where is my sister?" Her voice sharpened with rising panic, her exhaustion temporarily forgotten as adrenaline surged through her system.

Before Alexander could respond, the enormous doors at the opposite end of the hall swung open with a resonant groan of ancient hinges. The sound echoed dramatically through the space, drawing every eye toward the entrance. Nikolai entered the room again with purposeful strides, his pale features set in a grim expression, followed by several more vampires in impeccably tailored dark suits. They moved with that unsettling fluid grace that marked them as inhuman, their footsteps unnaturally quiet against the marble floor as they spoke in hushed tones, their expressions grave.

Alexander straightened beside her, his posture shifting from casual escort to alert security chief in an instant. The transformation was remarkable. His shoulders squared, his stance widened slightly, and his entire presence became more commanding and authoritative.

"Wait here," he instructed, his tone brooking no argument as he moved to intercept the group, leaving Cassie suddenly alone in the vastness of the hall.

Cassie watched as they conferred in a tight circle, their voices too low for even her enhanced hearing to detect from this distance. The tension radiating from their gathering was palpable, like the heavy air before a thunderstorm. Alexander's shoulders tensed visibly as Nikolai spoke, his hand rising to stroke his neatly trimmed beard, a gesture she was beginning to recognize as a sign of concern. The repetitive motion seemed unconscious, his fingers working through the dark strands as Nikolai continued speaking, occasionally gesturing with sharp, contained movements.

Fighting against both exhaustion and mounting anxiety, Cassie decided she had had enough of being kept in the dark. Once again, her mind demanded data, facts, information, anything to combat the growing unease that twisted in her stomach. With determined steps that belied her fatigue, she approached the group.

"What's going on?" she demanded, injecting as much authority into her voice as she could muster. The botanical knowledge that allowed her to nurture the most delicate of greenhouse specimens hadn't prepared her for navigating vampire politics, but her nature refused to be sidelined.

The vampires fell silent at her approach, exchanging meaningful glances that made Cassie feel like an unwelcome specimen under a microscope. Alexander turned to her, his expression carefully controlled, though she caught the slight tightening around his eyes. "There's been a complication."

"What kind of complication?" Panic edged into her voice, her usual methodical thought process fracturing under stress. Her hands curled into fists at her sides, nails digging into her palms. "Where's Claire?"

Before Alexander could answer, the doors at the far end of the hall opened once more, the sound somehow more commanding than before. The vampires around her straightened perceptibly, their attention instantly redirected. An impeccably dressed woman entered, her bearing regal and commanding in a way that made everyone else in the room, even Alexander, seem somehow diminished. She wore a tailored charcoal suit with a deep burgundy blouse that complemented her olive complexion, her jet-black hair pulled back in an elegant chignon without a single strand out of place. Her eyes, dark and penetrating like polished obsidian, fixed immediately on Cassie with an intensity that felt almost physical.

The woman approached with measured steps, the click of her heels against marble echoing through the cavernous space like a metronome. The vampires around Alexander parted respectfully, creating a path for her approach, their deference obvious even to Cassie's untrained eye. The woman moved with the confidence of someone accustomed to immediate compliance, her posture perfect, her movements economical yet graceful.

"Miss Marlow," she greeted, her voice cultured and precise, carrying a hint of an accent Cassie couldn't quite place, something European, maybe French, but aged and worn smooth like river stones. "I am Elise Beaumont, the King's seneschal."

Cassie straightened despite her fatigue, instinctively responding to the woman's authority. Her mind quickly cataloged the term 'seneschal' and thought it was an unusual way to say manager, or essentially the King's right hand. It made Elise appear cold and formal. "Where is my sister?"

Elise's expression remained impassive, but something in her eyes softened slightly, a momentary flicker of what might have been sympathy crossing her features before disappearing behind her professional mask. "That is precisely what I've come to discuss." She gestured toward the seating area with a manicured hand adorned with a single platinum ring bearing a dark red gemstone. "Please."

Reluctantly, Cassie followed her back to the arrangement of elegant chairs, her body moving automatically while her mind raced with possibilities, each more alarming than the last. Alexander and Nikolai joined them, their faces grim, taking positions that seemed strategically placed. Close enough to intervene if necessary, but not so close as to crowd the conversation.

"I regret to inform you," Elise began once they were seated, her posture perfect as she perched on the edge of her chair, "that the vessel carrying your sister and Sam has not arrived as scheduled."

The words hit Cassie like a physical blow, knocking the air from her lungs. Her horticultural training had taught her that even the hardiest plants could wither without warning if their root systems were compromised, and in that moment, she felt her own foundations crumbling. "What do you mean 'not arrived'? Where are they?"

"We believe they encountered difficulties during their journey north," Elise replied, her tone measured and diplomatic, each word carefully chosen. Her hands rested in her lap, perfectly still in a way no human's could be. "Our last communication with Sam indicated they were taking an alternate route to avoid witch patrols after receiving intelligence about increased activity along the coast."

"Are you saying they're lost?" Cassie's voice rose, panic threatening to overwhelm her carefully cultivated self-control. Her mind, usually ordered and methodical like her greenhouse diagrams, scattered in a thousand directions. "That my sister is lost at sea?"

Alexander leaned forward, his large frame casting a shadow across the polished floor. "We don't know that for certain," he said, his deep voice pitched low, as if trying to soothe a frightened animal. "Communications can be disrupted for many reasons, including weather conditions, technical failures, and security protocols requiring radio silence."

"The King has diverted considerable resources toward locating them," Elise added, her perfectly manicured fingers making a slight, elegant gesture. "Including our most advanced tracking methods and several search vessels equipped with both technological and magical detection capabilities."

Cassie's hands trembled in her lap, her fingers twisting together like the vines of her most aggressive climbing plants. The greenhouse metaphor felt hollow now. There was no controlled environment here, no careful regulation of temperature and humidity, just the cold reality of her sister missing in a world far more dangerous than she'd ever imagined.

"This is your fault," she whispered, glaring at Alexander, her eyes bright with unshed tears and accusation. "You separated us. You put her on a different boat."

"It was standard protocol," he replied, though his voice lacked its usual confidence. A muscle twitched in his jaw, betraying tension beneath his controlled exterior. "For security reasons," he began, but the words seemed to falter on his lips.

"I don't care about your protocols!" Cassie stood abruptly, her fatigue momentarily forgotten in her anger. The chair scraped loudly against the marble floor, the sound harsh and discordant in the formal space. Her deep auburn hair fell forward, partially obscuring her face as she leaned in toward Alexander. "My sister is missing because of you!"

"Miss Marlow," Elise interjected firmly, though she hadn't raised her voice. There was power in her tone nonetheless, the kind that commanded immediate attention. "I understand your distress, but I assure you that finding your sister is our highest priority at present. Assigning blame does nothing to expedite her recovery."

"Where's the King?" Cassie demanded, turning her attention to Elise. Trained from a young age by her mom to seek solutions rather than dwell on problems, she pushed through her emotional turmoil. "I want to speak to him in person. He's responsible for all of this."

Elise's expression remained carefully neutral, though something like surprise flickered in the depths of her dark eyes, at Cassie's boldness. "I'm afraid that won't be possible at the moment. The King has been called away to address this situation personally, along with other diplomatic matters that require his immediate attention."

"Called away?" Cassie echoed incredulously, her voice rising with each word. Her hands gestured expansively, a rare display of physical animation from her typically reserved demeanor. "He orders us kidnapped and then doesn't even bother to stick around? What kind of leader abandons his responsibilities like that?"

"The King does not explain his movements to anyone," Elise replied, a hint of steel entering her voice, her spine straightening imperceptibly. "Not even to me. But I can tell you that he has instructed me to ensure your comfort and safety until his return, and that he personally oversees the search efforts."

"I don't want comfort. I want my sister!" The words burst from Cassie with unexpected force, echoing slightly in the cavernous hall. The outburst was uncharacteristic for her, but the events of the past days had stripped away her usual composed exterior.

Alexander rose and placed a hand on Cassie's shoulder, his touch surprisingly gentle for someone of his imposing stature. "Cassie," he said, using her first name with a familiarity that would have bothered her under different circumstances, "the King is putting his best resources toward finding Claire. If anyone can locate her, it's him. He has capabilities and connections that extend far beyond what you can imagine."

She shrugged off his touch, wrapping her arms around herself as if to hold her fragile composure together. The enormity of the situation crashed down upon her. Her sister missing, her mother left behind in Harmony without explanation, and herself a prisoner in a strange city among creatures she barely understood. The weight of it all pressed down on her like the heaviest greenhouse humidity on a summer day, making it difficult to breathe.

"In the meantime," Elise continued, her voice returning to its measured, professional tone, "the King has ordered that you be held under close guard for your own protection."

"Protection?" Cassie's laugh was bitter, a harsh sound devoid of humor that seemed to surprise even herself. "You mean imprisonment. Let's not dress it up with pretty euphemisms. I'm a prisoner here."

"Call it what you will," Elise replied evenly, smoothing an invisible wrinkle from her immaculate suit. "But there are those who would harm you if they knew what you are, what you represent. The King has ordered you to be kept safe, and that is what we shall do, whether you appreciate our methods or not."

Cassie swayed slightly where she stood, the combination of emotional turmoil and daytime-induced fatigue finally taking its toll. The room seemed to tilt around her, the ornate ceiling and polished floors momentarily blurring. Her eyes clouded with exhaustion as she fought to maintain her balance, the stress of Claire's disappearance and her own captivity weighing on her like physical chains. The sunlight filtering through the windows only amplified her discomfort. Even indirect daylight sapped her strength in ways she was still learning to manage, like a shade-loving fern suddenly exposed to harsh afternoon sun.

Alexander moved closer, his tall frame tensing as if he was preparing to catch her if she fell. "You need rest," he said quietly, his voice pitched for her ears alone. "You're exhausted, and pushing yourself won't help Claire. You need your strength for what's ahead."

"I need to find my sister," Cassie insisted, though her voice had lost some of its fire. The words came out slightly slurred, her usual precise diction blunted by fatigue. She pressed her fingertips against her temples, as if trying to physically hold her thoughts together.

Elise signaled to someone behind them with a subtle gesture of her elegant hand. "Quarters have been prepared for you," she said, her tone softening marginally. "You'll be comfortable there while we search for your sister. Everything has been arranged with your specific needs in mind."

"And if I refuse?" Cassie challenged, though she knew it was futile. She recognized the inevitability of the situation, calculating probabilities and outcomes even as her heart rebelled against acceptance.

"That would be unwise," Elise replied simply, the understatement carrying more weight than any elaborate threat could have.

Two vampire guards approached from the periphery of the hall, materializing as if from nowhere. Their expressions were neutral, but their postures conveyed clear authority, their movements synchronized with military precision. They wore the same dark suits as the others, but something in their bearing marked them as security rather than advisors.

"Alexander and Nikolai will be accompanying the King," Elise explained, gesturing toward the two vampires. "These gentlemen will escort you to your quarters and ensure your safety in their absence. They are under strict orders regarding your well-being."

Cassie turned to Alexander, betrayal and accusation in her eyes. The realization that he too would be leaving hit her with unexpected force. Despite everything, he had become a strange sort of constant in the chaos of recent days, a known quantity in an increasingly unknown world. "You're leaving too?"

Something like regret flickered across his features, softening the hard planes of his face momentarily. "The King requires my expertise in this situation. I've been tracking your sister's vessel since it departed. I know its specifications, its intended route. I'm the most qualified to find it, and it's my job."

"Then find her," Cassie whispered, her anger giving way to desperation. Her strong facade crumbled completely, leaving only raw emotion in its place. "Please."

Alexander nodded, his dark eyes meeting hers with unexpected intensity. Something passed between them in that moment, an unspoken communication that transcended their adversarial relationship. "I will."

Nikolai stepped forward, breaking the moment. His pale features remained impassive, but there was an urgency in his movements. "We should depart immediately. The King is waiting."

Alexander hesitated, then reached into his pocket and pressed something into Cassie's hand. She felt the smooth, cool surface of a stone against her palm, its texture worn by time and handling. Looking down, she saw a small rock with a hole in the middle, a natural perforation that caught the light strangely. A witch's stone, or hag stone as they were also known, an object of power in her mother's tradition.

"For luck," he said quietly, his voice pitched low so only she could hear. His fingers lingered against hers for a moment longer than necessary. "It's always brought me both luck and security. My grandmother gave it to me, centuries ago."

Before Cassie could respond, he turned and followed Nikolai toward the exit, his broad shoulders set with determination. She watched them go, the stone clutched tightly in her fist, and she felt more alone now than she had since this nightmare began. The two vampires moved with purpose through the grand hall, their footsteps silent against the marble floor, until they disappeared through the enormous doors.

Elise gestured to the waiting guards, her movement elegant and economical. "They will take you to your quarters now. I suggest you use this time to rest and recover your strength."

Too exhausted and overwhelmed to argue further, Cassie allowed herself to be led from the grand hall. They guided her through a maze of corridors, each more elegant than the last, vaulted ceilings giving way to intimate archways, marble floors transitioning to plush carpets in deep jewel tones. The architecture seemed to shift subtly as they moved deeper into the complex, ancient stonework blending seamlessly with more modern elements in a way that made it impossible to determine the building's true age.

After what seemed like an eternity of twisting passages seemingly designed to confuse and disorient, they reached a heavy wooden door reinforced with ornate iron bands. Intricate symbols had been worked into the metal, protective sigils that Cassie recognized from her mother's grimoire, though these were far older, their design more primal.

One guard unlocked it with an ancient-looking key and stepped aside. "These will be your quarters for the duration of your stay. Everything has been prepared according to the king's specifications."

Cassie entered reluctantly, and she braced for a cell despite the elaborate journey to reach it. Instead, she found herself in a luxurious suite that reminded her of an upscale hotel room, though with distinctly old-world touches. A four-poster bed dominated one wall, draped with rich fabrics in deep forest greens that reminded her of her greenhouse. Comfortable seating arranged around a marble fireplace, bookshelves filled with leather-bound volumes, and a writing desk of polished mahogany filled the remaining space. Fresh flowers, all carefully selected non-toxic varieties, she noted with her botanist's eye, adorned various surfaces in elegant arrangements.

Large windows overlooked a meticulously maintained garden, the formal hedges and statuary visible in the distance, though Cassie noticed the subtle shimmer of magical reinforcement on the glass. Her fingers traced the nearly invisible runes etched into the window frame, recognizing containment and warding spells. Beautiful, but still a prison. But not her prison. She knew immediately these wards were weak to a witch with her abilities, and she looked forward to being alone to test them further. Her mind was already cataloging their structure, identifying potential weaknesses in the magical architecture.

"Is there anything you require?" the guard asked from the doorway, his expression professionally blank.

"My sister," Cassie replied flatly, turning to face him with her arms crossed protectively over her chest.

The guard's expression remained impassive, though something like discomfort flickered briefly in his eyes before disappearing. "A meal will be brought shortly. There are fresh clothes in the wardrobe, selected for comfort and practical use."

With that, he withdrew, closing the door behind him. Cassie heard the distinct sound of a lock engaging, followed by a subtle hum that suggested magical reinforcement activating. She stood motionless for several moments, listening to the receding footsteps until silence enveloped her completely.

She moved to the window, pressing her palm against the cool glass as she gazed out at the unfamiliar landscape. The gardens below were immaculate, their geometric precision reminding her of Renaissance designs she'd studied in her horticulture courses. Beyond them, she could see the edge of a forest, and further still, the glint of water, or the sea, though she couldn't be certain from this distance. Somewhere out there, Claire was lost, possibly in danger. The thought was unbearable, like a physical pain lodged beneath her ribs.

"I'll find you," she whispered, her breath fogging the glass. "I promise."

Exhaustion finally overcame her, the weight of the past days crushing down like an avalanche. Cassie sank onto the edge of the bed, the mattress yielding beneath her weight with unexpected softness. The stone Alexander had given her dug into her palm where she still clutched it tightly. She opened her hand to examine it, a small, oblong, and unevenly shaped surface, worn smooth by water and time, with a hole in the center that caught the light unusually. It had to be tilted slightly to see through the hole, the perspective shifting depending on the angle.

She traced its edges with her fingertip, feeling the subtle energy that hummed within the stone, faint but detectable to her witch senses.

She wondered why he had given it to her and what it might mean. A gesture of reassurance? A promise? Or simply a momentary impulse from a vampire who had already demonstrated more complexity than she'd initially given him credit for? Her mind searched for patterns, for meaning, even as her body cried out for rest.

The bright morning sunlight streaming through the windows grew heavier, more oppressive, the beams like physical weights pressing down upon her. Cassie's eyelids drooped despite her determination to stay awake, to plan, to find a way out. Her vampire nature demanded sleep during daylight hours, a biological imperative she'd fought against her whole life, and after the events of the past few hours, her body could no longer resist the pull toward unconsciousness.

She curled onto the bed, still fully clothed, not bothering to pull back the covers or change into the provided garments. The smooth stone remained clutched against her heart, its cool surface gradually warming against her skin. As consciousness slipped away, her last thoughts were of Claire. She wondered where she might be, whether she was safe, and how she would find her way back to her sister's side.

"I'll find you," she murmured again as sleep claimed her, the words a promise and a prayer. "No matter what it takes."

CHAPTER NINE

Alexander Ross strode purposefully down the long corridor toward the map room, Nikolai a half-step behind him. Their footfalls were nearly silent against the polished marble floor, a habit born from centuries of moving undetected among humans. The morning light filtering through tall windows cast long shadows across their path, a reminder that every minute spent indoors was precious time lost in the search for Claire Marlow.

The majority of the vampires were asleep at this hour, their bodies yielding to the pull of daylight. Only the older and more powerful bloodline vampires, those with centuries of resistance ingrained in their veins, remained active throughout the compound. Alexander could sense their movements, the subtle vibrations of ancient beings who, like him, had transcended the more debilitating limitations of their kind. The compound was not cloaked in darkness, and those who were not resilient to the effects of the day remained in their quarters until nightfall.

Alexander's mind was racing, calculating routes and probabilities. Sam was methodical and experienced. He wouldn't have deviated from the planned course without good reason. The yacht had excellent communication systems and multiple backup devices. Their sudden silence suggested something catastrophic.

"You're worried about the girl," Nikolai observed quietly.

"I'm worried about the mission," Alexander corrected, though without conviction. "Sam knows his responsibility."

"I meant the one who is probably planning her own escape at the moment."

Alexander's jaw tightened. Cassie's accusing eyes had haunted him as he'd walked away, bright orbs filled with fear and betrayal. He'd given her his witch stone, an impulsive gesture he still couldn't fully explain to himself. The stone had been his talisman for over two centuries, a connection to his human past that he rarely acknowledged. His grandmother had given it to him as a child for his passage to the New World with his father.

They reached the massive oak doors of the map room, an architectural marvel that commanded reverence from all who approached. The ancient wood was carved with intricate scenes of naval battles from centuries past: triremes clashing near Marathon, Spanish galleons exchanging broadsides with English vessels, and more modern engagements where steam and sail competed for dominance. Alexander's fingers traced a particularly detailed frigate, remembering similar ships from his early days as a vampire. Calim often decorated in ways to honor the past, creating spaces that served as both functional rooms and historical archives. The vampire king's millennia of existence had given him a profound appreciation for preserving history in tangible forms, particularly the military victories that had shaped human civilization. These doors, commissioned over a century ago from a master woodcarver who had later been rewarded with immortality for his skill, stood as a testament to Calim's belief that power must acknowledge its foundations.

Alexander pushed the doors open, and he and Nikolai entered the cavernous chamber. It was dominated by an enormous table with a large flat screen that displayed a detailed map of the Pacific Northwest coastline. Modern technology had been seamlessly integrated with ancient craftsmanship, holographic projections hovering above the wooden surface, displaying weather patterns, shipping lanes, and territorial boundaries.

At the far end of the table stood Callimachus, the Vampire King of Western Canada. Even from a distance, his presence commanded the room. Over two thousand years old, Calim retained the powerful physique of the Greek general he had once been. His auburn hair was cropped short in a style reminiscent of ancient military commanders, and his dark eyes held the weight of millennia. He wore modern clothing: a tailored charcoal suit that did nothing to diminish his warrior's bearing.

"Alexander, Nikolai," Calim acknowledged without looking up from the map.

Alexander approached, noting the other vampires gathered around the table, all senior members of the security council. Their expressions were grave.

"No communication from Sam's vessel since 0300 hours," the vampire to the left of the King, named Thomas, reported. "Last known position was here." He pointed to a spot along the coastline. "He reported changing course to avoid increased witch patrol activity in this sector." His finger traced a new path that veered further west into open waters.

"And the storm?" Alexander asked.

"Appeared suddenly, according to coastal monitoring. Not seasonal, and localized to this area," indicated a swirling pattern on the holographic overlay. "It bears the signature of witch weather manipulation, but far more powerful than standard patrol capabilities."

Alexander's eyes narrowed. "A different patrol than the one we encountered?"

"Yes. The patrol you encountered would have still been unconscious when this storm formed. This was something else," Thomas explained. "The timing is too precise to be coincidental."

"Someone knew Sam's route," Nikolai suggested. "Or was tracking him specifically."

Calim straightened to his full height, his gaze sweeping the assembled vampires. "Show me your encounter with the patrol."

Alexander nodded to a technician who brought forward a tablet. Moments later, the holographic display shifted to show footage from the yacht's security cameras: the storm, the boarding, Cassie's unexpected appearance on deck, the confrontation with the witch, and finally, the unconscious patrol being returned to their vessel.

Calim watched without comment, his expression unreadable. When the footage ended, he turned to Alexander.

"The hybrid's abilities are even more impressive than your initial report suggested," he observed. "She neutralized a trained witch patrol officer with minimal effort, despite having no formal combat training."

"She was defending herself," Alexander found himself saying. "And she was horrified when she realized what she'd done."

Calim raised an eyebrow at his defensive tone but didn't comment on it. Instead, he returned his attention to the map.

"The pattern is clear," he said. "Sam's vessel disappeared precisely when it entered this zone." His finger circled an area of open sea. "If the Northern Witch Patrol knew of our operation, others may have as well."

"The High Coven Council," one of the other vampires suggested.

Calim nodded slowly. "Perhaps. Though they typically operate with more... diplomatic approaches."

"Unless they discovered or knew what the Marlow sisters are," Nikolai pointed out.

A heavy silence fell over the room. The implications were enormous. If the High Coven Council had learned of the hybrids' existence, they might take extreme measures to eliminate what they would consider an abomination. Or, if they were aware of their existence, they might be trying to protect them or prevent their discovery by darker forces.

Alexander leaned over the map, studying the currents and surrounding islands. "We need to deploy search teams immediately. If the yacht was disabled rather than destroyed, they could have drifted here." He indicated a small archipelago. "These islands are uninhabited but could provide shelter."

"Already in progress," Calim confirmed. "Three vessels departed at first light, equipped with both technological and magical detection capabilities."

Alexander straightened, meeting his king's gaze directly. "I request permission to join the search, sir. I'm familiar with Sam's tactical preferences and contingency protocols."

Calim studied him for a long moment. "Your expertise would be valuable, yes. I'll have you oversee the operation from here, and Nikolai will assist with the search on the Artemis under your direction. But there's another matter requiring attention first." He gestured to an aide who approached with a sealed document bearing the distinctive wax seal of the High Coven Council, a triple spiral pattern that seemed to move when viewed from different angles.

"This arrived an hour ago," Calim said, opening the document. "The High Coven Council is requesting permission to send emissaries into our territory."

Alexander felt a chill run down his spine. "What do they want?"

"To discuss, and I quote, 'a matter of mutual concern regarding certain individuals recently transported from witch territory to vampire jurisdiction.'" Calim's voice was neutral, but his eyes were sharp. "They specifically mention the Marlow sisters."

"They know," Nikolai muttered.

"They suspect," Calim corrected. "If they knew with certainty, they would not be requesting a diplomatic meeting."

Alexander's mind raced. "The timing can't be coincidental. If they're aware of the Marlows, they could be behind Sam's disappearance."

"Or they could be genuinely concerned about a treaty violation and seeking to resolve it through proper channels," Calim countered. "We can't assume hostile intent without evidence."

"With respect, Your Majesty," Alexander said carefully, "the witches have never shown interest in diplomatic solutions when it comes to perceived threats to their bloodlines."

Calim's expression hardened slightly. "Neither have we, historically speaking. Yet here we stand, maintaining a peace that has lasted centuries." He set the document down on the map table. "I will meet with their emissaries. It may provide insights into what happened to Sam and the younger Marlow."

Alexander knew better than to argue further. Callimachus had not survived two millennia by making rash decisions. If he believed a diplomatic approach was warranted, he had his reasons.

"In the meantime," Calim continued, "I want you and Nikolai to lead the search effort. Use whatever resources you need. Finding Sam and Claire Marlow is our priority."

"And the older sister?" Alexander asked, trying to keep his tone professional.

"Cassie Marlow will remain here under guard. Her safety is paramount, especially now that the High Coven Council has shown interest." Calim's eyes narrowed slightly as he studied Alexander. "You seem particularly concerned about her welfare."

Alexander kept his expression neutral. "She's a valuable asset and potentially crucial to understanding the nature of these hybrids."

"Indeed." Calim didn't sound entirely convinced. "Before you depart, I'd like a private word." He gestured toward a door at the far end of the chamber that led to his personal study.

Alexander followed his king, acutely aware of the curious glances from the other vampires. Once inside the wood-paneled study, Calim closed the door and moved to a sideboard where a decanter of dark liquid sat. It was not wine, but a special blend of blood and rare herbs that helped older vampires maintain their strength without feeding directly from a beating heart.

"You've served me faithfully for centuries, Alexander," Calim began, pouring two glasses. "Your loyalty has never been in question."

"Thank you, Your Majesty."

Calim handed him a glass. "Which is why your behavior regarding the Marlow woman intrigues me."

Alexander accepted the drink but didn't immediately respond. Denying any special interest would be futile. Calim was too perceptive.

"There's something about her," he admitted finally. "Something familiar that I can't quite place."

"A connection from your human life, perhaps?" Calim suggested, sipping his drink.

"Impossible. That was over two centuries ago, and she's barely into her twenties." Alexander shook his head. "It's something else. When I first saw her in that shop, working with plants and humming that old melody... it felt like recognition."

Calim's expression sharpened with interest. "What melody?"

Alexander frowned, trying to recall. "Something ancient. I couldn't place it, but it seemed to reach inside me, like a memory I didn't know I had."

"Interesting." Calim set his glass down and moved to a bookshelf, running his fingers along the spines of ancient tomes. "The Marlow sisters represent something unprecedented, Alexander. Not just hybrids of witch and vampire. That alone would be remarkable, but something more specific."

"You know who their father is," Alexander realized.

Calim turned, his eyes reflecting the weight of his age. "I have suspicions. Suspicions that, if proven correct, could change everything we understand about our relationship with the witches."

"Who?" Alexander couldn't help asking.

"That's not relevant at the moment," Calim replied, his tone making it clear the subject was closed. "What matters is finding Claire Marlow and ensuring Cassie remains safely in our custody until we understand exactly what they are."

Alexander nodded, recognizing the dismissal. "We'll depart immediately."

"One more thing," Calim said as Alexander reached the door. "You gave the Marlow woman your witch stone."

Alexander froze, surprised that Calim had noticed such a small detail. "Yes. It seemed... appropriate."

"As you well know, the old stones that have been magically imbued with additional protective properties are rare and hold significant power for the witches, especially a stone as old as yours." Calim's expression was unreadable. "An interesting choice of gift for someone you've known less than a day."

"It was impulsive," Alexander admitted. "She seemed to need something to hold onto."

"Perhaps." Calim's gaze was penetrating. "Or perhaps some part of you recognized something in her that your conscious mind has yet to comprehend. A mate, perhaps?"

Before Alexander could respond, Calim returned to the map room, effectively ending the conversation. Alexander followed, his mind troubled by the king's cryptic words. What did Calim suspect about the Marlow sisters' parentage that he wasn't sharing? Why would he suggest a mate? Vampires mated only once, and finding a mate was rare. Cassie was also a witch, an unusual choice for a partner.

Back in the map room, Nikolai was already organizing the search operation, directing teams to specific sectors and coordinating with the vessels already deployed.

"I'll be ready to depart in twenty minutes," he informed Alexander. "The Artemis is being prepared as we speak."

The Artemis was their fastest vessel, equipped with the latest technology and magical enhancements. While the vampires didn't have the full magical abilities of the witches, they had their own limited abilities that they used quite often to imbue objects with enhancements. If anyone could find Sam's missing yacht, it would be with the assistance of the Artemis.

"Good. We'll start with the last known coordinates and work outward in a standard search pattern." Alexander studied the map one final time, committing the relevant details to memory. "Have we checked for any unusual witch activity in the area?"

"Our intelligence network reports increased movement among the Northern Covens, but nothing definitive," Nikolai replied. "They're being careful."

Alexander nodded grimly. "They always are."

As he assisted Nikolai with preparations to leave, Alexander found his thoughts returning to Cassie, alone in her luxurious prison. The stone he'd given her was more than just a talisman. It was a connection, a way to sense her presence even at a distance. His grandmother had given it to him when he was young, and he'd learned through the years that it was more than it appeared.

"She'll be safe here," Nikolai said quietly, reading his thoughts. "The King's protection is absolute."

"I know." Alexander straightened his shoulders, focusing on the mission ahead. "Let's find her sister and Sam."

"Will do." Nikolai gave Alexander a small smirk and an exaggerated salute.

Alexander ignored him and leaned back over the map. "The Artemis should be ready now. Shouldn't you be leaving?"

Chapter Ten

Cassie woke with a jolt, her body instantly alert despite the sunlight still streaming through the windows. For a moment, she was disoriented, the unfamiliar surroundings causing a spike of panic before memory rushed back. Vancouver. Vampires. Claire missing.

Claire.

The thought of her sister sent a fresh wave of anguish through her. Somewhere out there, Claire was lost at sea, possibly hurt or worse. She was the sister who'd always been the cautious one, who preferred books to adventures, who'd dreamed of faraway places but in reality never really desired to leave. Cassie was the one who dreamed of adventure and finding a place in the world where she belonged. Not Claire.

Cassie's fingers tightened around Alexander's witch stone, which she'd somehow managed to keep clutched in her hand even while sleeping. Its smooth surface had warmed against her skin, and she could feel a faint pulse of energy emanating from it, like a distant heartbeat.

She sat up, swinging her legs over the side of the bed. Her body felt unusually alert, adrenaline overriding her normal lethargy. A quick glance at the ornate clock on the mantelpiece showed it was just before sunset. She'd slept through most of the day.

"I'm coming, Claire," she whispered, determination hardening her voice. "I won't let them keep me here while you're lost out there."

Cassie moved to the window, pressing her palm against the glass as she surveyed her surroundings with renewed focus. The perfectly manicured garden below was deserted. Beyond the formal hedges and fountains lay a dense canopy of trees.

She could see no guards patrolling the grounds, though that didn't mean they weren't there.

Her attention shifted to the window itself. Earlier, her exhausted mind had registered the magical wards etched into the frame, but now she examined them with a botanist's precision. Each symbol was meticulously carved into the wood, creating an interlocking pattern of containment and alarm spells.

It was minor magic compared to what she had learned in her up-bringing, and to the spells she knew instinctively.

"You don't understand what I am," she murmured, a bitter smile touching her lips. "None of you do."

Cassie placed both hands against the glass, closing her eyes to better sense the magic. Her mother had taught her to recognize wards from an early age, drilling her on their structures and vulnerabilities. These were powerful but conventional.

She concentrated, reaching for that strange dual power she'd accessed during her fight with Alexander and the witch patrol. It came more readily now, flowing through her veins like electricity, making her fingertips tingle with potential. Her eyes snapped open, glowing with an inner light as she whispered words of unmaking, ancient witch phrases twisted with something darker, hungrier. The desire to modify the method should have surprised her, but it didn't. Turning to darker forces more easily should have terrified her, but it didn't. Instead, it sent a thrill coursing through her at the discovery. She felt powerful.

The wards shimmered, becoming briefly visible as lines of blue-white energy before flickering like a dying bulb. Cassie pushed harder, and the wards resisted, designed to withstand assault, but they hadn't been created to withstand magic infused with vampire strength.

With a sound like breaking glass, though the window remained intact, the wards shattered. Cassie staggered back, momentarily dizzy from the exertion. But unlike her previous experiences with this power, she didn't feel completely drained. The sunset was approaching, feeding her vampire side, balancing the energy she'd expended.

She waited, breath held, for alarms to sound or guards to come running. Nothing happened. The room remained silent except for the ticking of the clock and her own quickened breathing.

"They really don't know what I am," she whispered, relief and determination mingling in her voice.

Cassie turned her attention to the door. It would be locked, possibly guarded. She needed another way out. Her gaze returned to the window. The drop to the garden below was substantial, at least three stories. For a human, it would be potentially suicidal. For a witch, dangerous without proper preparation, it was still risky. But for whatever she was becoming, it was worth a try.

She moved to the wardrobe, quickly changing into the provided clothes. There were dark jeans, a fitted black sweater, and sturdy boots that fit surprisingly well. Practical clothes for movement. She tied her auburn hair back into a tight ponytail and slipped Alexander's stone into her pocket. She was starting to get used to dressing in clothes that weren't hers. Cassie shook her head at the number of times she'd changed her clothing within the past two days.

Back at the window, Cassie examined the latch. It was old but well-maintained, designed to open inward. She unlatched it and pushed, feeling the cool evening air rush in. The scent of pine and distant ocean filled her lungs as she leaned out, scanning the façade of the building.

The vampire stronghold was an architectural marvel, its stone walls adorned with decorative ledges and balconies. To her right, perhaps fifteen feet away, was another balcony, slightly lower than her window. It would require a leap that no human could manage, but Cassie was beginning to understand she was far from human.

"Stupid or brave?" she muttered to herself. "Claire would definitely say stupid."

The thought of her sister steeled her resolve. Claire needed her. And staying here, waiting for Alexander or the mysterious King to return, wouldn't help find her. She didn't know the vampires' intentions, and maybe leaving her sister lost at sea was their intent. She didn't want to risk that eventuality.

Cassie climbed onto the windowsill, crouching like a cat preparing to pounce. The stone wall beneath her window offered minimal handholds, but the adjacent balcony was close enough that she might make it with a running start. Might.

She took a deep breath, focusing on that strange new strength flowing through her body. What if it wasn't enough to make the jump? What if she fell, because her arrogant trust in her new abilities wasn't enough to make the leap? The powerful strength surging through her overpowered her doubts. Before she could reconsider, she launched herself from the window.

For one heart-stopping moment, she was airborne, the ground dizzyingly far below. Then her feet hit the balcony railing, her hands grasping the cold stone with preternatural strength. She teetered precariously for a second before pulling herself over, landing in a crouch on the balcony floor.

"I did it," she whispered, half-disbelieving. The jump should have been impossible, yet she'd made it with room to spare. Her heart hammered against her ribs, not from exertion but from the thrill of discovery. This power, this strength, it was hers to command. Once this was all over, she had to explore it more.

The balcony led to another room, its French doors closed but unlatched. Cassie peered through the glass, confirming the room was empty before slipping inside. It was another guest suite, similar to her own but decorated in shades of blue rather than green. The bed was made, the room pristine and clearly unoccupied.

She moved silently to the door, pressing her ear against the wood. No sounds came from the hallway beyond. Slowly, she turned the handle, easing the door open just enough to peek through.

The corridor was empty, lit by wall sconces that cast a warm glow over the gleaming floors. Cassie slipped out, closing the door behind her. She had no idea which way led to an exit, but she needed to keep moving. Standing still meant getting caught. Each moment she waited was another moment she didn't find her sister. If she got caught now, it would also mean potentially losing Claire.

She chose left, keeping close to the wall and moving with the silent grace of her newfound abilities. The corridor curved gently, leading to a grand staircase that descended to a lower floor. Cassie paused at the top, listening intently. Her hearing picked up distant voices, two male vampires discussing security rotations somewhere below.

Descending the stairs would put her directly in their path. She needed another route.

A service door caught her eye, partially concealed behind an ornate tapestry. Everything in this place was ornate. Staff quarters or storage, perhaps, but potentially a way to avoid the main corridors. Cassie slipped behind the tapestry and tested the door. It opened silently, revealing a narrow stairwell that appeared to run the height of the building.

"Perfect," she whispered, stepping through and pulling the door closed behind her.

The service stairs were utilitarian, lacking the opulence of the main areas but well-maintained. At least she'd found a place less ornate. Cassie descended quickly, her footsteps eerily silent even to her own hearing. Two floors down, she paused outside a door, listening carefully before easing it open.

She found herself in a side corridor lined with paintings of landscapes, forests, mountains, and seascapes rendered in exquisite detail. The hallway appeared empty, but voices drifted from around a corner ahead. Cassie froze, pressing herself against the wall as the voices grew louder.

"We should check on the hybrid," a male voice was saying. "The King wants hourly reports on her condition."

"She's sleeping," another voice replied. "Dr. Levin said the transition is taxing her system, and he'd introduce himself and check on her later this evening. Better to let her rest."

"Orders are orders. Besides, I want to see this for myself. A natural-born witch-vampire hybrid. Who'd have thought it possible?"

The voices were approaching her position. Cassie glanced frantically around, spotting a door across the hall. She darted across, turning the handle with a silent prayer that it wasn't locked.

The door opened, and she slipped inside, easing it closed just as the owners of the voices rounded the corner. Through the thin crack she'd left, she watched two male vampires in dark suits pass by, continuing their conversation as they headed toward the stairs she'd just descended.

They were going to check on her. The empty room. The broken wards. Her escape would be discovered within minutes. She tried not to panic, to think clearly.

Cassie turned, taking in her surroundings. She'd entered some kind of study or library, with walls lined with bookshelves and a massive desk dominating the center of the room. Large windows offered a view of the darkening sky, the last rays of sunlight fading into twilight. Claire would love this room.

No time to admire the décor. She needed to keep moving, to get out of the building before the alarm was raised. Cassie crossed to the door on the opposite side of the room, which led to yet another corridor. This one was broader and again more ornate, with marble floors and ceiling frescoes depicting what appeared to be ancient battles.

She was moving deeper into the complex rather than toward an exit. Frustration gnawed at her as she tried to orient herself. The building was a maze, as if it were deliberately designed to confuse outsiders. Without a map or guide, she was wandering blindly.

A distant shout echoed through the corridors, followed by the sound of running feet. They'd discovered her empty room. Damn it, she had to move, and fast.

Panic threatened to overwhelm her, but Cassie forced it down. Panic wouldn't help Claire. She needed to think clearly, to use her mind rather than give in to fear.

She noticed a subtle change in the air, a fresh breeze carrying the scent of pine and earth. An open window or door had to be nearby. Cassie followed the scent, moving swiftly down the corridor toward what she hoped was freedom. It was odd being able to smell with heightened senses, but also something she was beginning to like.

The corridor ended at a T-junction. The breeze was coming from the right, so she turned that way, finding herself in a gallery overlooking an interior courtyard. Large arched windows lined the gallery, some open to the evening air. Through them, Cassie could see a fountain surrounded by carefully tended flowerbeds, and beyond that, what appeared to be a service gate in the outer wall.

An exit. If she could reach the courtyard and cross to that gate, she might escape before the entire compound was alerted.

Cassie approached one of the open windows, judging the distance to the ground below. It was another substantial drop, but the courtyard was paved with flagstones rather than the hard marble of the interior floors. She might survive the fall with her abilities.

Before she could act, voices erupted from both ends of the gallery. Cassie whirled to see four vampires approaching from each direction, their movements coordinated to cut off her escape. They wore the same dark suits as the guards she'd seen earlier, but their expressions were hard and predatory.

"Miss Marlow," one called out, his voice deceptively calm. "Please step away from the window. The King has ordered you kept safe, and that drop would cause you considerable harm."

"I need to find my sister," Cassie replied, backing closer to the open window. "She's lost out there, and I won't sit in a gilded, stupidly ornate cage while she might be dying."

"The King has deployed his best resources to locate your sister," another vampire said, moving slowly closer. "Alexander Ross himself is leading the search. You have our word that everything possible is being done."

"Your word means nothing to me," she snapped. "None of you cared about our safety when you kidnapped me and my sister and separated us. Why should I believe you care now?"

The vampires were closing in from both sides, moving with the practiced coordination of predators who had hunted together for decades, if not centuries. Cassie glanced behind her at the courtyard below. The drop was daunting, but staying meant capture.

She made her decision in an instant, gathering that strange dual power within her. The vampires must have sensed the change because they lunged forward simultaneously, trying to reach her before she could act.

Too late. Cassie unleashed a wave of energy that sent the nearest vampires staggering backward. In the moment of confusion, she spun and leaped through the open window.

The air rushed past her as she fell, the ground approaching with terrifying speed. Instinctively, she tucked and rolled, hitting the flag-stones with bone-jarring force. Pain exploded through her shoulder and hip, but nothing felt broken. Her hybrid nature had absorbed the impact that would have shattered human bones.

Gasping, Cassie staggered to her feet, ignoring the shouts from the gallery above. She sprinted across the courtyard toward the service gate, her body already healing from the fall. The gate was her only chance. Beyond it lay the trees she'd seen from her window, dense enough to provide cover for her escape.

She was halfway across the courtyard when the vampires dropped from the gallery, landing with far more grace than she had. Four of them formed a line between her and the gate, while the others spread out to surround her.

"This is pointless, Miss Marlow," the lead vampire said, his hands raised in a placating gesture. "You can't outrun us, and fighting will only result in injuries the King specifically ordered us to prevent."

"Get out of my way," Cassie snarled, feeling her fangs extend as adrenaline and anger surged through her system. "I won't ask again."

"Please, be reasonable. Come back inside, and we can discuss your concerns about your sister."

Cassie didn't waste breath on further argument. She charged, feinting left before diving right, using a burst of vampire speed that surprised even her. She slipped past two of the guards, her momentum carrying her toward the gate.

A hand caught her arm, spinning her around. Cassie reacted instinctively, lashing out with witch-fire that blazed from her fingertips. The vampire released her with a cry of pain, the sleeve of his suit smoldering where her magic had burned through.

Another guard grabbed her from behind, pinning her arms to her sides. Cassie stomped on his instep with crushing force, then drove her elbow into his solar plexus when his grip loosened. She whirled, palm striking upward to connect with his jaw in a blow that sent him staggering.

Two more vampires rushed her. Cassie ducked under the first's grasp, using his momentum to send him tumbling over her shoulder. But the second caught her in a bear hug, lifting her off her feet. She kicked and struggled, but his strength exceeded hers.

"Enough!" he growled in her ear. "You'll only hurt yourself."

Cassie felt that strange dual power surging within her again, responding to her desperation. With a wordless cry, she released it in all directions, a pulse of energy that sent her captor flying backward. The other vampires were knocked off their feet, creating a momentary opening.

She ran for the gate, her lungs burning and muscles screaming from exertion. The burst of power had cost her, but freedom was just yards away. She could make it. She would make it.

Something heavy slammed into her from behind, sending her sprawling across the flagstones. Cassie rolled, coming up in a defensive crouch to face her attacker. One of the vampires had recovered faster than the others, tackling her from behind.

Before she could react, three more were upon her, their combined strength overwhelming. Cassie fought with everything she had, unleashing bursts of witch-fire and vampire strength in desperate combination. One vampire reeled back with a scorched face. Another clutched a dislocated shoulder. But there were too many, and her hybrid powers were still untrained and unpredictable. She was losing control of her power again, of herself. That scared her more than the vampires capturing her did.

A fifth vampire joined the struggle, grabbing her flailing legs. Together, they forced her down, pinning her against the cold stone. Cassie bucked and twisted, refusing to surrender even as her strength began to fade.

"Hold her steady," one ordered. "We need to get her inside before she hurts herself or someone else."

"Let me go!" Cassie shouted, her voice raw with frustration and fear. "My sister needs me!"

"Your sister needs you alive and unharmed," the vampire holding her shoulders replied, his voice strained with effort. "This isn't helping her."

Cassie's struggles intensified at the mention of Claire, a fresh surge of desperate energy flowing through her. She managed to free one arm, swinging wildly at the nearest vampire. Her fist connected with his jaw, the impact sending a shock of pain up her arm.

He barely flinched, capturing her wrist in an iron grip. "Enough," he repeated, more firmly this time.

In her frenzy to escape, Cassie failed to notice how close they had moved to the edge of the fountain. As she twisted violently, trying to break free of their combined hold, her balance shifted. The vampire restraining her legs lost his grip as she kicked out, and suddenly she was falling backward.

Time seemed to slow as Cassie realized what was happening. She was falling toward the fountain's edge, the hard stone rim rushing up to meet her. Her hybrid strength and resilience might protect her from many injuries, but a direct impact to the head at this angle...

She tried to turn midair to protect her head, but it was too late. It was too late to shield herself from injury, and too late to escape. The last thing Cassie saw was the vampires' faces, their expressions transforming from determination to horror as they realized they couldn't catch her in time.

Then darkness claimed her as her head struck the stone with sickening force.

Chapter Eleven

Alexander Ross was halfway through his analysis of search patterns when the sensation hit him, a sharp, visceral pull that made him straighten abruptly. He was in motion before he understood why. The witch stone he'd given Cassie was sending out a distress signal, its magic pulsing with an alarm that only he could feel. Something was wrong. Not with the stone, but with her.

"Alexander?" Nikolai's voice came through the communications system, sounding distant beneath the roaring in his ears. "We've identified a potential debris field at the coordinates you suggested."

Alexander barely registered the words. The connection to the stone had suddenly intensified, then wavered alarmingly, like a heartbeat growing erratic.

"Sir?" One of the technicians looked up from his monitoring station, concern etching his features. "Are you alright?"

Alexander gripped the edge of the map table, his knuckles whitening. "Get me Elise. Now."

The command in his voice sent the technicians scrambling. Within seconds, Elise's face appeared on the main communication screen, her expression perfectly composed as always.

"Alexander, we're in the middle of preparations for the High Coven delegation. This had better be good."

"Something's happened to Cassie," he interrupted, the formality between them dissolving under his urgency. "I can feel it."

Elise's mask of composure slipped momentarily. "What do you mean, you can 'feel' it?"

"The witch stone I gave her, it's connected to me. It's been activated." He straightened, already moving toward the door. "I need to see her, immediately." Alexander knew this was unusual and breaking protocol. Yet he had to see her, and all the logic he had practiced over the past few centuries could be damned. There was nothing logical about how he was feeling at this moment.

"That won't be necessary," Elise replied, her voice taking on a careful neutrality that instantly heightened his suspicion. "Miss Marlow experienced a minor incident, but Dr. Levin is attending to her now. Everything is under control."

"What incident?" Alexander demanded, freezing mid-stride.

Elise hesitated, something she rarely did. "She attempted to escape. During the... restraint process, she sustained a head injury."

The temperature in the room seemed to drop several degrees as Alexander's expression darkened. "How severe?"

"Dr. Levin assures me it's not life-threatening. Her vampire side is already accelerating the healing process."

Alexander turned to the senior technician. "Nikolai will keep you updated. I'll return once I've assessed this new situation."

"Alexander," Elise's voice sharpened. "The King explicitly ordered you to coordinate the search effort. Finding Claire Marlow and Sam remains your priority."

"Nikolai can handle the search coordination temporarily," Alexander replied, his tone leaving no room for argument. "I'll return once I've assessed the situation personally."

It should bother him that he could so quickly and easily abandon his responsibility. He didn't even hesitate, and that should cause him to pause and ask himself why. Why was he abandoning his duty, as second in command, for someone he barely knew?

Before Elise could object further, he cut the communication link. The technicians kept their eyes carefully averted, busying themselves with their tasks as Alexander strode from the room, his footsteps echoing like thunder against the marble floor.

Within moments, he had marched down the extended corridor toward the compound's private living areas.

As darkness descended, more vampires emerged and became visible. Alexander disregarded them in his urgency, and they swiftly cleared from his path. Approaching the residential section, he veered toward the stairwell, ascending the stone steps three at a time. The guards stationed outside the chamber where Cassie was snapped to attention as he approached, their expressions carefully neutral.

"Open the door," he demanded without preamble.

"Sir, Miss Marlow is receiving medical attention, and Dr. Levin has instructed us to prevent any visitors from entering," one of the guards responded.

"Do you take your orders from Dr. Levin or me?" Alexander didn't wait for a reply. He pushed open the door and entered.

The sitting room was empty, but voices drifted from the bedroom. Alexander moved silently across the space, his senses heightened by concern. Through the partially open bedroom door, he could see Dr. Levin, a vampire turned in his sixties during the Civil War era, who had been a field surgeon, bending over the bed where Cassie lay motionless.

"The fracture is already knitting," Levin was saying to someone out of Alexander's line of sight. "Remarkable regenerative capacity, especially for one so young. If she were fully vampire, I'd estimate her at least a century old based on healing rate alone."

Alexander pushed the door open fully, causing both Levin and his security chief, Marcus, who reported directly to him, to turn sharply.

"Alexander," Levin straightened, his expression betraying mild surprise. "We weren't expecting you."

Alexander barely acknowledged him, his attention fixed on Cassie. She lay pale against the dark sheets, her auburn hair spread across his pillow like spilled wine. She was still, too still. She was full of fire and determination, and her being in this position felt wrong. A bruise darkened the side of her face, though even as he watched, the edges were fading from purple to yellowish-green, healing at an accelerated rate. Her breathing was steady but shallow.

"What happened?" he asked, his voice dangerously quiet.

Marcus stepped forward. "She broke the wards on her window, something that should have been impossible. By the time we discovered her absence, she had already made it to the courtyard. We attempted to contain her without force, but she... resisted."

"She fought like someone with decades of combat training," another guard added from the doorway, rubbing his arm. "Witch-fire and vampire strength combined. We've never seen anything like it."

"And the head injury?" Alexander moved closer to the bed, noting the dried blood that still matted some of her hair despite attempts to clean it.

"During the struggle, she fell backward against the fountain rim," Marcus explained, his tone carefully professional. "It was accidental. We tried to catch her, but she moved too quickly."

Alexander's jaw tightened as he reached out, gently brushing a strand of hair from Cassie's face. Her skin was cool to the touch, but not with the alarming chill of severe vampire injury. "Why is she unconscious if she's healing?" He would never forgive himself if she didn't wake.

"I administered a mild sedative, one that should have worked immediately, but apparently her dual nature countered it, so I had to increase the dose, and it has caused her to be out longer than expected," Dr. Levin replied, closing his medical bag. "More for her comfort than necessity. The healing process can be... uncomfortable, especially for one unaccustomed to vampire recovery. She should wake within the hour."

"I want her transferred to my quarters immediately," Alexander ordered, his eyes still on Cassie's face.

Marcus and Levin exchanged a surprised glance.

"The security wards here aren't designed for someone like her," Alexander explained. "Given her unique abilities, we need something stronger. My quarters have the most sophisticated protection systems in the compound, after the King's own."

He told himself this was about her safety. Not about him claiming her, or wanting her to be close to him. But deep down, he knew it was about those things.

They hesitated, and Alexander's temper flared. "Leave us. I'll personally move her," he ordered, his tone allowing no argument. "All of you. I'll call if her condition changes."

The guards filed out silently. Dr. Levin lingered a moment longer, his experienced eyes assessing Alexander with clinical detachment.

"The head injury would have killed a human instantly," he said quietly. "Even a full witch would likely have suffered permanent damage. Her hybrid nature saved her life, but she'll be disoriented when she wakes. Possibly agitated."

Alexander nodded once, acknowledging the warning. "I'll handle it."

When the door closed behind Levin, Alexander pulled a chair to Cassie's bedside and sat, studying her with an intensity that would have unsettled most beings. In repose, with the fierce determination and defiance temporarily erased from her features, she looked younger and more vulnerable. The bruising on her temple had already faded to a faint yellow, barely visible against her pale skin.

He reached out, carefully taking her hand. The witch stone was clutched in her palm, its surface warm despite her cool skin. The moment he touched it, the connection between them strengthened. He could sense her more clearly now. The steady rhythm of her heartbeat, the swirling currents of her unconscious mind as it worked to heal her body.

"You are full of surprises, Cassie Marlow," he murmured, his thumb tracing small circles on the back of her hand. "Breaking wards that should have contained creatures ten times your age. Fighting off trained security guards. What else are you capable of?"

Her eyelids fluttered slightly at the sound of his voice, though she didn't wake. Alexander continued to hold her hand, finding unexpected comfort in the simple contact. The pull he felt toward her defied logical explanation. Over the course of many centuries, he'd never experienced anything like it. This sense of recognition, of connection that transcended their brief acquaintance.

Calim's words echoed in his mind: *A mate, perhaps?*

Yet as he sat beside her, watching the steady rise and fall of her chest, Alexander couldn't deny the protective instinct surging through him. The desperate need to ensure her safety that had pulled him from his duties, driving him back to the compound against all logic and protocol.

He reached out, gently brushing his fingertips across her forehead, tracing the fading bruise. Her skin was warming now, another sign of her rapid healing. The contact sent a jolt of awareness through him, like static electricity but deeper, more resonant.

"What are you doing to me?" he whispered, more to himself than to her.

He gathered her delicately into his embrace, one arm supporting her shoulders and the other cradling beneath her knees. Her weight felt almost insubstantial against his vampire strength, yet he took extraordinary care, mindful of her injuries. Carrying her against his chest, he could feel the subtle warmth of her body seeping through the thin fabric of her clothing, a stark contrast to his own cooler temperature. He moved to the door and pushed it open while maintaining his careful hold, ensuring her head didn't loll uncomfortably against his arm.

In his lifetime, and that of his immortal years as a vampire, he'd carried countless bodies. Some lifeless, some companions, but he'd never felt the weight of them press upon him like now. Carrying her felt immeasurably more heavy, in that it felt like he was carrying his future.

He proceeded down the corridor with measured steps, his footfalls nearly silent on the polished floor. Then he made his way down the stairwell, his movements fluid and controlled despite Cassie's weight. At the landing, he veered right and continued along the hallway, passing several unmarked doors until he reached the heavy oak doorway of his personal rooms, a sanctuary he rarely invited others into.

Upon entering, he crossed the spacious living area with its minimalist furnishings, a reflection of his practical nature and centuries of learning to travel light. The bedroom beyond was similarly austere but comfortable, dominated by a large bed with dark linens. With extraordinary gentleness, he placed Cassie onto his mattress, carefully arranging her limbs in what he hoped was a comfortable position before stepping back to assess her condition.

To his surprise, Cassie stirred, her eyelids fluttering again before slowly opening. Her eyes were unfocused at first, clouded with confusion as she tried to orient herself. Then her gaze found his face, and awareness dawned.

"Alexander?" Her voice was raspy, uncertain.

"I'm here," he replied, instinctively tightening his hold on her hand. "You're safe."

Cassie blinked several times, as if trying to clear her vision. "Where am I?"

"My quarters," Alexander explained. "You were injured during your escape attempt. I brought you here because the security is better."

Memory flooded back into her eyes, followed quickly by anger. Her vulnerability and lack of control made her susceptible, and waking up in unfamiliar surroundings terrified her. She tried to sit up, only to wince as the movement caused pain. Alexander placed a gentle but firm hand on her shoulder, easing her back against the pillows. His calm, composed demeanor made it worse.

"Careful. Your body is still healing."

"Claire," she said, her voice stronger now, edged with determination. "I need to find Claire. That's why I was trying to leave."

"I know." Alexander's tone softened. "But nearly killing yourself won't help her."

Cassie's eyes narrowed. "I thought you were supposed to be leading the search for her. Why are you here instead?"

It was a fair question, one Alexander wasn't entirely sure how to answer. The truth, that he'd sensed her distress through the witch stone and abandoned his post to rush to her side, seemed too revealing, too vulnerable.

"I felt the stone activate," he said finally, nodding toward her hand where she still clutched it. "It's connected to me. I knew something was wrong." He almost lied to her, told her it was only the stone and not his raw, instinctual desire to ensure she was unharmed.

Surprise flickered across her face, followed by understanding as she looked down at the stone in her palm. "You didn't mention that part when you gave it to me."

"It didn't seem relevant at the time."

"So it's what, a tracking device? A way to spy on me?" There was no accusation in her tone, just tired curiosity.

"It's a protection talisman," Alexander corrected. "The connection works both ways. You can use it to call for help if you're in danger. It was a gift from my grandmother long ago."

Cassie studied him for a long moment. "You came back because you thought I was in danger?"

"You were in danger. You fractured your skull."

She wanted to believe that was the reason, but she was afraid to trust that he was worried about her. She was their prisoner, and he needed to ensure she was safe, and nothing more. She wanted it to be more, but the desire caused confusion and she didn't want to trust herself when she couldn't even control herself right now.

"But I'm healing," she countered, reaching up to touch her temple where the bruise had almost completely faded. "You could have stayed with the search team. Finding Claire should be the priority."

Alexander leaned back slightly, creating distance between them as he tried to sort through his own conflicted thoughts. "Nikolai is perfectly capable of coordinating the search temporarily. I'll return once I'm sure you're stable."

"I'm fine," Cassie insisted, though the strain in her voice betrayed her. "Just a headache."

"A headache from a skull fracture that would have killed a human instantly," Alexander pointed out. "Your hybrid nature is the only reason you're alive, much less conscious right now."

This information gave her pause. She closed her eyes briefly, as if taking internal inventory of her injuries. When she opened them again, there was a new wariness in her expression.

"The security guards," she said. "Did I hurt any of them badly?"

Alexander took a few moments before he responded to her. Cassie's cheeks heated, and she resisted the urge to squirm, and hang her head in shame. She had hurt more people.

"A few dislocated joints, some minor burns from your witch-fire. Nothing permanent. They are already healing, too." He tilted his head, studying her. "You're concerned about them? The vampires who were keeping you prisoner?"

Cassie shifted uncomfortably against the pillows. "I don't want to hurt people. I just want to find my sister." Her voice caught slightly on the last word, betraying the emotion she was trying to contain.

Alexander felt something twist in his chest at her obvious distress. Without thinking, he reached out, brushing a strand of hair from her face. "We will find her, Cassie. I promise you that."

She caught his wrist, her grip surprisingly strong given her condition. "Don't make promises you can't keep."

Their eyes locked, and for a moment, everything else seemed to fade away: the room, the compound, the complicated politics swirling around them. Alexander was acutely aware of the warmth of her touch, the slight tremble in her fingers, the faint scent of herbs and earth that clung to her despite everything.

"I don't," he said softly.

Something shifted in Cassie's expression, a subtle softening around her eyes. She released his wrist slowly, her fingertips trailing across his skin in a way that sent an unexpected current of awareness through him.

"Why am I in your room?" she asked, changing the subject. "There must be medical facilities here."

Alexander hesitated, unsure how much to reveal. "The security systems here are tailored to my specific requirements. Given your demonstrated abilities, I thought it would be more appropriate."

"In other words, a better prison," Cassie concluded, a hint of bitter amusement coloring her voice.

"With good reason, it seems. You broke through wards that should have been impenetrable for someone your age." Alexander couldn't quite keep the admiration from his tone. "How did you do it?"

Cassie shrugged, then winced at the movement. "I don't know, exactly. I just... felt the structure of the magic and pushed against it differently than it was designed to resist. Like finding a weak spot in a plant cell wall."

Her botanical analogy was unexpectedly apt. Alexander had never considered magical barriers in such terms, but it made sense. All structures had inherent weaknesses if approached from the right angle.

"You continue to surprise me, Cassie Marlow," he said, echoing his earlier thought.

A faint smile touched her lips, the first he'd seen since her awakening. "Good. I'd hate to be predictable while being kidnapped and held against my will."

Despite the gravity of the situation, Alexander found himself returning her smile. "You're not a prisoner. You're a guest of significance."

"A guest of significance," she mimicked, rolling her eyes. "So you keep saying. Yet here I am, locked in a room with magical barriers, unable to leave."

"For your own protection," he reminded her, "as your recent injury demonstrates."

"I wouldn't need protection if I weren't here in the first place," she countered, though without the heat he might have expected. She seemed too tired for real anger.

Alexander studied her for a moment, noting the fatigue that shadowed her eyes despite her rapid healing. "You should rest more. Your body is still recovering."

"I've rested enough," Cassie insisted, pushing herself up to a sitting position with visible effort. "I want to know what's being done to find Claire. Real details, not vague reassurances." Each moment she rested, Claire might be spending those moments experiencing something worse. Her request wasn't simply demanding details, it was desperation for her sister. If she wasn't focusing on action finding her, she wouldn't be able to hold it together. She didn't want to lose control again.

Alexander recognized the determination in her expression, the same unyielding resolve he'd seen in her from the beginning. She wouldn't be put off with platitudes or empty assurances and promises.

"Nikolai is coordinating three search vessels from aboard the Artemis," he explained, his tone shifting to something more professional. "They're focusing on the area where Sam's yacht was last detected, expanding outward in a standard search pattern. We've also deployed aerial reconnaissance and are monitoring all communication channels for any sign of them."

Cassie absorbed this information with a small nod. "What about the witches? Could they have taken Claire?"

It was the question Alexander had been wrestling with since Sam's disappearance. "It's possible. The magical storm that coincided with their last communication bears hallmarks of witch weather manipulation. But if the High Coven Council was involved, they wouldn't have requested a diplomatic meeting afterward."

"Unless it's a trap," Cassie suggested.

"Perhaps. But that would be an extreme escalation, even for them." Alexander leaned forward slightly. "The King is taking their request seriously. A delegation is expected tomorrow."

This caught Cassie's attention. "Witches are coming here? To Vancouver?"

"Under diplomatic protection, yes. To discuss matters of mutual concern regarding certain individuals recently transported from witch territory.'"

Understanding dawned in her eyes. "They mean Claire and me."

"So it would seem."

Cassie fell silent, processing this new information. Alexander could almost see the calculations happening behind her eyes, the strategic assessment of what this might mean for her and her sister.

"I want to be there," she said finally. "When they arrive."

Alexander had anticipated this request. "That's not my decision to make. The King will determine who attends the diplomatic meeting."

"Then I want to speak to the King," Cassie insisted, her voice strengthening. "These witches might know something about Claire. They might even be responsible for what happened to her. I need to be there."

Cassie surprised herself with her bold demand. She was in no position to be demanding concessions. Yet she wouldn't back down.

Before Alexander could respond, a soft knock at the door interrupted them. He rose smoothly, moving to answer it with vampire speed that still seemed to startle Cassie slightly.

One of the compound's messengers stood in the hallway, his expression carefully neutral. "Sir, the King has requested an update. He requests your presence in the map room immediately." The messenger's eyes flickered briefly to the bed where Cassie sat. "Alone."

Alexander nodded once, dismissing the messenger before turning back to Cassie. "I need to go."

"To meet with the King? I need to see him." She immediately tried to stand, only to sway dangerously as her legs threatened to give way beneath her. Alexander was at her side instantly, steadying her with a hand at her elbow.

"You're not fully recovered," he said firmly. "You need to stay here and rest."

"But..."

"I'll speak to the King about your request," he promised, guiding her back to sit on the edge of the bed. "But you won't help anyone by collapsing in the middle of everything that is happening."

Frustration flashed across her face, but she didn't argue further. Instead, she looked up at him with an intensity that made something in his chest tighten. "Tell him I need to be there. Tell him Claire is my sister, and I have a right to know what happened to her. And I need to see him. I don't know why. I just feel that I really need to see and meet him." Cassie didn't feel a curiosity drawing her towards the king. It was something deeper, unexplainable. She had a primal draw, like he held the key to her future.

Alexander hesitated, almost saying more, then nodded. "I'll discuss it with him."

As he turned to leave, Cassie's voice stopped him at the door. "Alexander?"

He looked back, finding her watching him with an unreadable expression.

Cassie swallowed. She wanted to thank him, but she didn't want to seem ungrateful. None of this was easy for her, and thanking her captor felt unnatural.

"Thank you," she said quietly. "For coming back when you felt I was in danger."

The simple gratitude caught him off guard, warming something inside him that had been cold for centuries. "Rest," he said softly. "I'll return when I can."

As he closed the door behind him, Alexander tried to ignore the strange reluctance he felt at leaving her. He had duties to attend to, responsibilities that extended far beyond one hybrid woman, no matter how intriguing she might be. The king would be waiting, and he had responsibilities but all he wanted was to feel her touch, to be with her. It made him feel uncomfortable, uncertain. That was unsettling.

Yet as he made his way toward the map room, he found his thoughts returning to the image of Cassie sitting on his bed, her blue eyes fixed on his with that peculiar intensity. The witch stone had created a connection between them, but Alexander was beginning to suspect that something deeper, something more primal, had been awakened as well.

A mating bond? The possibility both thrilled and terrified him. In all his centuries of existence, he'd never expected to find a mate, certainly not one who challenged every assumption he'd ever held about witches, vampires, and the boundaries between them.

Straightening his shoulders, Alexander pushed these thoughts aside as he approached the map room. Whatever was developing between him and Cassie Marlow would have to wait. For now, finding Claire and dealing with the witch delegation took priority.

But even as he prepared to face his king, Alexander could still feel the subtle pulse of the witch stone's connection, tethering him to Cassie in ways he was only beginning to understand.

Chapter Twelve

Cassie paced the confines of Alexander's quarters, feeling stronger with each passing minute. The sedative had worn off completely, and the throbbing in her head had subsided to a dull ache. Her vampire side continued to amaze her. Injuries that should have kept her bedridden for weeks were healing before her eyes.

A soft knock at the door, similar to the one received earlier that pulled Alexander away, interrupted her thoughts. She tensed, expecting guards, but instead, a young vampire woman entered carrying a tray of food and fresh clothing. The tray contained a goblet of red liquid, fresh-sliced beets, and parsnips.

"Miss Marlow? I've been instructed to prepare you for an audience with the King."

Cassie's heart leaped. "Alexander spoke to him?"

"Yes, miss. The King has requested your presence." The woman set down the tray and gestured to the bathroom. "Perhaps you'd like to freshen up first?"

Thirty minutes, a shower, and yet another clothing change later, Cassie followed her silent escort through the labyrinthine corridors of the vampire stronghold. She'd changed into the provided clothes, which included dark tailored pants and a deep green blouse that complemented her auburn hair. The soft soles of the black penny loafers muffled her steps. She didn't know how the vampires kept getting her sizes correct, but she could become accustomed to this. Her nerves hummed with anticipation as they approached a set of imposing double doors. Cassie noticed these doors had no carvings.

"Well," she mused, "they sure missed an opportunity here to ramp up the ornate."

"Pardon me, miss?" The young woman at her side inquired.

"Oh, it's nothing," Cassie said with a dismissive shrug.

"The King is waiting inside," her escort said, stepping aside.

Cassie took a deep breath and pushed the doors open. The room beyond was smaller than she'd expected, intimate rather than imposing. A fire crackled in a stone hearth, casting dancing shadows across polished wood panels. Maps and ancient texts lined the walls, and a large desk dominated one end of the room. It was another chamber her sister would adore exploring. Cassie longed to position vegetation on the vacant surfaces, to introduce some verdant elements.

But it was the figure standing by the window that captured her attention. He turned as she entered, and Cassie felt an inexplicable wave of recognition wash over her.

The Vampire King was not what she'd imagined. She'd expected someone cold and intimidating, but instead, she felt an immediate sense of... safety. It was disconcerting. He was tall with a powerful build, his bearing unmistakably military. His auburn hair, the exact shade as her own, was cropped short, and his dark eyes studied her with an intensity that seemed to pierce through all pretense.

"Cassandra Marlow," he said, his voice deep and resonant, carrying the faint echo of an accent she couldn't place. "At last, we meet."

Cassie stepped further into the room, drawn forward by something she couldn't name. "You know who I am."

"I know more than you might expect." He gestured to a chair. "Please, sit."

As she moved closer, Cassie noticed his posture had changed. A subtle stiffening, a stillness that went beyond even vampire norms. His eyes had widened slightly, fixed on her face with an expression of what appeared to be shock.

"Is something wrong?" she asked, stopping short of the offered chair.

The King seemed to collect himself, though the intensity of his gaze never wavered. "No. Nothing is wrong. Quite the opposite, in fact." He moved around the desk, approaching her with measured steps. "I've waited a very long time for this moment, though I never truly believed it would come."

Confusion rippled through Cassie. "I don't understand."

He stopped before her, close enough that she could see the fine lines around his eyes, not from age, for vampires didn't age, but from experiences etched into his immortal features.

"Look at me, Cassandra," he said softly. "Truly look. What do you see?"

Cassie studied him, noting the high cheekbones, the strong jaw, the particular way his brow furrowed. Features that seemed oddly familiar, like looking at a masculine version of parts of herself.

Her breath caught. "Your hair," she whispered. "It's the same as mine."

"Yes." A single word, heavy with meaning.

"That's not possible," she said, even as a deeper truth began to unfold within her. "My father was a night witch. My mother told me he was."

"It seems your mother told you what she believed would keep you safe." The King's voice gentled. "She wasn't completely incorrect.

Vampires do contain minimal magical abilities and exist as beings of darkness. Though that description hardly captures the essence of my true nature."

The room seemed to tilt around Cassie as understanding crashed through her. "You're saying... Wait, are you saying that you're my father?"

"I am Callimachus," he confirmed. "And yes, Cassandra, I'm your father. It's a surprise to me also, but I see and sense both your mother and me within you."

Cassie staggered back, gripping the edge of a nearby table for support. The revelation should have felt like a lie, an impossible claim, yet something deep within her recognized its truth immediately. She searched his features again, seeing now what she'd missed before. The same shape to their eyes, though hers were silver-blue like her mother's. The same slight asymmetry to their smiles. The same auburn hair that had always set her apart from her mother's vibrant red.

"How?" she managed. "Vampires can't have children. Everyone knows that."

"It appears everyone is wrong." Callimachus, her father, moved to pour two glasses of a deep red liquid from a crystal decanter. "Or rather, they're right about ordinary vampires. But I am not ordinary, Cassandra. I was made from one of the First, the most ancient among us."

He offered her a glass, which she accepted automatically, her mind still reeling. "The First?"

"The original vampires, created through means lost to history. The children of these beings possess unique properties, different abilities." He gestured again to the chair. "Please, sit. This is a lot to absorb."

This time, Cassie sank into the offered seat, her legs suddenly unsteady. "My mother never told me. All these years..."

"Catherine did what she thought was right." Callimachus took the seat opposite her. "Our relationship was short and complicated. I met her during a rare diplomatic exchange with the High Coven. She was brilliant, fierce, much like you. We fell in love despite knowing it was forbidden and would be brief. She came to visit again a couple of years later, and then I never saw her again. If I had known those two meetings had produced offspring, I would have burned the world down to find you and your sister."

"But you didn't," Cassie said, an accusation slipping into her tone.

"I would have shattered the agreement had I been aware. Nothing would have prevented me from reaching you, or your sister and mother. Nothing." Callimachus was resolute, and Cassie trusted his words.

Cassie closed her eyes, memories flooding back. Her mother's evasiveness whenever she asked about their father, the strange abilities she'd never been able to explain, the instinctive connection she'd felt to the night. It had left her exasperated with social integration and unable to appreciate daylight hours, but now she questioned whether she had simply been misplaced, rather than awkward, in many situations and experiences.

"All this time," she whispered. "All those years of feeling different, wrong somehow. I wasn't broken. I was just..."

"Half vampire," Callimachus finished. "Half of me."

When Cassie opened her eyes, she found him watching her with an expression she couldn't quite decipher, pride, perhaps, or wonder.

"That's why you sent Alexander and Sam to bring us here," she realized. "You knew who we were."

Cassie swallowed. Her chest felt tight, and she struggled to not feel overwhelmed. She wanted to be angry at her mom for keeping this from her, from not telling her who she really was. But it was hard to be angry now that she was away from home, and vulnerable. She really wanted her mom here with her, to help guide her through this and help find her sister. She didn't know if she was relieved to know who she was, or scared to find out that she was more than she grew up believing herself to be.

"I suspected once Alexander updated me and provided the name of your mother," he corrected. "There were rumors of possible vampires living in witch territory. I couldn't be certain until I saw you." His expression darkened. "I never intended for you and Claire to be separated for long. That was a security precaution that went wrong."

At the mention of her sister, Cassie leaned forward urgently. "Where is she? What happened to Sam's yacht?"

"We're doing everything possible to find them," Callimachus assured her. "Alexander is our best tracker, and I've committed all available resources to the search."

"I need to help," Cassie insisted. "She's my sister. I just found out about you, but she is the sister I have always had by my side, and I cannot lose her."

"You will help, but not by rushing headlong into danger." Callimachus's tone held the unmistakable authority of someone accustomed to command. "The witch delegation arriving tomorrow may provide answers. They've requested this meeting specifically to discuss you and Claire."

Cassie absorbed this, working through the implications. "They know what we are."

"They suspect, at minimum." He nodded. "Which means they may know something about Claire's disappearance."

Cassie studied the face of the man who claimed to be her father, who was her father, she corrected herself, feeling the truth of it in her bones. His features had settled into her memory now, familiar despite their newness, like pieces of a puzzle finally clicking into place.

"I want to be at that meeting," she said firmly.

Callimachus considered her for a long moment. "It could be dangerous. The witches may not react well to your presence."

"I don't care. Claire is out there somewhere, possibly in danger. I need to know what they know." Cassie straightened in her chair, channeling the determination that had always driven her. "Besides, I'm your daughter, aren't I? Shouldn't I start learning how this world works?"

A smile spread across Callimachus's face, pride evident in his expression. "You are indeed my daughter." He nodded once, decisively. "Very well. You will attend the meeting, but you will follow my lead. The diplomatic balance between vampires and witches is precarious at best."

"Thank you." Cassie hesitated, then asked the question that had been burning in her mind. "Did you, or rather, do you want children?"

Something akin to remorse flashed in Callimachus's eyes. "I've been careful not to desire what was beyond my reach. But yes, without question, yes."

"Would you genuinely have sought us out if you'd been aware of our existence earlier?" Cassie asked. She wasn't trying to come across as needy or fragile, but she wanted to understand.

"The treaty between vampires and witches is maintained through strict separation. My presence in witch territory would have been an act of war," Callimachus replied, definitive in his answer.

"But you're here now," Cassie pointed out. She wanted to believe him. She really did. For so long she'd sought out answers to who her father was, and now that he was here, next to her, she was uncertain. The ache that she had long carried deepened.

"Because circumstances have changed. Your existence has already been discovered. The secret it appears your mother worked so hard to protect is out." He leaned forward, his expression intensifying. "Now my priority is keeping you and Claire safe while we determine what this means for our world."

Cassie fell silent, processing everything. The father she'd never known sat before her, not the banished night witch her mother had described, but an ancient, powerful vampire king. It explained so much about herself that had never made sense before.

She wondered if Alexander knew. If he didn't, would that change how he viewed her? She was afraid he would look at her different, and she wasn't sure how to feel about that. Her connection to him had felt real, but what if it wasn't? What if he was only doing his duty?

"There's so much I don't understand," she admitted finally. "So much I need to learn."

"And you will," Callimachus promised. "But first, we must find your sister and ensure your safety. The meeting tomorrow is just the beginning."

Cassie nodded, a new determination settling over her. She might be in unfamiliar territory, surrounded by creatures she barely understood, but she was no longer lost. She had found a piece of herself in this ancient being with her auburn hair and commanding presence.

"I'm ready," she said simply. She didn't quite know what came next, but she was ready for it.

Callimachus studied her with those ancient eyes that had seen millennia pass. "Yes," he agreed, something like pride warming his voice. "I believe you are."

Chapter Thirteen

C assie returned to Alexander's quarters, her mind reeling from the encounter with Callimachus, her father. The revelation still felt surreal, yet undeniably true. Each step through the corridors seemed to carry her between worlds. She was stepping between the one she'd known her entire life and this new reality where she was the daughter of an ancient vampire king.

The guards posted outside Alexander's door nodded respectfully as she approached, their demeanor subtly different now. Word traveled fast among vampires, apparently. They stepped aside without comment, allowing her entry into the now-familiar space.

Once alone, Cassie moved to the window, watching the night unfold in Vancouver. The city lights sparkled against the night sky, beautiful and foreign. She pressed her palm against the cool glass, grounding herself in the physical sensation while her thoughts whirled chaotically. The location of the compound gave a breathtaking view of the world outside.

The room was the same one she'd left not too long ago, but she wasn't the same person that returned to it. It was unnerving to be in the same space, yet to feel like it was completely different because she was.

"A vampire king," she whispered to her reflection. She looked far more composed in the mirror image looking back at her than she felt. "My father is a vampire king."

She began methodically searching the room, opening drawers and checking shelves. Alexander's quarters were surprisingly minimalist for someone who had lived for centuries. There were only a few personal items. Everything was arranged with precision. No photos, no mementos, just practical necessities and a small collection of books.

In the desk drawer, she found what she was looking for: a sleek smartphone, likely a backup. She grabbed it, fingers trembling slightly as she powered it on. The screen illuminated, revealing a lock pattern.

"Damn it," she muttered, trying a few simple patterns without success. The phone was more than just a phone. It was a lifeline and she couldn't access it.

The sound of the door opening made her freeze, the phone still clutched in her hand. She turned to find Alexander watching her from the doorway, his expression unreadable.

"Looking for something?" he asked, closing the door behind him.

Cassie didn't bother hiding the phone. "I need to call my mother."

Alexander's eyes flickered to the device, then back to her face. "The yacht has been found."

The phone suddenly felt insignificant. "Claire? Is she okay?"

"The yacht was empty," he said quickly. "Badly damaged but not sunk. The life raft is missing."

Cassie's knees weakened with a mixture of relief and renewed anxiety. She sank onto the edge of the bed. "So they abandoned ship? They could still be alive?"

"It's a strong possibility." Alexander moved further into the room, maintaining a respectful distance. "We're widening the search area, looking for the life raft. Every available resource has been deployed."

"I need to be out there helping," Cassie said, rising again. "Not sitting here uselessly."

"You're far from useless." Alexander gestured to the phone she still held. "Your mother might indeed have valuable information. Though I doubt my phone would be much help without the password or my fingerprint."

Cassie glanced down at the device, then set it aside with a frustrated sigh. "I just needed to do something. Claire's out there somewhere, maybe hurt, definitely scared. I'm here safe, and it doesn't seem right."

"We will find her," Alexander assured her, his voice gentler than she'd heard before. "Sam is resourceful and well-trained. If they made it to the life raft, he would know how to survive until rescue arrives. He's not going to let anything happen to your sister."

Cassie nodded, trying to take comfort in his words. She paced the length of the room, energy thrumming through her despite the minor, lingering effects of her injury.

"I met with the King," she said abruptly.

Alexander went still. "I know."

"He's my father." The words still felt strange on her tongue, both foreign and familiar simultaneously.

"Yes."

Cassie stopped pacing, turning to face him fully. "You knew? Before I did?"

"I suspected," Alexander admitted. "Calim shared his suspicions with me earlier today, though he wasn't certain until he saw you."

"Why didn't you tell me?"

"It wasn't my place." Alexander moved to the window, gazing out at the city lights. "Some truths need to be discovered, not delivered."

Cassie studied him, noting the tension in his shoulders, the careful way he held himself apart from her. "You're different now. Since learning who I am."

He didn't answer her right away.

"You're the daughter of my king," he replied simply.

"I'm still the same person I was yesterday." She stepped closer, challenging him with her proximity. "The same witch you kidnapped from her shop."

A flicker of something, amusement, perhaps, crossed his features. "You're far from the same and more than a witch. You've discovered who you are, where you come from. That changes a person."

"I suppose it does." Cassie ran her fingers through her hair, still damp from the shower she'd taken before meeting Callimachus. "I'm going to the meeting with the witch delegation also."

"Calim told me." Alexander turned from the window. "It's risky."

"So is breathing," she countered. "Besides, they might know something about Claire."

Alexander nodded, conceding the point. "Just follow your father's lead. The witches can be unpredictable when confronted with something that challenges their worldview."

"Like me." It wasn't a question.

"Like you," he confirmed.

They fell into silence, the space between them charged with unspoken thoughts. Cassie was acutely aware of his presence, the way he seemed to fill the room despite his stillness. There was something different about their dynamic now, something she couldn't quite name.

"Are you okay?" Alexander asked suddenly. "With everything. Learning about Calim being your father."

The question caught her off guard. She'd expected strategy discussions and plans for tomorrow's meeting, not personal concern.

"I don't know," she answered honestly. "It explains so much about my life, why I never fit in, why sunlight exhausts me, why I crave raw meat. But it also means my mother lied to me my entire life." She wrapped her arms around herself. "And now Claire is missing, and I can't even tell her what I've learned."

Alexander stepped closer, his movement hesitant, almost uncertain. "Your sister is resourceful. I saw that in the brief time I observed her before the operation."

"She is," Cassie agreed, a small smile touching her lips despite everything. "She's always been the practical one, the planner. She's also trusting and kind, and that makes me worry about her more, especially because she's my younger sister. We are so different. I'm the one who acts first and thinks later."

"Like jumping from a third-story window?" There was no judgment in his tone, only mild curiosity.

"That was a calculated risk."

"That nearly ended with your skull in pieces."

Cassie winced. "Fair point. But it worked until I was rudely interrupted."

To her surprise, Alexander chuckled, the sound warm and unexpected. "You are definitely Calim's daughter. He has the same determination."

The comparison to her newly discovered father sent a strange thrill through Cassie. She'd spent her entire life wondering about her paternal heritage, and now she had not just a name but a living connection to that mystery.

"Tell me about him," she requested, moving to sit on the edge of the bed. "What kind of king is he? What kind of man?"

Alexander considered the question, taking a seat in the chair across from her. "Calim is complex. He's ruled the Western Canadian territories for centuries with a combination of wisdom and strength. He values knowledge above all else, and collects it like others collect art or wealth."

"And as a person?"

"Fair but unyielding. Loyal to those who earn his trust. Merciless to those who betray it." Alexander's expression softened slightly. "He saved my life, not just by turning me but by giving me purpose when my human life ended on the battlefield."

Cassie absorbed this, trying to reconcile the powerful king with the man who had looked at her with such recognition, such pride. "He seemed pleased to learn I was his daughter."

"He was more than pleased," Alexander confirmed. "He was completely changed. I've been in his service for hundreds of years, and I've never witnessed him appear so luminous and full of optimism. Even though he is a King and a mentor, he's also become a close friend. It has been nice seeing this change."

A lump formed in Cassie's throat, unexpected emotion welling up. She'd spent so many years imagining her father as a distant figure, a night witch who'd abandoned them. The reality of Callimachus, powerful, ancient, yet seemingly genuine in his welcome, was overwhelming.

"We need to find Claire," she said, steering the conversation back to safer ground. "She's his daughter too. She deserves to know who she is."

Alexander nodded. "The search continues through the night. If they're out there, we'll find them."

"When," Cassie corrected firmly. "When we find them."

A small smile touched Alexander's lips. "When," he agreed.

Cassie's gaze fell on the phone she'd set aside. "I still need to talk to my mother. She has to know what's happening, that Claire is missing. And I have questions only she can answer."

"Understandable." Alexander studied her for a moment. "I'll see what can be arranged after tomorrow's meeting with the witch delegation."

"Thank you." The words felt inadequate for the unexpected ally he'd become, this vampire who'd kidnapped her just days ago and now sat across from her discussing her family with genuine concern.

Alexander rose, moving toward the door. "You should rest. Tomorrow will be challenging."

"Alexander," Cassie called as he reached for the handle. He paused, looking back at her. "Thank you. For everything you're doing to find Claire."

Something shifted in his expression, a softening around his eyes. "I made you a promise, Cassie. I intend to keep it."

The energy humming beneath her skin had been building for hours, a strange tingling sensation that demanded release. Her fingers twitched at her sides, and she could feel her heightened senses cataloging every small movement in the room, the slight shift of the curtains in the breeze, the almost imperceptible sound of footsteps several rooms away. "Do you have a training room or a workout room in this compound? I'm feeling a lot better, and I'd like to try out my new abilities and test them a bit. I don't want to get caught off guard again, and I feel restless," she said. She couldn't help Claire now, but she could be prepared.

Alexander's expression shifted to one of concern, his dark eyes studying her with the careful assessment of someone who had centuries of experience reading people. "Are you sure? You've gone through a lot very recently, and it might be better to rest and take it easy," he cautioned, leaning slightly against the doorframe. "The transition is still fresh, and pushing yourself too soon could have unpredictable consequences."

Cassie shook her head, pushing herself up from where she sat. The movement was faster, more fluid than she intended, and she found herself standing before she'd even fully processed the intention to rise. She needed to learn more about herself, because her strength didn't feel like it was hers yet. Once she learned more control, and what she was capable of, she might feel like she deserved the abilities that were developing. Right now, they felt unearned and chaotic.

"That's exactly why I need to do this," she insisted, running a hand through her auburn hair in frustration. "These new reflexes, this strength, it's all foreign to me. If I'm going to be any use in finding Claire, I need to understand what I'm capable of now. I can't afford to be surprised by my own body when it matters most."

Alexander examined her face, appearing to search for indications of fatigue and vulnerability. When Cassie felt the quiet had extended beyond comfort, he finally broke the silence. "I'll arrange for some exercise attire to be delivered to you, and I'll set up a training space. We should have a solid hour where I can coach you while simultaneously receiving updates on the search and supervising operations as necessary."

Cassie grinned, eager to test the limits of her capabilities and discover her new potential.

Alexander smirked wryly. "Why do I sense I'm going to wish I hadn't agreed to this?" He departed, pulling the door shut gently as he exited. Cassie spun around and performed a small celebration dance. She didn't necessarily want to dance. She wanted to hit something, do something more, but this was the next best thing. She was anxious to discover if she could surprise him, and perhaps even herself. The more she learned about herself, the better prepared she would be in the future.

Chapter Fourteen

A sharp knock at the door interrupted Cassie's thoughts. She opened it to find a middle-aged vampire woman standing in the hallway, her posture impeccable and expression neutral. She wore a knee-length black pencil skirt, a crisp white blouse, a tailored black blazer, and modest black pumps. Her hair was neatly secured in a tight bun.

"Miss Marlow," she said with a slight bow, "I've brought these for you." She extended a neatly folded stack of soft charcoal-colored exercise clothing, undergarments, black socks, and a pair of black running shoes balanced on top.

"Thank you," Cassie said, accepting the bundle. The fabric felt luxuriously soft against her fingers, lightweight but substantial.

"I'll wait outside while you change," the woman informed her. "Then I'll escort you to the training area."

Cassie nodded and closed the door. She quickly stripped off her current clothes and pulled on the exercise outfit. The pants fit snugly but comfortably around her waist and thighs, and the matching top was equally well-fitted. As she laced up the running shoes, she marveled at how perfectly everything fit.

"They didn't even ask my size," she muttered, flexing her foot inside the shoe. The fit was flawless, as if they'd been custom-made. She wondered if Alexander had guessed, or if vampires had some supernatural way of determining clothing sizes. Either possibility was slightly unnerving.

When she opened the door, energy sizzled through her in anticipation. The vampire woman was waiting as promised, her posture still perfect.

"This way, Miss Marlow."

Cassie followed her to an elevator she hadn't noticed before. They descended multiple floors, the display showing they were going deep beneath the compound. When the doors opened, they stepped into a long, tall hallway that seemed to stretch endlessly before them. The ceiling had to be at least twenty feet high, and the doors they passed were enormous, large enough to drive a semi-truck through.

"What's behind all these doors?" Cassie asked, curiosity getting the better of her.

"Various facilities," the woman replied vaguely. "Storage in some."

Cassie eyed the massive doors skeptically. Whatever they were storing must be enormous. She wondered if vampires hoarded artifacts from their long lives or perhaps kept more dangerous things locked away. The size of the doors suggested possibilities both fascinating and terrifying.

Finally, they stopped before one of the double doors. The woman placed her hand on a biometric scanner beside the entrance. A soft blue light swept beneath her palm, and the massive doors began to slide open with a whisper-quiet hydraulic hiss.

Cassie's jaw dropped as she took in the space beyond. "Gymnasium" seemed an inadequate description. The room was the size of an airplane hangar, with a ceiling that soared at least forty feet above them. The floor was covered in some kind of specialized material, not quite rubber, not quite wood, that seemed designed to absorb impact.

Various training equipment lined the walls, from weights to climbing ropes to what looked like specialized combat gear.

In the center of the vast space stood Alexander, dressed in fitted black training clothes similar to her own. He was stretching his arm across his chest, his movements fluid and precise. Despite the distance, he had to be at least fifty yards away. Cassie could see him clearly, another reminder of her enhanced vision.

Alexander noticed their arrival and pointed toward the wall beside the entrance. Cassie followed his gesture to see a table set up near the door, where the woman who had escorted her was now pouring a dark red liquid from a crystal pitcher into a glass.

"Here," the woman said, offering the glass to Cassie. "A little nourishment before training is recommended."

Cassie accepted the glass and took a tentative sip. The moment the liquid touched her tongue, she gagged, nearly spitting it out. The unmistakable metallic taste of blood filled her mouth.

"Don't worry," the woman said calmly, "it's not human blood."

Cassie stared at the glass with horror and fascination. "Why are you giving me this?"

"Alexander and your father would like to see if it helps nourish you and prevent energy depletion during the upcoming exercise," the woman explained matter-of-factly, as if offering someone blood was perfectly normal. Which, Cassie supposed, among vampires it probably was.

She glanced across the massive gymnasium to where Alexander waited, watching her. The distance between them emphasized the sheer size of the room. It was like standing at one end of a football field and trying to have a conversation with someone at the opposite goal line.

The room was brightly lit, almost painfully so to Cassie's sensitive eyes. She wondered if this was intentional, a way to test her abilities under less-than-ideal conditions. The vampire side of her nature preferred dim lights, but here she would need to function under these harsh lights.

Cassie looked back at the glass in her hand. The blood was dark, almost black in this light. Her stomach turned at the thought of drinking it, yet something deeper, more primal, stirred within her. It was a hunger she'd always suppressed, always denied.

Taking a deep breath, she raised the glass to her lips again and forced herself to take a proper swallow. This time, she was prepared for the taste. It slid down her throat, and to her surprise, a pleasant warmth began to spread through her body almost immediately. The effect was similar to the raw meat she'd always craved, but more intense, more direct.

"Animal?" she asked, gesturing to the glass.

"Deer," the woman confirmed. "Fresh from this morning's hunt."

Cassie nodded and took another sip. It was still revolting on some level, but the effect was undeniable. The lingering fatigue from her injury seemed to recede further with each swallow, replaced by growing senses of strength and alertness.

By the time she finished the glass, Cassie felt more energized than she had since before her kidnapping. Her senses seemed sharper, and her body felt lighter, as if the blood had awakened something long dormant.

"Thank you," she said, handing the empty glass back to the woman.

"You're welcome, Miss Marlow. Alexander will take it from here." With that, the woman exited, the massive doors sliding closed behind her.

Cassie turned her attention to the center of the gymnasium where Alexander waited. The distance between them seemed like both a challenge and an opportunity. She wanted to test just how fast she could move with this new energy coursing through her veins.

Without consciously deciding to do so, Cassie found herself sprinting across the gymnasium floor. The speed took her breath away. She was moving faster than she ever had before, covering ground at a rate that should have been impossible. The air rushed past her face as her feet barely seemed to touch the floor.

She came to a stop in front of Alexander, not even winded despite having just sprinted what had to be at least fifty yards in seconds.

Alexander's eyebrows rose slightly, the only indication of his surprise. "I see the blood helped."

"That was," Cassie searched for words, "incredible. I've never moved that fast before."

"It's one of the basic vampire abilities," Alexander explained. "Enhanced speed, strength, and senses. The blood accelerates and amplifies these traits, especially in younger vampires."

"What else can I do?" Cassie asked, unable to keep the excitement from her voice. Despite the circumstances that had brought her here, there was something exhilarating about discovering these new capabilities.

"That's what we're here to find out." Alexander gestured to the space around them. "Your dual nature makes you unique. You have abilities from both bloodlines, but they may manifest differently than they would in a pure vampire or witch."

Cassie nodded, flexing her fingers as energy continued to hum through her veins. "Where do we start?"

"Basic physical capabilities," Alexander said, moving toward an open area of the floor. "Speed, strength, agility. Then we can explore how your witch abilities might interact with your vampire nature."

For the next hour, Cassie pushed her body to limits she'd never imagined possible. She sprinted across the gymnasium in seconds, lifted weights that should have been impossible for someone her size, and jumped heights that left her momentarily breathless. Alexander proved to be a patient but demanding instructor, pushing her to try more, reach further, and tap deeper into the well of power within her.

"Your reflexes are exceptional," he noted after she'd completed a complex agility course he'd set up. "Even by vampire standards."

Cassie grinned, wiping sweat from her brow. Despite the exertion, she didn't feel tired. If anything, the activity left her more energized with each new discovery.

"Now," Alexander said, moving to stand across from her, "let's see how you handle yourself in a controlled combat situation."

Cassie's smile faltered slightly. "You want me to fight you?"

"I want you to try," he corrected, a hint of challenge in his voice. "You've already proven you can hold your own in a real confrontation. Now let's see what you can do when you're not running on pure instinct and adrenaline."

Cassie took a fighting stance, trying to remember the evening self-defense classes she'd taken in college. Alexander circled her slowly, his movements predatory yet controlled.

"Don't think too much," he advised. "Your body knows what to do. Trust your instincts."

He lunged, his movement so fast it was almost a blur. Cassie reacted without thinking, sidestepping his attack with supernatural speed. Alexander pivoted instantly, coming at her from a different angle. This time, she blocked his arm with her forearm, the impact sending a jolt through her body.

"Excellent form," he said approvingly, not breaking his rhythm as he continued his relentless assault, his movements fluid and purposeful, each strike calculated to test her newfound reflexes. "But remember to keep your guard up while counterattacking."

They moved across the floor in a deadly dance, Alexander attacking, Cassie defending. At first, she was purely reactive, responding to his movements rather than initiating her own. But as the session continued, something shifted. She began to anticipate his attacks, to see openings in his defense. Her body moved with increasing confidence, vampire strength merging with witch instinct in a way that felt both foreign and natural.

When she finally managed to land a solid hit, catching Alexander in the shoulder with enough force to make him step back, surprise flashed across his face.

"You're a quick learner," he said, rubbing his shoulder.

"I have an excellent captor, I mean instructor," Cassie responded, failing to hide her pleased grin.

Alexander relaxed briefly, a glimmer of admiration and humor visible in his gaze. Then he attacked again, faster and harder than before. Cassie met his assault with growing confidence, no longer just defending but counterattacking, pushing him to work harder.

They were so engrossed in their training that neither noticed the massive doors sliding open, nor the figure that entered and stood watching them from the entrance.

It wasn't until Alexander had Cassie pinned briefly to the floor, only for her to use a burst of witch-fire to force him to release her, that a slow clapping echoed through the gymnasium.

Both of them froze, turning toward the sound. Callimachus stood by the entrance, an expression of undisguised pride on his face.

"Impressive," he said, his voice carrying easily across the vast space. "Most impressive."

Cassie scrambled to her feet, suddenly self-conscious. Alexander straightened beside her, his posture shifting subtly from combat instructor to royal guard.

"Your Majesty," he acknowledged with a slight bow. "We were just finishing."

"Don't stop on my account," Callimachus said, walking toward them with that fluid grace that Cassie now recognized in herself. "I came to see how my daughter's training was progressing. It appears Alexander has been an excellent instructor."

"She's a natural," Alexander said, and Cassie felt a strange warmth at the compliment.

"Of course she is," Callimachus replied, stopping before them. His eyes, so similar to Cassie's, studied her with unmistakable pride. "She's my daughter."

The simple declaration sent a thrill through Cassie. After a lifetime of wondering about her father, of feeling like half of her identity was missing, here he was, claiming her openly and proudly. The feeling of success she had sparring with Alexander was a rush that made her feel invincible. But the feeling faded fast. It was no use if she couldn't protect the ones she loved, while she was safe and they weren't.

"The witch delegation will arrive at noon," Callimachus continued, his tone shifting to something more formal. "I want both of you well-rested and prepared. This meeting could provide crucial information about Claire's whereabouts."

"Have there been any updates on the search?" Cassie asked, her momentary elation dimming at the thought of her missing sister.

"Debris has been sighted," Callimachus informed them, his expression grave. "We've narrowed the search area considerably. It's proving challenging, as it is in witch territory, near the islands off the coast of Washington."

Hope and fear warred within Cassie. The hope was that Claire and Sam had likely made it to shore somewhere, but it also meant they were still missing, possibly injured or worse.

"I need to be out there," she said, the words escaping before she could stop them.

"You need to be here," Callimachus countered firmly. "The witch delegation may have information we lack. Your presence could be crucial in extracting it."

Cassie wanted to argue, but she recognized the logic in his words. If the witches knew something about Claire, her best chance of helping her sister was to be at that meeting.

"I understand," she said finally. Admitting it hurt more than she had expected. She didn't want to be reasonable and understanding.

Calim inclined his head, pleased. "Excellent. Now, I think you two deserve some downtime. Dawn approaches rapidly, and we must be ready."

As they prepared to leave the gymnasium, Cassie caught Alexander watching her with an expression she couldn't quite decipher. There was respect there, certainly, but something else too, something that made her pulse quicken in a way that had nothing to do with their training session.

Whatever this evening brought, whatever challenges the witch delegation presented, Cassie felt more prepared to face them. She was no longer just Cassie Marlow, the strange witch who couldn't function in daylight. She was the daughter of Callimachus, Vampire King of Western Canada, and she was beginning to understand just what that meant. She followed Alexander out of the training area, her muscles pleasantly sore from the intense session. They walked in companionable silence through the corridor. The elevator ride up was quiet, the soft hum of machinery filling the space between them as Cassie tried not to notice how the enclosed space amplified his scent, something earthy and distinctly male that made her eyes dart away whenever they accidentally met his gaze.

When they reached his floor, Alexander led the way down a hallway toward his quarters. Cassie followed a few steps behind, her eyes tracing the broad set of his shoulders, the confident stride that spoke of centuries of existence. She observed the subtle way he moved, fluid yet powerful, like a predator completely at ease in his territory.

She sensed he was acutely aware of her scrutiny and was deliberately permitting it, perhaps even inviting it in his own understated way. The corners of his mouth occasionally twitched upward when she lingered too long on a particular feature, though he never turned back to catch her in the act. Something about him attracted her on a level she couldn't articulate properly. It wasn't merely his physical appearance, though that was certainly striking. It was a visceral, primal attraction that resonated in her very cells. A yearning of nature itself, as though some ancient part of her recognized something equally ancient in him.

The silence between them felt charged yet comfortable, like the air before a summer storm, electric with possibility but not threatening. Cassie found herself wondering what it would be like to touch him. The notion made her shiver, despite herself.

Chapter Fifteen

At the entrance to his quarters, Alexander swung the door wide and gestured for Cassie to step inside, his movements precise and controlled. The doorway framed his tall figure, the dim lighting of the room accentuating his hard lines.

"I'll have a change of clothing sent to you so you can shower and relax," Alexander said, his deep voice softening as he watched Cassie walk through. His gaze followed her every motion with meticulous scrutiny, his interest nearly ravenous.

Cassie wandered over to the couch, her fingers trailing along the back of a nearby chair. She lowered herself onto the couch's soft cushions, feeling vibrant and alert but disinclined to relax.

"I will return later to check on you," Alexander promised, his hand still resting on the door handle. A moment of hesitation crossed his normally stoic features, as though he wanted to say more but thought better of it. "Try to relax. You're safe here."

Cassie watched Alexander leave, the door closing behind him with a soft click that seemed to emphasize her isolation. She sank back against the pillows, marveling at her amplified healing abilities. She'd been hurt earlier but felt better than ever now. Being alone in Alexander's personal quarters felt strangely intimate, the space austere yet comfortable, reflecting his practical nature. She got up and went to the door, opening it just enough to poke her head out into the hall.

"Alexander?" she called out softly, just as his footsteps began to fade down the corridor. Cassie regretted calling out to him and quickly closed the door. She felt suddenly like a teenager, nervous around a first crush. It wasn't an easy feeling. She disliked how quickly she felt like she needed him. But the feeling that remained outweighed her uncertainty.

The footsteps paused, then returned. The door opened, and Alexander stood at the threshold, his expression questioning her intentions.

Cassie looked up at him for a moment, not sure what to say. This second-guessing of herself hadn't given her a lot of time to think about what to say if he came back.

"Do you have to leave right away?" Cassie asked, surprising herself with the request. "Could you stay, just for a little while?"

Alexander hesitated, his gaze flickering toward the corridor where duty called. "I have a team in operation, conducting a search-and-rescue effort. Although I've been maintaining contact with them, I ought to be present to supervise."

"I know," she said quickly. "It's just..." She gestured vaguely around the unfamiliar room. "I have so many questions, and I don't want to sit here full of restless energy, wondering and worrying about my sister." She returned to the couch and sank back into the cushions.

Something in her expression must have reached him because Alexander stepped back inside, closing the door quietly. "Others are capable while I'm away," he said, his voice softening slightly. "I have a little more time. My crew will contact me if there are any developments."

Relief washed through her. "Thank you."

Alexander moved to the desk across the room and pulled out the chair, sitting down with the fluid grace that marked all his movements. "What would you like to know?"

Cassie shifted restlessly against the cushions, pushing herself back up to a full sitting position. "I don't know precisely. I have all this restless energy, despite everything. I feel like I need to be active, not just sitting in a room questioning if my sister is alive or injured or something more terrible. When we were practicing, it distracted my thoughts from fretting about circumstances beyond my ability to control or change."

The raw honesty in her voice hung between them. Alexander's expression remained neutral, but something in his eyes softened.

"Is there anything that would help you feel more settled?" he asked. "I could have more food brought up if you're hungry."

"I'm not hungry," Cassie said, though she wasn't entirely sure. Everything felt unsettled, her emotions raw and her body still adjusting to its newly-awakened abilities.

She stood and crossed to the window, needing movement. The view outside showed the same manicured gardens she'd tried to escape through earlier, now bathed in moonlight. Somewhere beyond those gardens, beyond the city, Claire was out there. Lost. Possibly afraid. The thought made her chest ache.

"I hate feeling helpless," she admitted, her back to Alexander. "I've always been the one who takes action, who finds solutions. Now I'm just waiting. I don't think I'm very good at waiting."

She turned, crossed back toward the couch, and stopped at the small table where the witch stone rested. Picking it up, she approached him, intending to return it.

"Here," she said, extending her hand. "I should give this back to you."

As Alexander reached out to take it, their fingers brushed. The contact sent a jolt of electricity coursing through Cassie's entire body, a sensation so intense it made her gasp. It wasn't pain. It was something else entirely, a sudden awareness that seemed to awaken every cell in her body.

Alexander's eyes widened slightly, telling her he'd felt it too.

"I want to touch you," Cassie said, the words tumbling out before she could stop them. Maybe it was the wrong thing to say, but she pushed the feeling of doubt aside. So much that had occurred had been beyond her control, even the changes in herself. This was something that she wanted and could control. She wanted to touch him and wanted to let herself feel hope.

Alexander's expression tightened. "That's not a good idea."

Instead of backing away, Cassie took a step closer. The energy between them was palpable now, like static electricity but deeper, more primal. "Why not?"

"You've been through a traumatic experience," Alexander said, his voice carefully controlled. "Your emotions are heightened. Your body is still adjusting to its dual nature. This reaction... It's just biology."

"Is it?" Cassie challenged, taking another step forward. She was standing between his knees now, close enough that she could feel the coolness radiating from his immortal body. "It doesn't feel like just biology."

"Cassie." Her name was a warning on his lips.

She ignored it, reaching out to trace the line of his jaw with her fingertips. His skin was cool beneath her touch, but not unpleasantly so. She felt him tense, his control evident in every rigid muscle.

"You should stop," he said, though he made no move to pull away.

"I don't want to stop," she whispered.

For a moment, they remained frozen, Cassie standing between his legs, her fingers against his skin. Alexander was rigid with restraint. Then, with a movement too swift for her to track, he reached up and caught her hand, drawing her face down toward his.

Their lips met in a kiss that was anything but tentative. Heat exploded between them, a fire that seemed to consume all rational thought. Cassie stepped closer, deepening the kiss as her hands found his shoulders, then slid into his hair. Alexander's arms encircled her waist, pulling her closer until she was pressed against him, the contact sending waves of sensation through her body.

The kiss seemed to last forever, yet ended too soon. Alexander pulled back abruptly, his eyes darker than usual, his breathing uneven despite not needing to breathe.

"This is not a good idea," he repeated, though his hands still rested on her waist.

Cassie remained where she was, standing between his legs, her heart racing. "Why? Because I'm part witch? Because I'm the daughter of your king?"

"Because a lot has happened in a very short time," Alexander said, his voice rough. "Your entire world has been upended. You're in a strange place, surrounded by beings you barely understand. You're worried about your sister. Complicating matters further would be unwise."

Cassie leaned forward, resting her forehead against his. "Everything is already complicated. Maybe that's okay."

Alexander's hands tightened slightly on her waist, as if he was fighting with himself. Then, with a sudden decisiveness, he stood, sweeping her into his arms in one fluid motion. Before Cassie could process what was happening, he had crossed through the space to the adjoining room and was setting her gently on the bed.

"Are you sure about this?" he asked, his expression serious as he looked down at her.

Cassie wasn't confused. She wanted this. It was her choice. It might ruin everything later, but right now, she didn't care. She wanted this moment.

Cassie reached up, pulling him down for another kiss that answered his question more eloquently than words ever could. This time, Alexander didn't resist. His control, so carefully maintained for centuries, seemed to unravel beneath her touch.

Chapter Sixteen

Alexander lowered himself over her with controlled restraint, his body hovering just inches above hers. Cassie felt the coolness radiating from his skin, a delicious contrast to the heat building within her. She shivered slightly, and he caught the motion. His eyes, dark and intense, searched her face and let his gaze linger on her.

"You're shivering," he murmured, his voice deeper than she'd heard before.

"It's not fear," Cassie whispered, reaching up to trace the strong line of his jaw.

His hand caught hers, bringing her palm to his lips. The gentle press of his mouth against her sensitive skin sent shivers cascading through her body. When his eyes met hers again, they burned with a heat that took her breath.

"I'll be gentle," he promised, his thumb stroking across her wrist where her pulse raced beneath the skin.

Cassie looked up at him and held her breath for a moment. She could stop it all now, walk away and not complicate things between them. He wasn't taking, only offering, only waiting. The longer he held her, the more her resolve disappeared. His patience only made her want him more. She ignored the hesitation and lifted her head to capture his lips again.

The kiss deepened instantly, his restraint giving way to something more primal. His tongue swept into her mouth, claiming her with a thoroughness that caused her to moan. Her hands slid beneath his shirt, exploring the cool, hard planes of his back, marveling at the contrast between his marble-like exterior and the responsive way his muscles tensed beneath her touch.

Alexander broke the kiss to trail his lips along her jaw, down the sensitive column of her throat. His teeth grazed her skin, not breaking it, but the hint of danger in the gesture sent a thrill through her core. Her body arched instinctively, pressing against his.

"Alexander," she gasped, her fingers tangling in his hair.

He lifted his head, his eyes now glowing with an otherworldly light. "Say it again," he commanded softly.

"Alexander," she repeated, understanding intuitively that something about hearing his name on her lips affected him deeply.

With deliberate slowness, he began lifting her shirt, his fingers sure and steady despite the tension radiating from him. Each newly exposed inch of skin received his devoted attention, a brush of his fingertips, the press of his lips, the gentle scrape of teeth. By the time he'd pulled her shirt off, Cassie was writhing beneath him, her body humming with need, her lace-covered breasts rising and falling with each rapid breath. Alexander's gaze darkened further as he took in the sight of her.

"Beautiful," he murmured, tracing the edge of her bra with one finger, the light touch sending sparks across her skin.

Cassie reached for the hem of his shirt, tugging impatiently. "Your turn."

A smile touched his lips, not his usual controlled expression but something warmer, almost playful. He sat back on his heels, pulling the shirt over his head in one fluid motion.

Cassie's breath caught at the sight of him. His chest was broad and perfectly defined, like a sculpture brought to life. A few old scars marked his skin, remnants from his human life, she realized, preserved in his transformation. Without thinking, she reached out to trace one that curved across his ribs.

"Battle of Agincourt," he explained quietly, watching her face. "The mace wound that would have killed me if Calim hadn't found me."

Cassie leaned up, pressing her lips to the ancient scar. "I'm glad he found you."

Something shifted in Alexander's expression, a softening, a vulnerability she hadn't seen before. He lowered himself to her again, this kiss deeper, more consuming than the ones before. His weight settled partially against her, his body fitting perfectly against hers despite their differences in size.

His hands slid beneath her, finding the clasp of her bra with practiced ease. The garment loosened, and he drew it away, his eyes darkening at the sight of her bare breasts. When his mouth closed around one sensitive peak, Cassie cried out, her back arching off the bed.

"You're so responsive," he murmured against her skin, his voice tinged with wonder.

"Only with you," she admitted, though she had no way of knowing if that was true. It simply felt right, as if her body had been waiting for his touch specifically.

His hands skimmed down her sides, finding the waistband of her pants. He looked up, seeking permission, and Cassie nodded, lifting her hips to help as he slid the fabric down her legs. Her underwear followed, leaving her completely exposed to his gaze.

Alexander sat back, his eyes traveling the length of her body with such intensity that Cassie could almost feel it as a physical touch. "Perfect," he whispered.

His hands returned to her skin, starting at her ankles and working slowly upward, mapping every inch of her with reverent attention. When he reached her inner thighs, his touch grew even gentler, teasing the sensitive skin there until she was trembling with anticipation.

"Alexander, please," she gasped, beyond pride or patience.

"Please what?" he asked, his voice a low rumble that she felt more than heard.

"Touch me," she demanded, her piercing eyes meeting his dark ones.

A smile curved his lips. "I am touching you."

"You know what I mean," she said, frustration and desire making her voice sharper.

Instead of answering, he lowered his head, pressing a kiss to her inner thigh. His cool breath against her heated center made her shiver. Then his mouth was on her, his tongue finding the most sensitive part of her with unerring accuracy.

Cassie's cry echoed through the room as pleasure shot through her, sharp and overwhelming. Her hands fisted in the sheets, and she strained toward his mouth as he continued his intimate exploration. The way he touched her scattered her thoughts and melted her control.

When he slid one finger inside her, curling it in a way that made her see stars, Cassie felt herself rapidly approaching the edge. Her breathing grew ragged, her muscles tensing as the pressure built within her. It was almost too much, as if her body couldn't decide what to do. Every part of her was tense.

"Let go," Alexander murmured against her, the vibration of his voice adding another layer to the sensations overwhelming her. "I've got you."

His words, combined with a particularly clever movement of his tongue, sent her crashing over the edge. The pleasure was intense, sudden and all consuming. She wanted to cry out, but the intensity stole her voice. She uncoiled beneath him, boneless and gasping. Alexander stayed with her through it all, his touch gentling as the aftershocks rippled through her.

When she finally opened her eyes, he was watching her with an expression that made her heart stutter in her chest. Pride, desire, and something deeper, more complex that she couldn't name.

"You're still dressed," she said, her voice slightly hoarse.

"An oversight I intend to correct," he replied, standing to remove his remaining clothing.

Cassie propped herself up on her elbows, watching as he undressed with efficient grace. When he stood naked before her, she couldn't help but stare. He was magnificent, every inch of him perfectly proportioned, powerful without being bulky. His arousal was evident, impressive in its size and obvious readiness.

"Come here," she said softly, holding out her hand to him.

Alexander rejoined her on the bed, his cool skin a delicious contrast to her overheated body. He settled between her thighs, his weight supported on his forearms as he looked down at her.

"Are you certain?" he asked one last time, his control visibly strained but still intact.

In answer, Cassie wrapped her legs around his hips, drawing him closer until she could feel him pressing against her entrance. "Completely certain."

With agonizing slowness, Alexander pushed forward, entering her inch by careful inch. He filled her slowly, and the sensation sent ripples through her. As her body opened around him, she felt herself opening on a deeper emotional level too. When he was fully seated within her, they both paused, breathing heavily, adjusting to the overwhelming sensation of their bodies joined so intimately.

"You feel incredible," Alexander murmured, his voice strained with the effort of remaining still.

Cassie rolled her hips experimentally, drawing a groan from deep in his chest. "So do you."

Taking her movement as permission, Alexander began to move, establishing a rhythm that started slow and deliberate. Each thrust was measured and controlled, his eyes never leaving her face as he watched for any sign of discomfort. But Cassie felt only mounting pleasure, her body responding to his as if they'd been lovers for centuries rather than minutes.

"More," she urged, her nails digging into his shoulders.

Something flashed in his eyes, a primal hunger he'd been keeping leashed. "Hold onto me," he warned, his voice dropping to that inhuman register that sent shivers down her spine.

Cassie wrapped her arms more securely around him as Alexander increased his pace, his thrusts becoming deeper and more powerful. The bed frame creaked beneath them, the headboard thumping rhythmically against the wall as he drove into her with controlled force.

The pleasure built rapidly, tighter with each thrust. Cassie felt herself approaching another peak, her inner muscles clenching around him as the tension mounted. Alexander seemed to sense it, one hand sliding between their bodies to find where they were joined, his thumb circling the sensitive bundle of nerves in a way that made her cry out.

"Alexander!" His name was a plea, a demand.

"Let go," he commanded again, his voice rough with his own approaching release. "Come again for me, Cassie."

His words pushed her over the edge. Her body clenched around him as she unraveled in his arms, breathless, heated and barely aware of herself. Through the haze of her own release, she felt Alexander's rhythm falter. His control finally broke, and he shuddered in his own completion.

For several long moments, they remained locked together, both trembling with the aftershocks of shared pleasure. Alexander's forehead rested against hers, their breaths mingling in the small space between them. Despite not needing to breathe, his chest heaved as if he'd run for miles.

Slowly, carefully, he withdrew from her body, rolling to the side to avoid crushing her with his weight. Before Cassie could mourn the loss of contact, he gathered her against his chest, one arm wrapped securely around her waist, the other stroking gently through her tangled hair.

"Are you alright?" he asked softly, his lips brushing her temple.

Cassie nestled closer, her body feeling pleasantly heavy and relaxed despite the circumstances that had brought them to this moment. "More than alright," she assured him, pressing a kiss to his chest, directly over where his heart would beat if he were human.

They lay in comfortable silence for a while, their bodies cooling, her heartbeat slowing, and in Alexander's case, remaining in its customary stillness.

Cassie traced idle patterns on his skin, marveling at the contrast between his hard exterior and the gentle way he held her.

"I shouldn't have..." He paused. "I should have waited," Alexander said finally, his voice rumbling beneath her ear where it rested against his chest. "Given you time to adjust to everything that's happened."

Cassie lifted her head to look at him, her silver-blue eyes once again meeting his dark ones. "I don't need time to know what I want," she said firmly. "And right now, this is exactly what I needed and wanted."

His expression softened, one hand coming up to cup her cheek. "You continue to surprise me, Cassie Marlow."

"Good," she replied with a small smile. "I'd hate to be predictable while being kidnapped and held against my will."

Alexander chuckled, the sound vibrating through his chest against her skin. "A guest of significance," he corrected, echoing their earlier conversation.

"Is that what I am to you now?" she asked, her tone light but her eyes searching his face. "A significant guest in your bed?"

Something shifted in his expression, a seriousness replacing the momentary humor. "You're more than that, though I'm not sure what it is yet."

Cassie nodded, understanding the complexity of their situation. In the span of days, she'd gone from witch to hybrid, from captive to the daughter of a king, from Alexander's prisoner to his lover. Labels seemed inadequate for the connection forming between them.

"We'll figure it out," she said, but her voice didn't sound as certain as she wanted. Saying it didn't make it true. But it sounded good for now. Cassie wanted to say more, to try to say what this meant to her, but the emotion she felt made it hard to talk. She settled back against his chest instead, seeking out his comfort. She didn't want to worry or overthink the situation. She left things unspoken.

His arms tightened around her, secure and protective. "Yes," he agreed quietly. His words didn't elaborate but they held a promise.

As Cassie drifted toward sleep, comforted by Alexander's cool strength surrounding her, she found herself thinking of Claire again. Her sister was still out there somewhere, possibly in danger. But for the first time since their separation, Cassie felt a little hope. It made her fear sharper, not softer. She wasn't at peace, but she wasn't drowning anymore. With Alexander and her newfound father searching for Claire, perhaps there was reason to believe they would find her and bring her home safely.

And when they did, Cassie would have quite a story to tell her sister about their true heritage, their vampire king father, and the unexpected connection she'd formed with the very vampire sent to capture her. Claire would love the story if they can find her in time.

Chapter Seventeen

Late morning found Cassie awake, her body humming with renewed energy as the sun's rays spilled through the compound. The day's lethargy had lifted like a veil, replaced by a clarity and focus that felt almost intoxicating. She'd spent the early morning hours drifting in and out of consciousness, her vampire nature demanding rest when the sun rose, but now she was fully alert, her mind racing with preparations for the witch delegation's arrival.

Alexander had left hours ago, called to an emergency strategy session with Callimachus. He'd kissed her before departing, a lingering touch that held promises neither of them had voiced aloud. The memory of their night together sent warmth spreading through her body. Still, Cassie pushed those thoughts aside. Tonight was about Claire, about finding answers that might lead to her sister.

A soft knock at the door announced the arrival of a vampire attendant bearing formal clothing for the diplomatic meeting. The garments were laid out with meticulous care. A deep emerald dress that complemented her auburn hair, paired with a fitted black jacket embroidered with subtle silver patterns that caught the light as the fabric moved.

"The King thought you might appreciate something that reflects both heritages," the attendant explained, gesturing to the silver embroidery. "The patterns contain protective sigils from both vampire and witch traditions."

Cassie examined the intricate designs, recognizing some of the witch symbols her mother had taught her, while others, presumably vampire in origin, remained unfamiliar. "It's beautiful," she admitted, running her fingers along the delicate stitching.

As she dressed, Cassie mentally rehearsed what she knew about witch diplomatic protocols. Growing up on the periphery of witch society, she had absorbed more than she realized. The High Coven Council operated with rigid formality, every gesture and word laden with significance. They would be watching her closely, searching for weaknesses or inconsistencies.

The attendant returned to escort her to the war room where the meeting would take place. Unlike the ornate public spaces of the compound, this chamber was designed for function rather than intimidation. A massive oval table dominated the center, surrounded by high-backed chairs. Maps and strategic displays lined the walls, some digital, others ancient parchments protected behind glass.

Callimachus stood at the head of the table, deep in conversation with a group of vampires. Alexander stood slightly apart from the group, his posture rigid with tension. When he caught sight of her, something flickered in his eyes, a warmth quickly masked as he nodded in formal acknowledgment.

Her father turned as she entered, and for a moment, his carefully controlled expression softened. "Cassandra," he greeted, extending his hand to draw her closer. "You look rested."

"I am, and it's just Cassie. I have never used my full name," she confirmed, acutely aware of the room's attention shifting to her. "Have there been any updates about Claire?"

"Nothing conclusive, Cassie," Callimachus replied, acknowledging her preferred name, his tone carefully measured. "But tonight may bring answers from unexpected sources."

He guided her to a seat at his right hand, a position of honor that wasn't lost on the assembled vampires. Several exchanged glances, their expressions ranging from curiosity to barely concealed disapproval.

"The witch delegation will arrive within the hour," Callimachus announced, addressing the room at large. "Before they do, we must establish our position clearly. The existence of Cassie and her sister represents a significant development in vampire-witch relations, one that could either strengthen or shatter centuries of careful diplomacy."

"With respect, Your Majesty," an older vampire with silver-streaked hair spoke up, "is it wise to reveal the hybrid's existence so openly? The witches may see her as a violation of the treaty."

"They already know," Alexander interjected. "Or at least suspect. That's why they've requested this meeting."

"Then perhaps we should consider limiting her involvement," another advisor suggested, not quite looking at Cassie. "Her presence could be provocative."

Cassie straightened in her chair, her eyes flashing. "I'm not going to hide while you discuss my sister's fate," she stated firmly. "I have as much right to be here as anyone."

A tense silence fell over the room. Callimachus studied her for a moment, something like pride flickering in his dark eyes.

"My daughter speaks for herself," he declared, emphasizing the relationship deliberately. "And she will participate fully in these proceedings."

The term "daughter" sent a ripple through the assembled vampires. Though they must have heard rumors, this public acknowledgment from their king left no room for doubt or challenge.

"The question remains," Elise Beaumont said from her position at Callimachus's left, "how much do we reveal about Claire Marlow's disappearance? If the witches are responsible, showing our hand too early could be disadvantageous."

"We need information more than we need to protect our pride," Alexander countered. "If they know something about Sam's yacht, that takes priority over diplomatic posturing."

"Alexander is right," Callimachus nodded. "Claire's safety comes first. However," he raised a hand to forestall further comments, "we will approach this strategically. The witches have requested this meeting to discuss what they term 'unauthorized extraction of individuals from witch territory.' We will hear their grievances before revealing our concerns."

Cassie leaned forward, her mind processing the political dynamics unfolding around her. "The witches value reciprocity in negotiations," she offered, drawing on memories of overheard conversations between her mother and visiting coven members. "If we acknowledge their concerns first, they'll feel obligated to address ours with equal consideration."

Several advisors turned to her with surprise, clearly not expecting such insight from someone they still viewed as an outsider.

"Precisely," Callimachus confirmed, his exterior revealing nothing of his own surprise at her knowledge. "We acknowledge without conceding, listen without revealing, and then present our own concerns as a natural extension of the dialogue."

Alexander's eyes met Cassie's across the table, a flash of approval in his gaze before he returned his attention to the king. "The delegation will be limited to three representatives, as agreed. High Priestess Morgana leads them, and she's known for her strict adherence to tradition but has maintained relatively balanced relations with our kind."

"She's also my mother's second cousin," Cassie added quietly. "Though I've only met her twice at major sabbats."

This information caused another stir among the advisors. Family connections, even distant ones, carried significant weight in supernatural politics.

"That connection could prove useful," Elise noted. "Or dangerous, depending on how they view your unique situation."

Cassie nodded, understanding the double-edged nature of her heritage. To the witches, she might represent either a bridge between worlds or an unforgivable transgression. Her very existence challenged centuries of carefully maintained boundaries between supernatural communities, and she knew firsthand how many covens kept themselves isolated and secret to protect and ensure their survival. Her father was including her now, but would that always be the case? What if her magic was something she couldn't control? Would he see her as more of a dangerous witch than his daughter?

"I have another connection on the High Coven Council, my grandmother Camila," Cassie added, absently twisting a strand of her deep auburn hair around her finger.

Elise nodded in approval.

As the discussion continued, a subtle shift in energy alerted Cassie to a new presence before the door opened. A young vampire entered, bowing respectfully.

"Your Majesty, there's an urgent communication from King Augustus of the Eastern Territories. He requests an immediate audience."

Callimachus frowned, the timing suspicious. "Augustus rarely involves himself in Western affairs unless compelled by significant self-interest. What reason does he give?"

"He claims to have information regarding the witch delegation and similar situations in his own territory."

The room fell silent as implications rippled through the assembled vampires. Augustus, the Vampire King of Eastern Canada, maintained his own court in Quebec City, historically keeping his distance from Vancouver's politics.

"Similar situations?" Alexander repeated, his voice carefully neutral. "Did he elaborate?"

"No, sir. He requested privacy and indicated the matter was of utmost sensitivity."

Callimachus considered for a moment, then nodded decisively. "Prepare the secure communication chamber. Alexander, Cassandra, you will join me. The rest of you, continue preparations for the witch delegation."

As the room emptied, Cassie caught Alexander's questioning glance. She lifted her shoulders some, equally puzzled by this unexpected development. She wasn't sure what role fit her in that moment. She was a worried sister, but she was also now the daughter of a king. A king of creatures who had always been her mortal enemy.

Callimachus waited until they were alone before speaking. "Augustus's timing is rarely coincidental," he explained, leading them toward a smaller chamber adjacent to the war room. "If he's reaching out now, on the eve of witch negotiations, he either knows something vital or wants something significant."

"Could he know about Claire?" Cassie asked, hope flickering despite her caution. The thought of anyone having information about her sister sent a familiar ache through her chest, a mixture of longing and dread that never quite subsided.

"It's possible, though unlikely. Augustus rarely ventures into Pacific waters." Callimachus paused at the door, his ancient eyes narrowing as he considered the implications. His hand rested on the ornate handle, fingers tracing the intricate carvings that had been worn smooth by centuries of use. "The Eastern Territories maintain their own intelligence networks, but they seldom extend this far west without our knowledge."

He turned to face Cassie fully, lowering his voice. "Whatever he reveals, follow my lead. Eastern politics are complex, and Augustus has his own agenda." Callimachus's visage hardened, the military commander momentarily visible beneath his composed exterior. "He's survived nearly as long as I have by playing multiple angles simultaneously. Remember that every word he speaks serves a purpose, and often several purposes at once."

The secure communication chamber was surprisingly intimate, dominated by a large screen on the far wall. Sophisticated equipment hummed quietly, monitored by a technician who quickly established the connection before discreetly withdrawing.

The screen flickered to life, revealing a man whose aristocratic features contrasted sharply with Callimachus's military bearing. Where her father exuded ancient strength, Augustus projected cultivated refinement. His medium brown hair was cropped close to his head, and his tailored suit was impeccably European in cut.

"Callimachus," he greeted, his Latin-laced accent subtle but unmistakable. It surprised Cassie. She had been expecting a French-Canadian accent and some type of response such as, "It's been too long, mon ami."

"Augustus," Callimachus responded with careful neutrality. "Your call is unexpected but timely. We are preparing to receive a witch delegation within the hour."

Augustus's pale blue eyes flickered with interest. "Yes, I've heard. News travels quickly when the High Coven mobilizes." His gaze shifted to Cassie, sharpening with sudden intensity. "And this must be the cause of their concern. Your daughter, I believe?"

The slight hesitation before "daughter" carried volumes of meaning. Cassie felt Alexander tense beside her, his protective instinct palpable.

"Cassie Marlow," Callimachus confirmed, neither confirming nor denying the relationship explicitly. "She has a significant interest in our discussions with the witches."

"I imagine she does," Augustus murmured, studying Cassie with undisguised fascination. "The resemblance is remarkable, particularly around the eyes. Though I see her mother in her as well."

Cassie straightened under his scrutiny. "You knew my mother?"

A thin smile crossed Augustus's face. "Catherine Marlow's reputation extends beyond Californian and Western Canadian territories. A formidable witch from a distinguished lineage." He turned his attention back to Callimachus. "Which brings me to the purpose of my call. It seems we share a delicate situation."

"Explain," Callimachus commanded, his patience visibly thinning.

Augustus leaned back, steepling his fingers. "The High Coven's sudden interest in your affairs coincides with certain developments in my own territory. Specifically, regarding my witch companion, Eleanora."

"Ellie," a soft voice off-screen corrected.

Augustus gave a small smile and said, "Ellie."

"Your witch companion?" Alexander clarified, surprise evident in his tone.

"Indeed. Though 'companion' hardly captures the full nature of our relationship." Augustus's face softened momentarily. "Ellie comes from a prominent Connecticut coven. Our association has been discreet but not entirely secret in Quebec."

Cassie glanced at her father, noting the slight narrowing of his eyes. "What does this have to do with the current situation?"

Augustus met Callimachus's gaze directly. "Ellie is my mate, and she is pregnant."

The statement landed like a thunderbolt in the small room. Cassie felt her breath catch, the implications staggering. Not just one hybrid lineage, but potentially two, on opposite coasts of the continent. The revelation sent her mind spinning, neurons firing rapidly as she processed this monumental information. Another vampire-witch pairing had produced a child in Quebec. The weight of this knowledge pressed against her chest, making her eyes widen slightly as she glanced between her father's tense form and Augustus's composed features on the screen.

A soft sigh drifted from off-camera. There was the sound of movement, and a small-statured woman with light blond hair, visibly pregnant, entered the video frame and sat directly in Augustus's lap. The king embraced his mate and drew her back firmly into his embrace.

"Hi, I'm Ellie, and I'm seven months pregnant with this rogue's kiddo," the woman smiled and waved. Cassie instantly liked her.

Seven months pregnant. A witch and a vampire, just like her parents. The statistical improbability of such a pairing resulting in conception once was astronomical; twice bordered on the impossible. Yet here they were, living evidence that the impossible had happened, was happening, again. Cassie's fingers curled against her palms, nails digging into skin as she considered the implications. Two hybrid bloodlines, separated by thousands of miles but connected by an unthinkable biological rarity. The coincidence seemed too profound to be mere chance. Maybe it wasn't such a rarity as it was taboo. Forbidden.

The air in the room felt suddenly thicker, charged with the electricity of revelation. Cassie wondered what this meant for her own existence, for the identity she was only beginning to understand. If there were others like her, or soon would be. Perhaps she wasn't the biological anomaly she'd believed herself to be. The thought was both comforting and terrifying. It also unmoored her even more. Ellie's pregnancy was being protected from the onset, but she and her sister had been hidden, and kept secret. Were they a shameful secret to hide, or children to protect? She wasn't certain how she felt in this moment.

"Interesting," Alexander breathed, though his eyes flickered to Cassie, living proof that it was indeed possible.

"Impossible was my first thought," Augustus agreed. "Until medical confirmation proved otherwise. The child shows both witch and vampire markers in preliminary testing."

Callimachus remained impassive, though Cassie sensed the turmoil beneath his controlled exterior. Her father never moved, but she felt the shift enough to understand that Augustus's words had an effect. "Do many know?"

"As you know, it's difficult to maintain absolute secrecy, and I suspect information has leaked to the High Coven. Their sudden interest in hybrid matters cannot be coincidental."

"Seven months," Cassie repeated, her mind racing. "And they're only confronting you now? That doesn't make sense."

Augustus inclined his head in acknowledgment. "A valid observation. Unless they've only recently connected the pieces. Or unless something has forced their hand."

"Me. Claire," Cassie breathed, the realization hitting her. "Our being taken and brought here might have triggered their response. But Claire's missing."

"A second hybrid?" Augustus raised an eyebrow, and leaned forward. "Fascinating. And currently missing?"

Alexander stepped forward slightly. "We're conducting an extensive search. Her vessel disappeared under suspicious circumstances that may involve witch intervention."

"Which explains the timing of their diplomatic overture," Augustus mused. "They're assessing how much you know while positioning themselves to control the narrative."

Callimachus's expression darkened. "If they've harmed Claire in any manner, I won't hold back my response."

"Caution, old friend," Augustus interrupted. "If the High Coven has indeed taken action against your family, then they've already committed to a course that might well shatter the treaty. We must consider the broader implications."

"The treaty already lies in tatters if vampires can reproduce with witches," Callimachus pointed out. "The entire foundation of our separate territories rests on the separation of the species based on deep distrust and hatred, including the biological improbability of such unions."

Augustus nodded gravely. "Precisely. Which is why I propose we coordinate our response. My Ellie faces similar dangers, and our child represents the same fundamental challenge to the established order."

Cassie watched this exchange with growing unease. The political maneuvering felt distant from her immediate concern of finding Claire. Yet she recognized that these ancient vampires were calculating centuries of consequences in each measured response.

"What exactly are you proposing?" Callimachus asked, his voice deceptively calm.

"An alliance. Formal recognition of hybrid offspring as legitimate members of both communities, with protected status under a revised treaty." Augustus leaned forward. "The witches will resist, of course. Their bloodline purity has been central to their identity for millennia. But faced with a united front from both Eastern and Western vampire territories, they may be persuaded to negotiate rather than risk open conflict."

"And if they already hold Claire as leverage?" Cassie interjected, unable to remain silent any longer. "What then?"

Augustus turned his cool gaze to her. "Then we negotiate from a position of strength. Two acknowledged hybrids and an unborn third represent a new reality they cannot simply eliminate, particularly when one of their own is carrying the heir to the Eastern territories."

The calculation in his voice chilled Cassie. He was using his unborn child as a political chess piece, just as he proposed using her and Claire.

"We need to find my sister first," she insisted, looking to her father. "Before any negotiations or alliances."

Callimachus relaxed his shoulders back a notch, softening slightly as he met her gaze. "Claire's safety remains our priority." He turned back to Augustus. "Your proposal has merit, but I make no commitments until my daughter is returned safely."

"Understandable," Augustus conceded. "But do not dismiss the strength our united position would bring to your negotiations. The witches must understand that harming any hybrid, including your missing daughter, would have consequences from both territories."

A subtle chime sounded, and Alexander glanced at his watch. "The witch delegation has arrived at the outer gates, Your Majesty."

Callimachus straightened, decision made. "Augustus, I will consider your proposal. For now, I agree any discussion regarding hybrids must include both Eastern and Western territories."

"A wise first step," Augustus smiled thinly. "I wish you success in tonight's negotiations and in finding your daughter."

The screen went dark, leaving the three of them in momentary silence.

"Do you trust him?" Alexander asked quietly.

"Augustus has never acted without self-interest," Callimachus replied. "But in this case, our interests may align. His unborn child faces the same threats as Cassandra and Claire."

Cassie processed this new information, her mind racing. "If vampires can reproduce with witches, even rarely, it changes everything. The entire power balance between our kinds..."

"Has been built on a fundamental misconception," Callimachus finished. "One that now threatens both my daughters."

The claim of parenthood, stated so definitively, sent warmth through Cassie despite the circumstances. She had spent her entire life wondering about her father, and now he stood beside her, acknowledging her publicly as his own.

"The witches will be waiting," Alexander reminded them, though his eyes lingered on Cassie with an intensity that made her heart quicken.

Callimachus nodded, his expression shifting back to the impassive mask of kingship. "Then let us not keep them waiting. Cassie, remember what we discussed. Observe the formalities, but watch for any reaction when Claire is mentioned. The slightest hesitation could reveal knowledge they're trying to conceal."

Cassie straightened, channeling both her analytical nature and the newfound strength of her hybrid heritage. "I'm ready."

As they moved toward the door, Alexander briefly touched her elbow, the contact sending a jolt of awareness through her. "Stay close to me," he murmured, his voice low and reassuring. His touch promised protection, should she be threatened.

She nodded, drawing comfort from his proximity as they prepared to face the witch delegation. Somewhere out there, Claire was waiting, possibly in danger. Tonight, Cassie would begin the process of bringing her home, no matter what it took. She would also meet the arriving witches as not one of them, but something more.

Chapter Eighteen

The grand reception hall had been transformed for the witch delegation's arrival. Gone were the usual trappings of vampire dominance. The ancient weapons and battle trophies that normally adorned the walls had been replaced with neutral artwork. Even the lighting seemed different, warmer somehow, less intimidating to visitors accustomed to natural magic rather than the cold power of immortality.

Cassie stood at her father's right hand, the position of honor making her acutely aware of the weight of expectation pressing down on her shoulders. Alexander remained slightly behind her, a reassuring presence she could sense without turning. The vampire court had arranged itself in a semicircle, their faces carefully composed into diplomatic masks that revealed nothing of the tension crackling beneath the surface.

"Remember," Callimachus murmured, his voice pitched for her ears alone, "the witches will be assessing you from the moment they enter. Stand tall. You have nothing to be ashamed of."

Cassie nodded, straightening her spine. The emerald dress her father had provided fit perfectly, its subtle protective sigils warming against her skin. She could feel the witch magic woven into the fabric responding to her own latent abilities, strengthening as she drew upon her dual heritage.

A series of chimes echoed through the hall, announcing the delegation's approach. The massive doors swung open silently, and Cassie felt the atmosphere shift as three figures entered. Their power preceded them like a wave, washing over the assembled vampires with the unmistakable signature of high witch magic. It was earthy, primal, and ancient in a way that differed fundamentally from vampire energy.

Leading the trio was High Priestess Miranda, her silver-streaked black hair swept into an elaborate knot adorned with small crystals that caught the light. Her midnight blue robes whispered against the marble floor as she advanced with regal confidence. Behind her walked two other witches, one male and one female, both dressed in the formal attire of the High Coven. They weren't representatives. They were also High Coven members.

Cassie's breath caught in her throat as she recognized the third figure. It wasn't just any witch, but her grandmother, Camila Marlow. She wanted to run to her, to sink into her arms, to be gathered close in the way only her grandmother could hug her. Her chest ached in seeing her familiar face. But she stood still, reminding herself that she was being closely watched.

Callimachus must have sensed her surprise, for his hand briefly touched her wrist in warning. Cassie fought to keep her expression neutral, though her heart raced. She hadn't expected her grandmother to be part of the delegation. This was no mere diplomatic mission. The High Coven had sent one of their most respected Council members, who also happened to be her own blood relative.

The witches halted at the prescribed distance, and Miranda stepped forward to perform a traditional greeting.

"King Callimachus," she intoned, her voice carrying the distinctive cadence of formal witch speech. "The High Coven Council extends its greetings and appreciation for your hospitality during this time of concern."

"High Priestess Miranda," Callimachus replied with equal formality. "Vancouver welcomes the representatives of the High Coven. May our discussions prove fruitful for both our peoples."

With words of greeting exchanged, Miranda's gaze shifted to Cassie, her dark eyes widening almost imperceptibly. A flicker of something, recognition, perhaps, or calculation, crossed her features before disappearing behind her diplomatic mask.

"And this must be Cassandra Marlow," she said, her tone carefully neutral, though her eyes betrayed intense interest. "Your presence here is quite unexpected."

Before Cassie could respond, Camila stepped forward, breaking protocol. Her grandmother had always been one to disregard formalities when they interfered with what she considered more important matters.

"Cassie," Camila said, her voice warm with genuine affection despite the tension in the room. "Are you well, child? Have they treated you properly?"

Cassie felt Alexander stiffen behind her, but Callimachus remained perfectly composed, watching the interaction with sharp attention.

"Grandmother," Cassie acknowledged, unable to keep a small smile from her lips despite the gravity of the situation. "I'm well. I've been treated with respect and acceptance." Cassie looked up at Callimachus and smiled.

Camila moved closer, ignoring the subtle shift in posture from the vampire guards. She reached for Cassie's hands, taking them in her own and squeezing gently. The familiar gesture sent a wave of comfort through Cassie, a reminder of solstice celebrations and quiet afternoons spent learning herb lore in her grandmother's section of their garden.

"Let me look at you," Camila said, her keen eyes examining Cassie from head to toe. Though appearing to be in her seventies, Camila Marlow was much, much older and retained the vigor and sharp intelligence that had earned her a seat on the High Coven Council decades ago. Her gray-streaked and lightly faded red hair and green eyes, so similar to Cassie's mother's, were pulled back in a simple braid, and her ceremonial robes couldn't quite hide her practical nature.

"I'm fine, truly," Cassie assured her, touched by the concern in her grandmother's eyes.

"And Claire?" Camila asked, her voice dropping to an urgent whisper. "Where is she? Is she safe?"

The question sent a chill through Cassie. If her grandmother was asking about Claire's whereabouts, then the witches didn't have her sister after all. The hope that the delegation might provide answers about Claire's disappearance began to crumble.

"We had hoped you might tell us," Callimachus interjected smoothly, his voice carrying just enough edge to remind everyone of the seriousness of the situation. "Claire Marlow's vessel disappeared a day ago under suspicious circumstances."

Camila's expression shifted from concern to alarm. She turned to Miranda, who had maintained her diplomatic composure throughout the exchange. "You said nothing of this. You told the Council both girls had been taken by vampires."

"That was our understanding based on initial reports," Miranda replied carefully. "Our intelligence indicated both Marlow sisters had been taken from witch territory by vampire operatives."

"One of whom is now missing," Callimachus stated flatly. "Along with one of my most trusted lieutenants. Both vessels encountered witch patrols on their way north."

A tense silence fell over the hall. Cassie looked between her grandmother and the other High Priestess, searching their expressions for any hint of deception. Camila's shock appeared genuine, but Miranda's carefully controlled features revealed nothing. The high priestess's features were as hard as stone and revealed nothing.

"Perhaps," Alexander suggested from behind Cassie, his voice measured, "we should continue this discussion in a more comfortable setting. The formal reception hall is hardly conducive to productive dialogue."

Callimachus nodded once. "A wise suggestion. Please, follow us to the council chambers where refreshments await."

As the group moved toward the adjoining room, Camila kept close to Cassie, her hand resting protectively on her granddaughter's arm. "Catherine is beside herself with worry," she murmured. "When we learned you and Claire had been taken, it was all I could do not to come here immediately. But that would have set off a diplomatic crisis had I done so."

"Mom is okay?" Cassie asked quickly, pushing down any feeling of guilt. She didn't have the luxury of spiraling into self-shame at that moment. "The sedative, she's okay?"

"Wore off after a few hours," Camila confirmed. "She contacted me immediately, and the High Coven has been in emergency session ever since."

"Did you know?" Cassie couldn't help asking. "About me? About what I am?"

Camila's eyes softened with understanding. "I've known since the moment your mom returned from a diplomatic visit outside of Seattle. She never told me all the details, but she told me enough. It was a miracle that she was going to have you, and I have treasured you from the moment I learned about you. Never doubt my love and support for you or your sister, Cassie. I worked with your mother to balance, carefully protect and nurture you considering your aversion to sunlight and your dietary needs. But Catherine refused to discuss your father, and I respected her wishes." She squeezed Cassie's arm gently. "I never imagined this, though. A vampire king..."

They entered the council chamber, a more intimate space with a circular table that eliminated the hierarchy of the reception hall. Callimachus gestured for everyone to be seated, and Cassie found herself between her father and grandmother, with Alexander positioned directly across from her. The strategic placement wasn't lost on her. She was literally between worlds, vampire and witch, with her hybrid nature the bridge connecting them.

Cassie watched as her father took a seat in a chair larger than the rest. To her, it resembled a throne.

Servants appeared silently, placing goblets of deep red liquid before the vampires and delicate crystal cups of herbal tea for the witches. Before Cassie, they set both options, a subtle acknowledgment of her dual nature that didn't go unnoticed by the witch delegation.

Once the servants had withdrawn, Callimachus addressed the gathering. "Let us speak plainly. The Marlow sisters represent something unprecedented. They are children born of vampire and witch bloodlines, a possibility long thought impossible."

"An abomination," Miranda said quietly, though without the venom Cassie might have expected. She also did not seem surprised as she added, "Or so our prior assumptions would have us believe."

"And yet here she sits," Callimachus countered, gesturing to Cassie. "Healthy, intelligent, with access to both witch magic and vampire abilities. Hardly an abomination, but rather a new possibility."

"A dangerous possibility," the male witch spoke for the first time, his voice carrying the distinctive accent of the New England covens. "One that threatens the very foundations of our separate societies. She should not be here but with the witches."

"Councilor Giles," Camila said sharply, "a reminder that you speak of my granddaughter."

"With respect, Councilor Marlow," Giles replied, not backing down, "your personal connection to this situation is precisely why many on the Council questioned your inclusion in this delegation."

"My 'personal connection' is why I insisted on coming," Camila retorted. "And the High Coven agreed that family representation was appropriate given the circumstances."

Miranda raised a hand, silencing the brewing argument. "We are not here to debate the ethics of hybrid existence but to address the violation of territorial sovereignty and the treaty terms." She turned to Callimachus. "Your operatives entered witch territory without permission and forcibly removed two individuals under witch protection. This constitutes a direct breach of our agreement."

"An agreement predicated on mutual understanding of separate societies and biological impossibilities," Callimachus pointed out. "We believed vampires were in witch territory and were removing them immediately, as we are required to do to keep the peace. We ensured that we kept to the waters and only entered briefly to extract and remove from your lands. All customs and laws were followed. The existence of my daughters has changed everything."

The deliberate use of "my daughters" sent a ripple through the witch delegation. Giles's mouth tightened into a thin line, while Miranda's eyes narrowed calculatingly.

"You claim paternity," she stated.

"It is not a claim, but a fact," Callimachus replied. "One confirmed by both physical resemblance and magical signature."

Cassie felt her grandmother's hand tighten on her arm. "Catherine never told me," Camila murmured, her voice barely audible. "All these years..."

"And now one of these hybrid children is missing," Miranda said, returning to the central issue. "Under circumstances you believe involve witch intervention."

"A magical storm appeared precisely where Sam's vessel was last reported," Alexander explained, leaning forward slightly. "A storm bearing the unmistakable signature of high witch weather manipulation."

Giles scoffed. "Northern California patrol witches don't have that level of weather control."

"Exactly," Alexander agreed. "Which suggests involvement from someone with considerably more power."

The implication hung heavy in the air. Coven leaders and High Coven members possessed the ability to generate and control magical storms of that magnitude. It's why they held leadership positions, due to their superior ability to manipulate and control the world and elements around them. It enabled them to keep others with lesser abilities safe in the human world and against other potential supernatural threats.

"The High Coven did not authorize any action against Claire Marlow or her vampire escort," Miranda stated firmly. "If such a storm was conjured, it was done without Council approval."

"But not necessarily without Council knowledge," Callimachus suggested, his voice deceptively gentle.

They were talking about her like she wasn't in the room, going back and forth as if she were an outsider, incapable of being part of them. Their barbed words made her want to scream. Instead, she reminded herself to observe, and let the rage that was building inside her dissipate.

Cassie forced herself to refocus and watched the witches carefully, remembering her father's instruction to observe their reactions. Miranda maintained her composure, but Giles shifted uncomfortably in his seat. Her grandmother's expression had darkened with concern and something that looked like suspicion.

"The Council is not monolithic," Camila said slowly, her eyes fixed on Miranda. "Individual members have been known to act independently when they feel the collective is moving too slowly."

"Are you suggesting a rogue element within the High Coven may have taken action against my daughter?" Callimachus asked, his tone sharpening.

"I'm suggesting it's a possibility we cannot dismiss," Camila replied. She turned to Cassie, her expression softening. "Child, when did you last see your sister?"

"When they took us." Cassie answered, grateful for her grandmother's direct approach. "Alexander brought me north on one vessel, while another vampire named Sam took Claire on a different route."

"A standard security protocol," Alexander added. "To minimize risk in case of interception."

"Which proved prescient, it seems," Callimachus noted dryly.

Camila's brow furrowed in thought. "Claire always had a particular sensitivity to magical currents. Even as a child, she could sense approaching storms before anyone else." She looked up at Callimachus.

"If she felt a magical attack coming, she might have taken action to protect herself."

"The life raft," Cassie breathed, the pieces clicking together in her analytical mind. "If Claire sensed danger, she might have convinced Sam to abandon ship before the storm hit."

"Which would explain why the yacht was damaged but not destroyed," Alexander agreed, his eyes meeting Cassie's across the table. "They could be adrift, or they might have reached one of the coastal islands."

Hope flared in Cassie's chest for the first time since learning of Claire's disappearance. If her sister had escaped the magical storm, there was a real chance she was still alive.

"I want to join the search," she declared, addressing her father directly. "Claire would sense me, just as I would sense her. Our connection might lead us to her."

Before Callimachus could respond, Miranda interjected. "That would be unwise. The waters between here and Northern California are contested territory. Your presence, a hybrid with untrained abilities, would only escalate tensions."

"My sister is out there," Cassie countered, unable to keep the edge from her voice. "Possibly hurt, definitely scared. I won't sit here discussing politics while she needs me."

"Cassandra," Callimachus said, using her full name as a gentle warning. "High Priestess Miranda raises a valid concern. However," he continued, turning to the witch delegation, "I propose a joint search effort. Vampire vessels with witch representatives aboard, combining our resources to locate Claire and Sam."

The proposal clearly caught Miranda off guard. She exchanged a glance with Giles before responding. "Such cooperation would be unprecedented."

"As are my daughters," Callimachus pointed out. "Perhaps it's time our people found new ways to work together."

"The High Coven would need assurances," Giles said cautiously. "Guarantees that this wouldn't establish a precedent for future territorial incursions."

"Naturally," Callimachus agreed. "Just as we would require assurances that Claire would be returned to us unharmed when found."

Cassie noticed her grandmother watching this exchange with a calculating expression. Camila had always been a shrewd political operator within the High Coven, known for finding compromise where others saw only conflict.

"I believe we can craft an agreement acceptable to both sides," Camila suggested. "A limited cooperation focused solely on finding Claire and Sam, with strict parameters that protect the broader treaty."

Miranda nodded slowly. "We are authorized to negotiate such terms, provided they don't compromise witch or vampire sovereignty."

"Then let us proceed," Callimachus said, his tone shifting to something more businesslike. "But first, I believe Councilor Marlow might appreciate some time with her granddaughter. Family matters deserve attention, even amid diplomatic concerns."

The consideration surprised Cassie, though she understood it was as much strategic as compassionate. Her grandmother was clearly the most sympathetic member of the witch delegation, and strengthening that connection could only benefit their position.

"Thank you," Camila said, inclining her head slightly to Callimachus. "I would indeed value such an opportunity."

As the others began discussing the technical details of a joint search operation, Camila drew Cassie slightly away from the table. Though they remained in the room, the arrangement of pillars and furniture created a small pocket of privacy.

"You've discovered much in a short time," Camila observed, her voice gentle but probing. "How are you truly, Cassie? Not the diplomatic answer, but the honest one."

Cassie hesitated, considering her response. Her grandmother had always been the one person she could speak to without reservation, the wise counsel who understood her better than anyone except perhaps Claire.

"Overwhelmed," she admitted finally. "Everything I thought I knew about myself has changed. I'm angry with Mom for keeping the truth from us, terrified for Claire. Everyone is watching me, expecting something from me, but I don't even know who I am anymore. And..." She glanced toward Alexander, who was engaged in conversation with the other vampires. "Confused about other things as well."

Camila's perceptive gaze followed Cassie's. "The vampire who brought you here. There's something between you."

It wasn't a question. Cassie felt heat rise to her cheeks. "It's complicated."

"I imagine it is," Camila said, surprising Cassie with the lack of judgment in her tone. "The heart rarely follows diplomatic protocols, my dear."

"You're not disappointed?" Cassie asked hesitantly.

Camila smiled, the expression warming her lined face. "Cassie, I've lived long enough to know that love finds its way into the most unexpected places. And I've seen how he looks at you. He's protective, and his eyes rarely leave you."

The observation sent a flutter through Cassie's chest. She hadn't allowed herself to name the connection forming between her and Alexander, but her grandmother's words resonated with truth.

"What happens now?" Cassie asked, redirecting the conversation. "With the rest of the witches and not just the High Coven, I mean. If they learn what I am, what Claire is, what happens next?"

"Many will resist," Camila acknowledged, her expression sobering. "Our laws regarding vampire-witch relations are ancient and deeply ingrained. But they were made at a time that demanded protection of our people. Laws can change when reality demands it." She squeezed Cassie's hands. "And you, my dear, are a new reality they cannot ignore."

"Are there more like us?" Cassie asked suddenly. She desperately wanted to tell her grandmother more, but it was not her place to reveal the secrets of the vampires.

Surprise flickered across Camila's features at Cassie's question. Her eyes narrowed thoughtfully. "There are certain rumors that have reached the Council from the New England covens. It appears there might be another witch who is with child, but she seems to have disappeared. Hybrid bloodlines emerging simultaneously after centuries of supposed impossibility... something fundamental has changed."

Before Cassie could respond, Alexander approached, his expression apologetic for the interruption. "Forgive me, but we've received word from one of the search vessels. They've found something that might be relevant to Claire's disappearance."

Cassie straightened immediately. "What is it?"

"Debris matching the yacht's life raft has washed up on a small island approximately thirty miles offshore." Alexander's eyes held hers, careful not to offer false hope. "And there are footprints leading inland."

"She's alive," Cassie breathed, certainty flooding through her. "I can feel it."

Camila studied her granddaughter's face intently. "You've always been connected, even as children."

Cassie looked at her grandmother. "We were always close."

"But connected nonetheless," Camila said. "Perhaps more strongly than we realized, given your unique heritage."

Alexander nodded toward the main group, where Callimachus was now examining a map projected onto the table's surface. "They're planning the search parameters now. With your permission, Councilor Marlow, I'd like to bring you along with Cassie into the discussion."

"Of course," Camila agreed, moving with them back to the table. "My granddaughter's insight may prove invaluable, and I will offer anything that I am able."

As they rejoined the others, Cassie felt a renewed sense of purpose. The diplomatic complexities remained daunting, the future uncertain, but for the first time since arriving in Vancouver, she had concrete hope of finding Claire. With vampires and witches working together, however tentatively, the impossible suddenly seemed within reach.

And as Alexander took his position across from her, Cassie felt his presence a steady anchor amid the swirling currents of supernatural politics. She allowed herself to believe that perhaps other impossibilities might prove equally attainable. Her grandmother put a hand on her shoulder and gave a soft squeeze, bringing her attention back to her grandmother, seated next to her.

"Abomination."

Cassie looked up and across the table, surprised at the soft venom the word contained. Miranda hadn't shouted it. She'd said it quietly, almost clinically, as though pronouncing a diagnosis. Yet the weight of the word struck Cassie in her chest, blooming into her ribcage like dark fire.

Cassie clenched her hands in her lap, tendrils of power itching at her fingertips, begging to answer the insult in kind. She swallowed it down, aware of every eye on her.

But before she could summon a defense, the air in the council chamber shifted.

It thickened as though the walls themselves tightened in around them. The soft lights lining the conference room chamber guttered low in unison. A cold weight pressed Cassie's shoulders into her chair, not physical, but spiritual, as if the very concept of her existence hung in some immense and ancient balance.

She looked up at the head of the table, but her father hadn't moved. The digital map in front of him illuminated his features in razor sharpness.

Callimachus remained where he sat at the head of the table, his posture perfect, his hands relaxed against the carved arms of his chair. His gaze changed. His dark brown eyes deepened, blackened, until they were endless wells swallowing all light.

The witches stiffened. Giles's lips parted, his earlier contempt gone, his throat bobbing in a swallow he couldn't quite stifle. Even Miranda, for all her brittle poise, flinched as if an icy hand brushed the back of her neck.

"Do you dare," Callimachus said, his voice low, so soft Cassie had to lean forward to hear, even with her enhanced hearing. Yet even though her father's voice was low, the words reached every corner of the hall, vibrating in the stone and in her bones.

"Cassie and Claire," he continued, his black gaze now fixed on Miranda, "are blood of my blood. Flesh of my flesh. Their existence is not an anomaly to be dissected. It is a warning and a promise."

The marble beneath their feet trembled. A long groan ran through the chamber walls, as though ancient stone remembered every death his hand had dealt upon it. Cassie's eyes darted up and watched as the lights around the room dimmed. Then the room and the lights were gone.

Images flickered in her mind. Not hers. His.

The battlefield. Dust. The cacophony of dying men. Bronze clashing with bronze, screams swallowed by war cries. She felt the impact of a spear thudding into his chest, pain that wasn't hers but lanced through her memory as though she'd lived it. Spear after spear raining down, his body collapsing, yet still upright, riddled and bleeding. And then, not too much longer after, she wasn't sure, there was the glimmer of fangs. The press of immortal teeth. Darkness, and rebirth in blood.

Her stomach lurched as she became witness to her father's death and birth.

She was back in the room, the lights no longer dim, images gone.

Beside her, Alexander had gone perfectly still, head bowed, eyes respectfully lowered. He and the King seemed to have a familiar relationship, but in this moment, it was changed. Alexander showed deep deference, to a King this time, and not the familiarity of a friend that Cassie had become accustomed to witnessing between them. Even Alexander didn't meet his King's gaze, acting as if looking directly at Callimachus in this state might flay the soul from the body.

"You speak of abominations so freely," Callimachus murmured, his voice heavy with restrained violence. "Do you think I do not know the weight of the word?"

The room darkened further, shadows climbing the walls though no light had died. Cassie realized she wasn't just seeing shadow; she saw his presence manifest around the room. It was an aura of power older than empires, saturating every breath of oxygen. It clawed the air itself into submission.

Callimachus leaned forward, fingers curling into the arm of his chair. The simple shift in his posture carried the menace of a predator who had watched countless centuries unravel and fed on the innards of kings and tyrants alike.

"You forget whose hall this is," Callimachus whispered. His teeth gleamed faintly. They were not fully bared, but Cassie glimpsed enough fang to flash-freeze her veins. "You sit here because I have allowed it. You breathe here because I permit it."

Silence fell around the room. No indrawn or exhaled breaths. It was the quiet in the sharpest moment of intense fear.

The witches' magic flickered instinctively around their hands, small defensive lights they probably hadn't meant to summon. But none of them dared raise them higher.

Cassie sat frozen, her heart hammering not from fear but from something stranger. The recognition she felt surprised her. This was her father. The ancient monster that witches whispered about in warning stories. The predator whose shadow had shaped centuries of uneasy peace. What she had feared as a child. But now, it wasn't fear she felt. It was the strength that was in her grandmother's gentle squeeze on her shoulder. It was the strength of unconditional paternal love and support.

And a part of him lived in her. A part of her that she was still learning. Part of her was becoming like him. There was also no going back. She was now part of this world, part of him. She always had been.

The weight of it pressed down until she thought she might shatter with the realization of what this meant. He was her defender, her father.

Then, as quickly as it came, the oppressive darkness receded. The shadows slunk back into corners. Callimachus sat back, composed once more, the picture of regal control.

He exhaled, slow, deliberate. His eyes softened, warming as they fell upon her. He did not smile, but there was something in his face, some recognition of what he had just shown her.

"A word of counsel, High Priestess," he said, in a tone sharp and crisp as iron. "I allowed you a grace with the word once before, but never again. Heed my warning well. Choose your words with more care. Else the next abomination you behold will not simply be my daughter."

A ripple of fear shuddered through the delegation.

Cassie drew a shaky breath, unable to tear her gaze from him. Her father. Her king.

Both man and monster, at once.

The dark fire in Cassie's chest blossomed into a gentle but strong hearth flame.

She looked over as the door to the room opened, and servers brought in more dark goblets for the vampires and silver-covered plates for the witches. A plate was set in front of Cassie, and the cover removed, revealing sliced parsnips and raw steak cubes. A goblet with dark liquid was set before her. A corner of her lip turned up, appreciating how her difficult dietary restrictions were met with ease. She turned her attention back to her father and whispered a silent thank you. He gave a slight, barely perceptible nod.

The meal was a mostly silent affair, with very little talking and restrained, limited observations and responses around the table. Cassie twirled her fork absentmindedly, trying to concentrate on the plate in front of her. Her body refused to cooperate, to eat like nothing had happened. The floor was still and solid now, but his voice still rang in her ears, louder than the muted sound of dining around her.

Callimachus had turned off the digital map and waited until the witches were nearly finished eating before he picked up his goblet, drained it, and addressed the room.

"When you are finished, take a moment, and then we will resume in the greater hall again." He turned and left the conference room.

Cassie felt her grandmother pat her leg under the table. Cassie turned her head and saw her grandmother watching the empty door. She had a sneaking suspicion her grandmother was enjoying the attention and support Callimachus was directing toward her.

Chapter Nineteen

Cassie sat beside her grandmother Camila, away from the others in the chamber, watching as vampire and witch representatives pored over detailed maps of the coastal waters. The unexpected alliance, born of necessity rather than goodwill, created a strange energy in the room, centuries of distrust temporarily set aside in the search for Claire.

"You know," Camila said quietly, her weathered hands wrapped around a cup of herbal tea, "our numbers have been declining for generations."

Cassie looked up, surprised by the abrupt change in topic. "The witches? But I thought we lived all over North America and were doing well."

"Doing well, yes. But thriving?" Camila's smile held little humor. "We've maintained that illusion carefully. The truth is far more concerning."

Camila set down her cup, leaning closer to Cassie. The privacy sigils she'd discreetly cast around their alcove shimmered faintly, ensuring their conversation remained private from even vampire hearing.

"A few hundred years ago, a witch might expect to bear four or five children in her lifetime. Now, we're fortunate if each family produces one at most, and two is rare. Some never have children." Her voice dropped further. "Some bloodlines have disappeared entirely. Along with them, ancient knowledge, lost forever."

Cassie processed this revelation, her analytical mind immediately calculating implications. "But witches live for 150 to 200 years. Wouldn't that compensate for fewer births?"

"It should, theoretically," Camila acknowledged. "But longevity doesn't help when fewer children are born each generation. We're slowly fading, Cassie. The High Coven has known this for decades."

"Is that why," Cassie hesitated, pieces falling into place. "Is that why Mom was allowed to keep us? Even though we're part vampire?"

Camila nodded. "The Council knew of your existence from the beginning. I made certain of it. If my family were to be in danger, then I would have pursued different options for you and your mother."

"You told them?" Cassie couldn't keep the shock from her voice.

"I had to." Camila's eyes held a fierce protectiveness. "If I hadn't brought it before the Council immediately, established a precedent for your protection, others might have discovered you and taken matters into their own hands. I wanted to be prepared for any eventuality."

The implications sent a chill through Cassie. She stared at her grandmother. All this time she and her mother had been hiding Cassie and Claire, their safety had strings attached. "They would have killed us?"

"Some would have tried," Camila admitted. "The hatred between witches and vampires runs deep, particularly among the older generations who remember the wars."

"Wars?" Cassie echoed. Her mother had mentioned conflicts but never elaborated.

Camila's expression darkened with memory. "The fighting reached its peak during the Seven Years' War and continued through the American Revolution. Vampires aligned with European powers, witches with colonial interests. The bloodshed was," she paused, "catastrophic."

"I had no idea," Cassie whispered.

"Few do, outside the High Coven. We lost nearly two-thirds of our population in those decades." Camila's fingers tightened around her cup. "Vampires could replenish their numbers by turning humans. We could only watch our bloodlines dwindle."

Understanding dawned on Cassie. "That's why the treaty was formed."

"Yes. When the American Revolution ended, we established clear boundaries. Vampires took the Canadian territories, witches the American colonies. Both sides agreed to strict non-interference." Camila's eyes drifted to where Alexander stood, conferring with her father. "The treaty saved what remained of both our peoples."

"But you allowed Claire and me to live, even though we were violations of that separation."

"The Council voted six to five," Camila revealed. "The deciding factor was our declining numbers. You and Claire represented something new, children with witch blood, regardless of your vampire heritage."

Cassie absorbed this information, suddenly understanding her isolated upbringing. "Is that why we lived so remotely? Why Mom kept us hidden?"

"The agreement was strict. You would be raised in witch territory, under Catherine's guardianship, but isolated from the general witch population." Camila reached for Cassie's hand. "Only the High Coven knew of your true nature. I helped your mother keep you protected and hidden. The Northern California patrol had no idea vampires existed within their territory."

"Which explains their reaction when they encountered me," Cassie murmured, remembering the witch's horror aboard Alexander's yacht.

Across the room, she caught Alexander watching her, his expression questioning. She gave him a small nod, indicating she was fine. The silent communication felt natural, as if they'd been reading each other's signals for years rather than mere days.

"There's something between you," Camila observed, following Cassie's gaze. "Something significant."

Heat rose to Cassie's cheeks. "Is it that obvious?"

"To a grandmother's eyes? Absolutely." Camila's expression softened. "The Council won't approve."

"I don't need their approval," Cassie said, more sharply than she intended.

"No, you don't," Camila agreed, surprising her. "But you should understand the world you're stepping into. The treaty has maintained peace for centuries, but it's a fragile thing, built on separation and mistrust. This changes everything."

Cassie glanced toward her father, who stood tall and commanding as he discussed search strategies with the witch representatives. "Things are already changing. Claire and I exist."

"Perhaps that's what frightens them most," Camila mused. "Not that the treaty might break, but that it was built on false assumptions from the beginning."

Before Cassie could respond, Alexander approached their alcove, his expression carefully neutral, though his eyes held an urgency that made her heart quicken.

"Forgive the interruption," he said, inclining his head respectfully to Camila. "But the King has requested Cassie's presence. We're finalizing the joint search parameters."

Camila waved a hand, dispelling the privacy sigils with practiced ease. "Of course. I believe I'll join you both."

As they moved toward the main table, Cassie leaned closer to Alexander. "Is there news about Claire?"

"Not yet," he murmured, his voice pitched for her ears alone. "But your father believes your connection to her might help narrow the search area."

The main table had been transformed into a detailed holographic display of the coastline between Vancouver and Northern California. Glowing markers indicated search vessels already deployed, while red indicators showed the last known position of Sam's yacht and the island where debris had been found.

"Cassandra," Callimachus acknowledged as she approached, using her full name in this formal setting. "The witch delegation has agreed to a joint search operation. Four vessels, each with both vampire and witch representatives aboard."

"I want to go," Cassie said immediately, her voice firm. She didn't only want to go, she had to go. She needed to be doing something, and staying behind would make her crumble. "Claire would sense me, just as I would her."

Miranda, who had been studying the map intently, looked up with a frown. "That would be unwise. Your hybrid nature makes you uniquely vulnerable if there are indeed rogue elements targeting your sister."

"All the more reason for me to be involved," Cassie countered. "If someone is specifically after hybrids, I'm already a target whether I'm here or on a search vessel."

"She makes a valid point," the male witch, Giles, admitted reluctantly. "And if there is a connection between the sisters, her presence could prove valuable."

Callimachus studied Cassie for a moment, his ancient eyes assessing. "Alexander will command the lead vessel," he decided. "Cassandra will accompany him, along with a witch representative of the High Coven's choosing."

"I volunteer," Camila said immediately, stepping forward. "As Claire's grandmother, I have the strongest magical connection to her after Cassie."

Miranda looked as though she might object, but after a moment's consideration, she nodded. "Councilor Marlow's experience and personal connection make her the logical choice."

"Then it's settled," Callimachus declared. "The ship Apollo will depart at midnight, with additional vessels following established search patterns." He turned to Cassie. "Prepare yourself. The waters will be rough, and we don't know what you'll find. The Apollo is not as fast as the Artemis, but it is larger and more equipped should any challenges arise. It will hold a larger crew and have more cargo and defenses."

"I'll be ready," Cassie promised, determination hardening her voice. Her fingers curled into tight fists at her sides, nails digging crescents into her palms. The weight of her sister's absence hung heavy on her shoulders, but it was a burden she would gladly bear if it meant bringing Claire home safely.

As the meeting began to disperse, with witches and vampires breaking into smaller groups to discuss technical details, the grand chamber filled with the low murmur of urgent conversations. Maps were unfurled across tables, and magical artifacts were brought forth from hidden compartments in the walls. The scent of ancient parchment and ceremonial herbs permeated the air as preparations intensified around them.

Alexander drew Cassie aside to a shadowed alcove near one of the room's tall windows. Moonlight filtered through the glass, casting silver highlights across his concerned features. His hand rested briefly on her elbow, the touch light but grounding.

"Are you certain about this?" he asked, his voice low with concern, his dark eyes searching hers intently. "If there is a rogue faction powerful enough to create a storm worse than we encountered, they could target the search vessels as well. We'd be sailing directly into dangerous waters, both literally and figuratively. Whoever took Claire might be expecting a rescue attempt and be preparing accordingly."

"I'm certain," Cassie replied without hesitation, her eyes meeting his with unwavering resolve. "Claire's out there, Alexander. I can feel it in my bones, like a constant pull beneath my skin. And she needs me. Every moment we delay means another day that something could happen. Something," She couldn't bring herself to finish the worrying thought. The possibilities were too horrifying to voice. She couldn't lose her sister.

Something in her expression must have convinced him, for he nodded once, his features softening almost imperceptibly. His hand briefly touched hers in a gesture too quick for the others scattered throughout the chamber to notice, but the contact sent warmth spreading through her arm and into her chest, a momentary respite from the cold dread that had settled there since Claire's disappearance.

"I'll keep you safe," he promised, his voice dropping to a whisper meant only for her ears, rich with conviction and something else, something that made her pulse quicken despite everything. "Both of you. Whatever forces are at work here, whatever power created that storm, they'll have to go through me first." His dark eyes held a dangerous glint that reminded Cassie of exactly what he was, not just a diplomat, but a predator centuries old, with the strength and cunning to match his words.

Cassie believed him. Despite everything, the kidnapping, the revelations, the diplomatic complexities swirling around them, she trusted Alexander Ross in a way that defied rational explanation. Perhaps it was the witch stone connection, or something deeper, more primal that her dual nature recognized.

"I know you will," she said softly.

Camila approached, her keen eyes missing nothing of the exchange between them. "The witches are preparing protective amulets for the search party," she informed them. "I'll need something of Claire's to strengthen the locator spells."

"I don't have anything," Cassie realized with dismay. "Everything was left behind in Harmony."

"Blood calls to blood," Camila reminded her gently. "You share the same parentage. That connection will be enough."

Alexander nodded in understanding. "I'll make sure the Apollo is fully prepared. We'll find her, Cassie." His confidence steadied her, a rock amid the turbulent sea of uncertainty.

As he moved away to oversee preparations, Camila studied her granddaughter with thoughtful eyes. "He cares for you deeply, in this short time," she observed. "More than duty or obligation would explain."

"I care for him too," Cassie admitted, no longer seeing any point in denial. "I know it's complicated, with everything that's happening."

"Life is always complicated," Camila interrupted gently. "Especially for those of us who straddle different worlds. You've spent your entire life caught between sunlight and shadow, never fully belonging to either. Perhaps it's fitting that you've found a connection with someone who understands living between worlds."

The insight struck Cassie deeply. She'd never considered that Alexander, turned from human to vampire centuries ago, might understand her sense of displacement better than most. The revelation settled into her bones like a profound truth she'd always known but never articulated. He existed between worlds too, once human, now immortal, carrying memories of a mortal life while navigating an eternal one. It might clarify why she experienced such an unexplainable bond with him, as he'd lived a previous existence before his current one and had struggled to integrate both identities into a cohesive whole.

"Cassie, vampires mate for life," her grandmother said softly. "You need to understand that, whatever you pursue." Camila's silver-threaded hair caught the dim light as she leaned closer, her weathered hands clasping Cassie's with surprising strength. "It's not like human relationships or even witch bonds. When they give their heart, it's an irrevocable choice that spans centuries. What might feel like an intense connection now becomes something far more permanent for their kind." Her grandmother's eyes, filled with ancient wisdom and concern, searched Cassie's face. "I don't say this to discourage you, only to ensure you recognize the gravity of what might develop between you two."

Cassie inclined her head, absorbing her grandmother's wisdom. The implications weighed heavily on her mind. She hadn't been looking for a future, or even that type of bond. Yet now that was more than a simple possibility, she wasn't sure she wanted to ignore it.

"Will the Council ever accept hybrids?" she asked, changing the subject slightly. "Truly accept us, not just tolerate our existence?"

Camila sighed, her age showing momentarily in the weariness that crossed her features. "Change comes slowly to those who measure their lives in centuries rather than decades. But necessity is a powerful motivator." She glanced toward Miranda and Giles, deep in discussion with several vampires. "Our numbers continue to decline. If hybrids represent a new future for witchkind, even the most traditional among us may eventually embrace that possibility."

"And if they don't?"

"Then we create our own path," Camila said simply. "As witches have always done when faced with impossible choices."

Across the room, Callimachus caught Cassie's eye, beckoning her to join him. As she moved to answer her father's summons, Cassie felt a strange sense of rightness settling over her. She wasn't fighting against what she was, like she had done before arriving here, but embracing the unique position it gave her. It was a bridge between ancient enemies, a new possibility in a world built on old divisions.

Chapter Twenty

The two SUV caravan glided through Vancouver's empty pre-dawn streets, carrying Cassie, Alexander, and four other vampires toward the harbor where the Apollo awaited. Cassie pressed her forehead against the cool window glass, watching shadows slip past as her mind raced with thoughts of Claire.

"We'll find her," Alexander said quietly from beside her, his hand covering hers where her hand rested on the seat between them.

Cassie turned to him, eyes reflecting the passing streetlights. "I know. I can feel her out there. It's like there's an invisible thread pulling me toward her."

In the front seat, two vampire security officers maintained a professional silence, though Cassie occasionally caught them exchanging glances in the rearview mirror. Word of her relationship with Alexander had clearly spread throughout the compound. To be fair, she hadn't considered discretion in the short time since she'd known him.

The lead SUV turned onto a wide boulevard that would take them directly to the harbor. Cassie's senses, still adjusting to their enhanced capabilities, registered a subtle wrongness in the air a split second before Alexander tensed beside her.

"Something's wrong," she began.

Her world exploded in a blinding flash and deafening roar. She barely registered what happened as the lead SUV went cartwheeling through the air in a ball of flame. Their driver swerved violently, tires screaming against asphalt as he fought to avoid the explosion.

"DOWN!" Alexander shouted, throwing himself over Cassie to shield her as their SUV skidded sideways.

The windshield shattered inward as bullets tore through the vehicle. The driver jerked multiple times, crimson blooming across his chest before he slumped forward, unable to keep a grip on the steering wheel. The SUV careened out of control, slamming into a concrete barrier with bone-jarring force.

Cassie's head struck the window, pain exploding behind her eyes. Alexander's weight pressed her into the seat, shielding her as more bullets punched through metal and upholstery. She tasted blood in her mouth, sharp and metallic.

"Stay down," Alexander commanded, his voice tight with pain. "Don't move. I can withstand this. You can't."

He shifted, and Cassie felt something warm and wet soaking through her jacket where his body pressed against hers. Blood. His blood was flowing so fast it was drenching her.

"You're hurt," she gasped, panic and fear rising in her throat. She'd scarcely spent a significant amount of time with him, but was terrified of losing him.

"Doesn't matter." Alexander reached inside his jacket, withdrawing a handgun. "When I move, stay low. Stay with me at all times. Understand?"

Before she could respond, the passenger door was wrenched open. The vampire security officer twisted in his seat, fangs bared as he lunged toward something outside. A flash of silver cut through the air, and his head separated from his body in a spray of dark blood. The silver flashed again, cutting across to the driver's side and beheading the driver.

Alexander fired three rapid shots through the open door. Someone screamed, the sound abruptly cut short. He shoved the gun into Cassie's hands. The coldness of the metal startled her.

"Safety's off. Point and squeeze," he instructed, his voice eerily calm despite the blood now soaking his shirt. "I need to get us out of here."

Cassie's fingers closed around the unfamiliar weight of the cold weapon in her hand, her mind racing to process what was happening. The scent of blood, smoke, and an unfamiliar odor she guessed was gunpowder filled the air, overwhelming her heightened senses.

Alexander kicked out the rear window, glass showering onto the pavement. "Go. I'll cover you."

"I'm not leaving you," Cassie insisted, gripping the gun tighter, trying to stay calm.

A shadow passed over the shattered windshield. Alexander moved with blinding speed, intercepting a figure that had been about to reach into the vehicle. The sound of breaking bones cut through the night as he snapped the attacker's arm, then drove a fist into their throat.

More gunfire erupted, bullets pinging off the SUV's metal frame. Cassie ducked lower, adrenaline sharpening her senses. She could hear multiple heartbeats approaching from different directions. They were human heartbeats, not vampire. Or maybe they weren't human.

"Witches," she whispered, recognizing the distinctive energy signature beneath the human-like vitals.

Alexander nodded grimly, pressing a hand against the wound in his side. "Vampires working with witches. They appear to be targeting you again."

"That's impossible," Cassie breathed. Centuries of hatred between the species made such an alliance unthinkable.

"Apparently not." Alexander's face contorted with pain as he shifted position. "We need to move. They're getting closer, and we need to get away from this wreckage before it becomes our coffin."

A bullet whizzed through the broken window, grazing Cassie's arm. She hissed in pain, then raised Alexander's gun and fired blindly toward the source. The recoil surprised her, the weapon bucking in her hands.

"Don't shoot until you have a clear target," Alexander advised. Blood now soaked the entire left side of his shirt, dripping onto the seat beneath him. His normally pale face had taken on an ashen quality that terrified Cassie. Vampires could heal from almost anything but beheading and fire that reduced them to ash, but blood loss of this magnitude would eventually incapacitate even one as old as Alexander.

"Can you run?" she asked, her mind working through their limited options.

"Not far," he admitted. "I've lost too much blood."

The implications chilled her. Their attackers knew exactly who they were targeting. They knew Alexander was a vampire, and so were the drivers. They wouldn't have beheaded them otherwise.

Another figure appeared at the shattered windshield, hands weaving in the distinctive patterns of a darker type of witch magic. Cassie recognized the spell immediately. It was meant to immobilize. Without thinking about who she was targeting, she raised the gun and fired.

The witch crumpled, the half-formed spell dissipating in the air. Cassie stared at the gun in her hands, shock and horror washing through her at what she'd just done. She didn't feel relief. She'd killed a witch. What type of witch killed their own, to defend their enemy? In doing so, she crossed a line that couldn't be uncrossed.

"They left you no choice, Cassie," Alexander said quietly, reading her expression. "This was an ambush."

Cassie nodded, pushing aside her horror to focus on their immediate survival. "Who would do this? Who even knew we were leaving?"

"Too many," Alexander grimaced. "The High Council witch delegation, the security team, anyone at the compound who overheard our preparations."

A new sound cut through the chaos, the rhythmic thump of helicopter blades approaching rapidly. Reinforcements, but for which side? Although vampires lived in the city, Vancouver was overwhelmingly human.

"Who do you think that is?" Cassie whispered.

Alexander tensed, listening intently. "We can't wait to find out. We need to move now."

He kicked out what remained of the driver's side window, then dragged the dead vampire from behind the wheel. With agonizing slowness, he pulled himself into the front seat, leaving a smear of dark blood across the console.

"Can you drive?" Cassie asked, following him through the gap.

"Better than I can run," he managed, his breathing labored as he settled behind the wheel. "Get in."

Cassie scrambled into the passenger seat, still clutching the gun. The dead security officer's headless body slumped against the door. She swallowed hard, forcing herself to focus on Alexander instead.

Alexander pushed the start button on the console. Nothing happened. He tried to push it again, with no results.

"Damaged in the crash," he muttered, slamming his fist against the panel in frustration.

The helicopter sounds grew louder, accompanied by shouts and the pounding of feet approaching from multiple directions. They were running out of time.

Cassie closed her eyes, reaching for that strange dual power within her. The witch magic responded first, flowing through her veins with familiar warmth. Then came the vampire strength, darker and more primal, surging up from some deep well she was only beginning to understand.

"I can feel them," she whispered, her eyes snapping open. "Three witches approaching from the east. Two vampires circling behind us." She turned to Alexander, determination hardening her features. "I can buy us time."

Before he could protest, Cassie flung open the passenger door and stepped out, raising the gun in one hand while gathering her hybrid power in the other. The draw on her power was easier now, the energy crackling between her fingers with electric intensity.

A figure darted from behind a parked car, moving with vampire speed. Cassie fired, the bullet catching them in the shoulder. They staggered but didn't fall, fangs bared in a snarl of rage.

Cassie whispered quickly, but the words were intentional as she released her power, sending a blast of energy that caught the vampire square in the chest. The vampire flew backward, crashing through a storefront window in a shower of glass.

"Cassie!" Alexander's voice was tight with pain and urgency. "Behind you!"

She whirled, catching movement in her peripheral vision. A witch had emerged from the shadows, hands already completing a complex casting pattern. Cassie felt the magic building, a suffocating pressure in the air around her.

She fired twice, the bullets going wide as the witch completed the spell. Invisible power slammed into Cassie, driving the air from her lungs and sending her sprawling across the pavement. The gun slid away from her reach.

The witch advanced, drawing a silver knife from beneath her robes. "Abomination," she hissed, her face contorted with hatred. "You should never have existed."

Cassie scrambled backward, her hand searching desperately for the gun. Her fingers closed around rough concrete instead.

The witch lunged, the silver of the knife flashing in the streetlight. Cassie rolled aside, the blade missing her throat by inches. She lashed out with her foot, catching the witch in the knee. Bone cracked, and the witch screamed, staggering backward.

Cassie seized the moment, surging to her feet and tackling the witch before she could recover. They struck the pavement hard, the blade sliding away across the concrete. Cassie pinned the witch's arms, her vampire strength giving her the advantage despite her injuries.

"Who sent you?" she demanded, her voice barely recognizable to her own ears. "Why are you working with vampires?"

The witch spat in her face. "We will purify both bloodlines. We'll not allow abominations like you and your sister to live."

Cassie's grip tightened involuntarily, making the witch gasp in pain. "Where is my sister? What have you done with Claire?"

A strange smile twisted the witch's features. "We will end her. And you too."

The witch's head jerked sideways, eyes widening in shock. Blood bubbled from her lips as she went limp beneath Cassie's hands.

"What have you done? We needed information to find Claire!" Cassie cried.

Alexander stood over her, his face a mask of pain and determination. Blood soaked his entire left side now, dripping steadily onto the pavement. In his hand, he held a silver knife, the witch's own weapon, the one he had used to cut her throat.

"We need to go," he said, swaying slightly. "More coming." The silver blade dropped from his grip, striking the pavement with a metallic ring.

Cassie scrambled to her feet, catching Alexander as he stumbled and nearly fell. She wrapped an arm around his waist, supporting his weight the best she could.

"Where to now?" she asked.

Alexander nodded toward a side street. "The alley, and hopefully to find cover."

They staggered forward together, Alexander leaning heavily against her. Each step left a dark smear on the pavement behind them. The helicopter was directly overhead now, its searchlight sweeping across the destruction.

"Alexander," Cassie said urgently, feeling him grow heavier against her. "Stay with me."

"Always," he murmured, his voice fading. "I just need a moment."

His legs buckled, and Cassie barely managed to control his descent as he slid to the ground. She caught his head with one hand and propped his back against the brick wall of the alley. His eyes fluttered, struggling to stay open.

"No, no, no," Cassie knelt beside him, frantically searching for the source of the bleeding. His shirt was soaked through, making it impossible to locate individual wounds. Her hands shook as she searched for injuries she didn't know how to treat. "Alexander, please. You can't do this."

He reached up, his bloodied fingers leaving a smear on her cheek as he touched her face. "Find Claire," he whispered. "Promise me."

"We'll find her together," Cassie insisted, tears blurring her vision. "Just stay awake." She needed him to stay with her. She couldn't lose him. Now not. Not after everything they'd been through in such a short time.

Footsteps approached from both ends of the alley. They were surrounded, with nowhere left to run. Alexander's eyes met hers, a lifetime of regret in their depths.

"I'm sorry," he said softly. "I failed to protect you."

"No," Cassie shook her head fiercely. "You didn't fail. We're still fighting."

She rose to her feet, standing protectively over Alexander's prone form. Her hybrid power gathered around her like a storm, energy crackling between her fingers as vampire strength surged through her muscles. If they wanted Alexander, they would have to go through her first. She started to murmur dark words, words her mother told her to use only in the most dire of situations. They weren't meant for defense. They were meant for ruin. It was an ending spell, one that would do more than immobilize. It was one of deadly intent.

As the shadows at both ends of the alley solidified into approaching figures, Cassie Marlow prepared to protect Alexander, her eyes glowing with supernatural light in the darkness. She felt her fangs elongate and bared them, hissing a warning.

Chapter Twenty-One

Three vampires emerged from the shadows at the end of the alley, their movements cautious but deliberate. They wore tactical gear similar to what Alexander had worn when he'd first kidnapped her, and each carried an M4 assault rifle pointed in her direction. Despite their weapons, they approached slowly, as if uncertain how to proceed against her. She radiated barely leashed power.

"Miss Marlow," the lead vampire called, his voice low and controlled. "We need to get you and Commander Ross out of here. King's orders."

Cassie didn't lower her hands, but she dropped the intention for the deadly spell. Instead, she whispered words that charged an immobilizing spell, preparing in the event it was needed. Behind the approaching vampires, she heard shouts and the distinct sound of fighting, more of their attackers being engaged.

"Stay back," she warned, her voice low from the power surging through her. "I don't know who you are."

The lead vampire stopped, raising one hand while keeping his rifle pointed downward. "I'm Matthew, and I've been sent to help you. We're part of the security team from the compound. The King sent us when communications with your convoy went dark."

Cassie remained in her defensive stance, her body positioned to shield Alexander. "Prove it," she demanded.

Matthew's eyes rapidly moved to Alexander's prone form, concern evident in his expression, then back to Cassie. "Your father calls you Cassandra despite your preference for Cassie. You were staying in Commander Ross's quarters. You drank deer blood before training in the underground facility yesterday."

The details were specific enough to give Cassie pause, but she didn't release her power. They'd already been betrayed once. "Anyone in the compound could know that."

One of the other vampires stepped forward, his movement triggering Cassie's defensive instinct. She unleashed a blast of hybrid energy that sent him flying backward, slamming into his companion. Both vampires crumpled to the ground, one lying deathly still, the other groaning in agony but swiftly rising to a standing position.

Matthew remained where he stood, hands now raised higher. "Miss Marlow, please. Commander Ross needs blood immediately. We're here to help, and we need to get both of you out of here."

A weak voice came from behind her. "Cassie, let them."

She glanced down to see Alexander struggling to lift his head, his eyes barely focusing. "It's Matthew, I trust him."

The confirmation from Alexander made her hesitate. She looked back at the vampire security team, then at the one she'd struck down, guilt washing through her as she realized she might have seriously injured one of their rescuers. She acted without hesitation, like when she and Alexander had trained. Seeing the crumpled vampires made her realize she needed a lot more training, if they ever got out of this situation. She needed to harness who she was becoming before she completely lost control.

Matthew moved slowly toward his fallen comrades, checking the unmoving vampire. "He's alive, but barely. Your power packs quite a punch, Miss Marlow."

"I'm sorry," she whispered, the deadly energy finally dissipating from her fingers. "I didn't know if you were with them."

"Understandable," Matthew replied, his attention now on Alexander. He quickly detached a small pouch from his tactical belt and approached cautiously. "May I?"

Cassie nodded, stepping aside but remaining close as Matthew knelt beside Alexander. He opened the pouch, revealing a vial of dark red liquid.

"Emergency blood supply," he explained, carefully lifting Alexander's head. "It's not much, but it will help stabilize him until we can get him proper treatment and more blood."

Alexander's lips parted as Matthew poured the thick blood into his mouth. The effect was immediate. Some color returned to his ashen face, and his eyes focused more clearly.

"Status?" Alexander demanded, his voice stronger though still strained.

"Area not secure," Matthew reported crisply. "Helicopter extraction two blocks north. Four hostiles neutralized. Three vampires, one witch, unknown number still active."

Alexander nodded, attempting to push himself upright. Matthew moved to help him, supporting his weight as he struggled to his feet. Cassie slipped beneath Alexander's other side and assisted in raising him further.

"Can you walk?" she asked, worry evident in her voice.

"I can now," he replied, though his body trembled with the effort of standing. "The blood helps, but I've lost too much. I'll need a more substantial feeding when we're secure."

Matthew gestured to the other vampire, who had recovered enough to stand. "Help Commander Ross. I'll take point with Miss Marlow."

The injured vampire moved to Alexander's other side, taking some of his weight. Cassie noticed how he kept a respectful distance from her, wariness evident in his posture.

"I'm sorry about that," she said, unsure of how to apologize.

"No apology necessary, miss," he replied stiffly. "You were protecting your mate."

The casual use of the term sent a jolt through Cassie, but there was no time to correct or question it. Her surprise at hearing the word from another vampire wasn't that it was wrong. It was because it felt right. It felt true. Matthew was already moving toward the far end of the alley, rifle raised and ready. The vampire was correct. She protected her mate, Alexander. She'd unpack the weight of it later.

"Stay close," he instructed. "The helicopter is waiting, but we have to cross open ground to reach it."

Cassie nodded, keeping one arm around Alexander's waist as they followed and kept pace with Matthew. The vampire who'd been unconscious was quickly gathered up by the third member of their team, carried over his shoulder like he weighed nothing.

As they reached the end of the alley, Matthew paused, scanning the street beyond. The sound of the helicopter blades was louder now, accompanied by shouts and occasional gunfire.

"Prepare to move," he said, his body tensing. "Move!"

They quickly moved from the alley. Two blocks away, a helicopter hovered just above street level, its searchlight sweeping the area. Between them and their extraction point, figures moved in the shadows, some with the unnatural speed of vampires, others with the distinctive energy signature of witches.

Matthew fired precise bursts from his rifle, providing covering fire as they moved forward. The vampire supporting Alexander kept pace with Cassie, while the one carrying their unconscious comrade brought up the rear.

A witch stepped into their path, hands already weaving a spell. Matthew dropped to one knee, firing three shots in rapid succession. The witch collapsed before casting a spell.

"Keep moving!" Matthew shouted over the gunfire. "Don't stop for anything!"

They'd covered half the distance when a vampire appeared seemingly from nowhere, tackling the security officer who carried their unconscious teammate. Both went down in a tangle of limbs, rolling across the pavement.

"Leave him!" Matthew commanded when Cassie hesitated. "Extraction is priority!"

The helicopter was close now, hovering just above the street with its side door open. A vampire in tactical gear manned a mounted gun, providing suppressing fire that kept their attackers at bay.

Alexander stumbled, nearly taking Cassie down with him. "Almost there," she encouraged, tightening her grip around his waist. "Just a little further."

They reached the helicopter as bullets pinged off its metal exterior. Matthew jumped in first, then turned to help Cassie with Alexander. Together, they hauled him into the cabin, where he collapsed against the far wall, breathing heavily.

"Go!" Matthew shouted to the pilot. "We've got them!"

The helicopter began to rise, the door still open as the last security officer made a desperate sprint toward them, his fallen comrade held tightly over his shoulder. A witch appeared behind him, hands glowing with deadly intent.

"No!" Cassie lunged toward the open door, gathering her hybrid power once more. She sent a blast of energy toward the witch, knocking them backward just as the security officer leaped for the helicopter.

Matthew caught his teammate's arm, hauling him and their fellow team member aboard as the helicopter climbed higher. Their power amazed Cassie, though she'd begun to experience similar capabilities herself. The door slammed shut, sealing them in relative safety as they rose above the chaos below.

Cassie crawled to Alexander's side, her hands trembling as she assessed his wounds. His shirt was soaked with blood, multiple bullet wounds visible through the torn fabric. They weren't healing very fast.

"He needs blood," she told Matthew. "A lot of it."

Matthew nodded grimly. "Medical team is standing by at the compound. We'll be there in seven minutes."

Alexander's eyes fluttered open, finding Cassie's face. "You're safe," he murmured, relief evident despite his pain.

"Thanks to you," she replied, taking his hand in hers. "Just stay with me, okay? We're almost home."

The sentiment slipped out before she could stop it. Somehow, in the span of a few days, the vampire compound had become a place that felt like home, a refuge rather than a prison. It was where Alexander and her father lived.

Alexander's lips curved in a weak smile. "Not getting rid of me that easily," he whispered, squeezing her hand with what little strength he had left.

As the helicopter sped toward the compound, Cassie remained by Alexander's side, her mind racing with questions. Who had organized this attack? How had they known about their departure? And what had they meant about Claire and ending her? Did they have her? Was it too late?

The implications chilled her to the bone. Whoever these people were, this alliance of rogue vampires and witches, they knew about her and Claire. They might even be holding her. And they were more than willing to kill them. As the evening had demonstrated, this alliance was determined to kill them.

Cassie looked down at Alexander's pale face, determination hardening within her. They would heal him, regroup, and then they would find Claire. No matter what it took, no matter who stood in their way, she would not rest until her sister was safe.

The helicopter banked sharply, heading toward the compound's lights glowing in the distance. Now that they were safe, Cassie felt a lethargy tugging at her, but she fought it off, focusing instead on Alexander's face and the promise she'd made to herself. Tears threatened to fall, but she refused to let them. She needed to stay aware and strong. Claire and Alexander needed her, and she wasn't going to fail them.

Chapter Twenty-Two

The helicopter descended rapidly toward the compound's landing pad, the whine of its engines competing with the steady thrum of rotors. Medical staff waited below, their forms silhouetted against the floodlights that illuminated the pad. Cassie clutched Alexander's hand, her own covered in his blood, watching as he mustered what little strength he had left. She knew he was a vampire and would survive, but it was hard seeing him hurt this badly.

"We're here," she whispered, leaning close to his ear. "Just hold on a little longer."

The moment the skids touched down, the door slid open, and the medical team swarmed in. They moved with practiced efficiency, transferring Alexander onto a stretcher while a doctor immediately began assessing his wounds.

"Multiple gunshot wounds, severe blood loss," the doctor called out. "Get him to the trauma unit, and have fresh blood ready!"

Cassie scrambled after them as they rushed Alexander across the landing pad toward the building. It wasn't yet dawn, but the attack and her fight caused a heaviness to settle in her limbs. She pushed through it, refusing to succumb to exhaustion while Alexander was hurt.

Inside, the bright lights of the medical facility momentarily blinded her. The antiseptic smell mingled with the metallic scent of blood that clung to her clothes and skin. The team wheeled Alexander through a set of double doors, a nurse stepping in front of Cassie when she tried to follow.

"I'm sorry, Miss Marlow, but you need to wait here," the nurse said firmly.

"No, I need to be with him," Cassie insisted, trying to push past.

A strong hand caught her arm. She turned to find Callimachus standing beside her, his ancient eyes filled with concern that seemed directed at both her and Alexander.

"Let them work, Cassie," he said, his voice gentle. "Alexander is strong, and they know what they're doing."

Cassie's resistance crumbled at her father's touch. The adrenaline that had sustained her through the attack suddenly drained away, leaving her trembling and disoriented. Callimachus guided her to a nearby chair, his arm supportive around her shoulders. She wanted to lean into him, but the blood on her hands surprised her. Her fingers trembled as she looked at the blood caked in her fingernails and crusted on her knuckles. It was Alexander's blood.

"Are you able to detail what happened, from your point of view?" he asked, studying her blood-stained clothes and the cuts on her face and hands.

"Ambush," Cassie replied, her voice hollow. "They knew we were coming. Vampires working with witches." She looked up at her father, anguish clear in her eyes. "They said they were going to end Claire. That they'd end me too."

Callimachus's expression hardened, the ancient warrior momentarily visible beneath his composed exterior. "Who said this?"

"One of the witches," Cassie explained, recalling the hatred in the witch's eyes. "She called me an abomination. Said they would purify both bloodlines."

Her father's jaw tightened, a muscle working beneath the skin. "Purists," he muttered, almost to himself. "They are extremists who believe in maintaining the separation between supernatural creatures, at any cost."

"But they were working together," Cassie pointed out. "Vampires and witches, fighting side by side. How is that maintaining separation?"

"Sometimes the most extreme elements of opposing factions find common cause in their hatred," Callimachus explained, his voice grim. "They see you and Claire as a threat to both species' purity."

The doors to the trauma unit swung open, and a doctor emerged, her scrubs already stained with blood. She approached Callimachus with a respectful bow.

"Your Majesty, Commander Ross has lost a significant amount of blood. We've removed three silver-tipped bullets and are treating multiple other wounds. He'll need substantial transfusions before he starts healing on his own."

"Whatever he needs," Callimachus commanded. "Spare nothing."

The doctor nodded, then turned to Cassie. "He's asking for you, Miss Marlow. Quite insistently, despite our efforts to sedate him."

Relief flooded through Cassie. If Alexander was conscious enough to be demanding, he was fighting. "Can I see him?"

"Briefly," the doctor conceded. "He needs rest and blood to heal properly."

Cassie rose, swaying slightly as exhaustion and daylight lethargy competed within her for dominance. Callimachus steadied her with a hand on her elbow.

"Go to him," he said softly. "I'm organizing our response to this attack."

"What about Claire?" Cassie asked, fear for her sister rising fresh in her mind.

"We'll redouble our search efforts," Callimachus promised. "And Cassie," his voice dropped lower, "whoever is responsible for this will pay dearly. No one threatens my daughters and lives."

The cold certainty in his voice should have frightened her, but instead, Cassie found it comforting. For the first time in her life, she had someone other than her mother and grandmother willing to move heaven and earth to protect her, a father who commanded the power to do exactly that.

She followed the doctor through the double doors into the trauma unit. Alexander lay on a bed surrounded by medical equipment, multiple IV lines running blood into his arms. His skin was ashen, but his eyes were open, searching the room until they found her.

"Cassie," he breathed, relief evident in his voice.

She moved to his side, taking his hand carefully to avoid disturbing the IV. "I'm here," she assured him. "You should be resting, not demanding to see me."

A ghost of a smile touched his lips. "Had to make sure you were safe. I needed to see you." His blood still covered her clothes, and cuts from the explosion stung across her skin. They were healing but still fresh. "You're the one who decided to use yourself as a human shield."

"Vampire shield," he corrected weakly. "More durable."

Despite everything, Cassie found herself smiling. "Not durable enough, apparently. Maybe you are better suited to kidnapping."

Alexander's expression sobered. "Someone knew our route, our timing."

"I know," Cassie said, squeezing his hand gently. "My father is already investigating."

"I need to be working with him, taking precautions," Alexander warned, his voice strengthening slightly with urgency. "If there's a traitor in the compound," he didn't finish.

"I'll be careful," she promised. "But right now, you need to focus on healing."

The doctor approached, checking one of the monitors. "That's enough for now," she said firmly. "Commander Ross needs rest, and you, Miss Marlow, should have your own injuries treated."

Cassie nodded, reluctantly releasing Alexander's hand. "I'll be back," she promised him.

"I know," he answered, his gaze already growing heavy as the specially formulated sedatives designed to subdue vampires at last began working.

Outside the trauma unit, Cassie found her father deep in conversation with several security officers. They fell silent as she approached, exchanging glances that spoke volumes.

"How is he?" Callimachus asked.

"Resting now," Cassie replied. "The doctor says he'll recover." She looked around at the grim faces surrounding her father. "What's happening? What aren't you telling me?"

Callimachus dismissed the security team with a nod before turning back to her. "We've found evidence that the attack was coordinated from within the compound. Someone with access to our security protocols and scheduling."

The implications sent a chill through Cassie. "A traitor."

"Yes," Callimachus confirmed. "And given the nature of the attack, silver-tipped bullets, the coordination between vampires and witches, someone with connections to both worlds."

"I didn't realize silver was something that harmed vampires," Cassie said.

"Although it won't cause our death, it prevents our regeneration and becomes dangerous for that reason," Callimachus explained.

"What do we do now?" Cassie asked, fatigue making her voice rough.

"First, you need to rest," her father said firmly. "You've been through a traumatic experience. Even with your abilities, after everything that has happened and what you've endured, you need some time to recover."

"I can't rest," Cassie protested. "Not with Claire still missing and Alexander injured. Not with traitors in our midst."

Callimachus placed his hands on her shoulders, his expression softening. "Cassie, I understand your determination. It reminds me of myself, in fact. But even vampires must rest to maintain their strength."

She wanted to argue further, but exhaustion was rapidly overtaking her. The adrenaline that had sustained her through the attack and its aftermath was gone, leaving her hollow and drained. She could barely keep her eyes open.

"What about Claire?" she asked, the words slurring slightly with fatigue.

"We will find her," Callimachus promised. "But to do that, we need you at your full strength. Get some nourishment. Rest now. When you wake, we will plan our next move together."

Cassie let her father guide her toward the elevator. As they rode up to the residential level, she leaned against the wall, spent.

"I want vengeance," she said suddenly, the words surprising her as much as they seemed to surprise her father. "For Alexander. For Claire. I want whoever did this to pay."

Callimachus studied her, pride mingling with concern in his ancient eyes. "Vengeance is your birthright as my daughter," he said softly. "But it must be tempered with strategy. Blind rage benefits only our enemies."

The elevator doors opened, and he led her down the corridor to a new suite of rooms. "These are more secure than Alexander's quarters," he explained. "And closer to my own."

Inside, the suite was elegantly appointed, with a large bed that looked impossibly inviting to Cassie's exhausted body. Fresh clothes awaited her, and the bathroom door was open, revealing a shower.

"Rest," Callimachus said again. "I will have guards posted outside your door. No one will disturb you."

Cassie turned to face her father, suddenly overwhelmed by the events of the past few days. "They want to kill us," she whispered. "Claire and me. Just for existing."

"They will not succeed," Callimachus replied, his voice hardening with resolve. "I will rain fire down upon anyone who threatens my daughters. The vampires of this territory answer to me, and they will hunt down these traitors. As for the witches involved," his eyes gleamed with dangerous intent, "they will learn why I was feared on the battlefield long before I became a vampire."

His words brought a strange comfort. This ancient being, this warrior king who had survived millennia, was her father. His protection wasn't just words. It was backed by centuries of power and the command of a supernatural kingdom.

"Once I'm refreshed, I want to find my sister," Cassie said, her voice strengthening despite her exhaustion.

Callimachus nodded, something like tenderness crossing his features. "We will find her," he promised. "Now rest, daughter. It won't take much to feel refreshed. Your strength will return."

As her father left, Cassie managed to shower mechanically, washing away Alexander's blood and the grime of battle. Clean clothes felt like a luxury after the horror of the night. She crawled into the bed, her body surrendering to exhaustion before her head even touched the pillow.

Her last conscious thought was of Claire, somewhere out there, possibly in the hands of the same people who had tried to kill her and Alexander. "I'm coming for you," she whispered into the darkness. "Just hold on. And please be alive."

Chapter Twenty-Three

Cassie woke up, her body refreshed. Her mind, though, was still heavy with worry. The digital clock beside the bed showed it was late in the afternoon, a few hours before sunset. She'd slept through most of the day, her hybrid nature demanding recovery time after the trauma and exertion. Every muscle felt renewed, the peculiar tingling sensation that always accompanied her accelerated healing process still lingering beneath her skin.

She stretched cautiously, taking inventory of her body. The wounds she'd sustained during the attack had closed completely, leaving behind only the phantom memory of pain. Her body healed more quickly than she was able to grasp, leaving her feeling as if something wasn't quite right.

Her eyes adjusted quickly to the darkness, another benefit of her unusual heritage. The sheets smelled of lavender and something clinical, reminding her that she was far from the comforting scent of her greenhouse back in Harmony. She longed for her plants and yearned for the aroma of fresh earth and the soothing sensation of burying her fingers in the soil.

Cassie ran her fingers through her tangled auburn hair, memories of the previous night's chaos flooding back in vivid detail. The attackers, Alexander's injuries, it all crashed down upon her consciousness with renewed urgency. She needed information. She needed to know what had transpired while her body had selfishly demanded rest. The hunger gnawing at her stomach told her she'd need to find raw sustenance soon. Her unique dietary restrictions wouldn't be suspended even in a crisis.

She sat up and noticed a high-covered tumbler on her nightstand. Her instincts informed her it contained exactly what her body required. She extended her arm, grasped the container, removed its lid, and swallowed the blood in several gulps. She was discovering it increasingly less repulsive and more soothing, even invigorating. That it helped so much, and went down so easily should be disturbing. Yet it wasn't, and she wondered if she was becoming accustomed to this different lifestyle with similar ease. Like drinking the blood, the lifestyle should have been repulsive, but it wasn't.

She rose quickly, dressing in the practical clothes that had been provided: dark jeans, a fitted black top, and sturdy boots. Her first thought was of Alexander, and she was heading for the door when a knock sounded. She pulled the door open, discovering Alexander propped against the doorframe, a gentle smile playing across his lips.

"Miss me?" he asked.

Cassie didn't answer with words. She rushed forward into his embrace, pressing her cheek against his chest. The familiar scent of him, pine needles, old books, and something uniquely Alexander, enveloped her, providing a momentary sanctuary from the chaos that had engulfed both their lives. She held him tightly. She wasn't ready yet to let him go and feel any absence from him, no matter how small.

Alexander hugged her for a moment, his strong arms encircling her with a protective gentleness that made her feel both vulnerable and safe. Then, with deliberate tenderness, he lifted her chin with his fingertips, his brown eyes meeting hers with an intensity that made her breath catch in her throat before he leaned in and kissed her deeply, pouring all the unspoken relief and longing that words couldn't adequately express into the connection between them.

Alexander lifted his head first, breaking their kiss reluctantly. His eyes searched hers, filled with equal parts concern and longing. The golden afternoon light filtered through the curtains, catching the angles of his face and softening his strong features. His thumb traced a gentle path along her jawline as he spoke.

"Would you like to rest for a few more hours with me?" he asked, his voice low and intimate as he guided them into a quiet room. There was no presumption in his tone, just a tender invitation born from the knowledge of all she'd been through. "The others won't expect us until later, and you could probably use more recovery time." His fingers brushed a strand of auburn hair from her face, tucking it carefully behind her ear.

Cassie inclined her head in agreement, a silent acquiescence that spoke volumes in the stillness of the room. The ease with which she accepted the invitation passed through her, and she refused to feel guilty for the small amount of time she wanted to spend with him. It wasn't so much a decision, as it was normalizing the moment. They would rejoin the world that was moving around them soon enough.

She raised her face toward his, her eyes half-lidded with desire and something deeper, and drew his lips to hers again. Alexander responded without hesitation, kissing her with a tenderness that contrasted with the strength evident in the set of his shoulders. His kiss was gentle yet consuming, acknowledging her fragility without treating her as fragile.

Then, with careful deliberation, he lifted her by the waist, his large hands spanning the curve where her slightly thin frame widened. Cassie instinctively curled her legs around him, her auburn hair cascading down her back as she wrapped her arms around his neck, trusting him completely with her weight and her vulnerability. The intimacy of the position wasn't lost on either of them, but there was something almost innocent in the protective way he cradled her against his chest.

He moved toward the bed with measured steps. His steps were quiet. When they reached the edge of the mattress, Alexander lowered her down with exquisite gentleness, as if she were made of something precious, his dark brown eyes never leaving her face as he set her onto the cool sheets. Trust fluttered through her, bright and promising. It wasn't a choice she was making anymore, and it was an acute awareness that was now there, present and fierce. He'd protected her with his life, and the rawness of that made the moment more intense.

Cassie savored the revelation, lying back against the pillows as Alexander lowered himself beside her, his weight creating a gentle depression in the mattress. His movements were careful as if he were handling something infinitely precious. In the dim light of the room, his eyes held an intensity that made her heart quicken.

"I thought I might lose you yesterday," she whispered, tracing the line of his jaw with her fingertips. "When I saw all that blood, I felt like I'd lost a piece of my heart."

Alexander caught her hand, pressing a kiss to her palm. "It would take far more than silver-tipped bullets to separate me from you."

His words sent warmth cascading through her. There was something profound in his tone, a depth of feeling that transcended their brief time together. Cassie shifted closer, needing to feel the solid reality of him against her.

Alexander's hands moved with reverent patience as he undressed her, each garment removed with unhurried care. His cool fingers trailed across her skin, leaving goosebumps in their wake. When she lay bare before him, his gaze traveled the length of her body.

"You're beautiful," he murmured, his voice rough with emotion.

Cassie reached for him, helping him shed his own clothing until there was nothing between them but the charged air of the room. His body was magnificent, all lean muscle and ancient strength. It was marred only by the old scars earned before he was turned, and faint pink lines where recent bullet wounds had nearly healed.

She traced one of these marks with gentle fingers. "Does it still hurt?"

"Not anymore," he assured her, capturing her hand and bringing it to his lips. "Not with you here."

When he lowered himself over her, the cool press of his skin against hers drew a soft gasp from her lips. His weight was perfectly balanced, present but never crushing as he settled between her thighs. Their bodies aligned with an instinctive rightness that made Cassie wonder how she'd ever felt complete before knowing his touch.

Alexander took his time, his mouth exploring the sensitive curve of her neck, the hollow of her throat, the swell of her breasts. Each kiss was a declaration, each caress a promise. When his lips closed around one nipple, Cassie arched beneath him, a soft moan escaping her.

"Alexander," she breathed, her fingers threading through his dark hair.

He looked up, his eyes meeting hers with an intensity that stole her breath. "I want to spend the rest of my existence with you, Cassie," he confessed, the words seeming to surprise even him with their sudden honesty. "I've lived centuries, but nothing has felt as right as being with you."

The declaration hung between them, momentous and perfect in its simplicity. Cassie felt tears prick at her eyes, overwhelmed by the depth of feeling his words evoked.

"I feel it too," she whispered. "Like I've been waiting for you without knowing it."

Alexander moved up to capture her lips, the kiss deep and consuming. When he finally pulled back, his expression was solemn despite the desire burning in his eyes.

"Be my mate, Cassie," he said softly. "Not just for now, but for all the time we have. Vampires mate for life, and it's rare and precious when we find someone who calls to our soul."

Cassie cupped his face between her palms, searching his eyes. The word settled heavily into her, threatening to choke her with indecision. It was a life-binding decision, and while there was no doubt in her heart, her mind wasn't convinced as quickly. She'd nearly lost him, and neither his life nor her life was certain. Waiting wouldn't bring resolution or guarantees. He also didn't ask her to choose between being a witch or vampire. He chose her just as she was. The thought of leaving him terrified her more than staying, choosing him. She didn't have to promise him forever. She was promising him now, and honesty. That was her choice, and it was freeing.

"We've known each other for such a short time," she said. "And there's so much uncertainty ahead of us."

"Time means little when you recognize what you've found," Alexander replied. "I knew from the moment I saw you in that shop, surrounded by your plants and humming that ancient melody. Something in me recognized you, Cassie Marlow."

She smiled, feeling a sense of rightness settle deep in her bones. The feeling was always there, and the words finally caught up in her head. "Yes," she answered simply. "I'll be your mate, Alexander Ross. Whatever comes, we'll face it together."

The joy that transformed his features was breathtaking. He kissed her again, this time with a passion that burned away all hesitation. His hands mapped her body with renewed purpose, learning every curve and plane as if he were committing her to memory.

When he finally joined their bodies, sliding into her with deliberate slowness, Cassie gasped at the perfect fullness. They moved together in a rhythm as old as time, each stroke building pleasure between them. Alexander watched her face as he moved, his dark eyes never leaving hers, witnessing every reaction, every flutter of pleasure that crossed her features.

"You're everything," he whispered against her lips.

Cassie wrapped her legs around him tightly, drawing him deeper. "And you're mine," she answered, the words both a claim and a promise.

Their pace quickened, the need between them growing. Alexander's control began to slip, his movements becoming more powerful, more primal. Cassie welcomed it, meeting him thrust for thrust, her nails scoring his back as pleasure built within her.

When her release came, it crashed through her like a tidal wave, her body arching and tightening around him as she cried out his name. Alexander followed moments later, his body shuddering against hers as he found his own completion.

They remained joined afterward, neither willing to break the connection. Alexander's forehead rested against hers, their breath mingling in the small space between them. The intimacy of the moment was profound, transcending the physical act they'd shared.

"I never expected to find you," Alexander murmured, brushing a strand of auburn hair from her face. "In all my centuries, I never thought I'd discover someone who could make me feel so alive."

Cassie smiled, her heart full. "And I never imagined my kidnapper would become my mate," she teased gently. "Life has a strange way of surprising us."

He chuckled, the sound rumbling through his chest against hers. "Indeed it does." His expression sobered slightly. "You know this won't be easy. There are those who will oppose us, who see our union as a threat."

"I know," she acknowledged. "But we can do it." Her determination hardened her voice. "Night's falling soon. We should join the others and see if there's been any progress."

Alexander nodded, reluctantly withdrawing from her embrace. "You're right. Your father will be waiting for us."

As they dressed, Cassie felt a new certainty settling over her. The bond between them wasn't just physical attraction or being thrown together by events. It was something deeper, more profound. A recognition between souls that surpassed the boundaries of witch and vampire, of centuries and moments.

Alexander paused at the door, turning back to her with an expression of such tenderness it made her heart ache. "Whatever comes next, Cassie Marlow, we face it as one."

She stepped into his embrace, drawing strength from his solid presence. "As one," she agreed, sealing the promise with a kiss. He had the confidence of centuries. Hers was newer, and lighter. Even if the future wasn't guaranteed, their togetherness was right.

Another knock at the door had Cassie turning away from Alexander and toward whoever waited outside. The sharp, insistent tapping cut through the intimate moment like a blade, three quick raps that demanded immediate attention. The interruption felt almost cruel, as it was ending their time together. She reluctantly pulled back from Alexander's warmth, her eyes darting to the door of the room. A flicker of annoyance crossed her features, mingling with the concern that had been her constant companion since Claire's disappearance. Whoever stood on the other side of that threshold was either bringing news or complications, neither of which could wait, despite the rare moment of connection she'd just shared with the vampire who'd become so unexpectedly central to her world.

Chapter Twenty-Four

Callimachus stood outside, his expression bemused but composed. He gave a quick nod of acknowledgment to Alexander before speaking to Cassie. "You're awake. Good. There have been developments."

Cassie swallowed her irritation. The world didn't care about her wants as it crashed back into her reality. The certainty she found and felt with Alexander only moments ago turned to fear. "Claire?" Cassie asked.

"Nothing concrete, but we've identified several of the attackers." Callimachus gestured for her to follow him. "The delegation from the High Coven is still here. Your grandmother wishes to speak with you."

Cassie followed her father through the corridors, noting the increased security presence. Every intersection had armed guards, and she spotted magical wards shimmering faintly along the walls. They were new protections added since the attack.

"How bad was it?" she asked quietly.

"Four of our security team dead," Callimachus replied, his voice tight with controlled anger. "Three of the attackers captured alive, two vampires and one witch. They're being questioned."

The euphemism wasn't lost on Cassie. "Questioned" likely meant methods she preferred not to contemplate. She trembled as she told herself it was necessary, considering what torments they could be suffering, but rapidly fortified her resolve. They had attacked her and Alexander, but the reassurance she was seeking wasn't there. Her body was whole, and she was rested and refreshed, as was Alexander. Four others were not. The disparity weighed like lead in her belly. They were dead and she wasn't.

They entered a conference room where Camila Marlow sat alone, her weathered hands clasped on the table before her. She looked up as they entered. Relief washing over her features at the sight of Cassie.

"Thank the Goddess," she breathed, rising to embrace her granddaughter. "When I learned of the attack, I was absolutely frantic."

"I'm okay," Cassie assured her, returning the embrace but not fully. She still struggled with the fact that others had been harmed while she escaped and didn't fully wrap her arms around her grandmother. "But Claire is still missing, and now we know someone is actively trying to kill us."

Camila pulled back, her expression hardening. "I've examined one of the witches involved in the attack," she said, turning to include Callimachus in the conversation. "With your permission, of course."

Callimachus inclined his head. "Your expertise was valuable."

"What did you find?" Cassie asked.

Camila's lips pressed into a thin line. "The witch bears the mark of the Purist Covenant, a splinter faction that broke from the High Coven nearly a century ago. They believe in absolute separation between supernatural species and have been particularly vocal about the dilution of witch bloodlines. This primarily concerned human-witch unions, not vampire-witch pairings, which were unprecedented before your parents. It appears this new turn of events has pushed them toward more radical and desperate actions."

"But they're working with vampires," Cassie pointed out, the contradiction bothering her.

"An alliance of convenience," Callimachus suggested. "United by their shared hatred of half-witch, half-vampire hybrids."

Camila nodded grimly. "The Purists have always been extreme in their methods. They despise any dilution of witch bloodlines and consider it a desecration of our ancient heritage. They've been suspected in the disappearance of several witches who married or consorted with humans. In three cases over the last decade, entire families vanished without a trace, mothers, fathers, and their half-blood children. The High Coven investigated, but evidence was always mysteriously absent or contaminated. When a witch has a child with a human, the witch heritage is weakened, and the child has less ability than her witch parent. The Purists saw this as a desecration of the witch bloodlines."

"And now they're targeting Claire and me," Cassie concluded, a cold dread settling in her stomach. She imagined those entire families that had disappeared being hers, with her sister, alone and terrified somewhere. She twisted her hair between her fingers, a nervous habit she'd developed in college. It rarely came out, except during the most stressful moments. As Cassie listened to her grandmother, she realized the threat wasn't new, and had existed long before she did. She'd only inherited it. "But why now? If they've known about us, why wait until we're adults?"

"What troubles me most is that they somehow knew of your existence at all. The High Coven kept your nature secret even from most of our own kind," Camilla said.

"Which suggests a leak within the High Coven itself," Callimachus said, his voice dangerously soft.

Cassie gasped. Witches would not be safe if their governing body was compromised. The world of people she could trust shrank to those surrounding her now.

Camila's expression tightened. "I've considered that possibility. It's why I've asked to speak with you three privately." She took a deep breath, her decision visibly weighing on her. "I believe the High Coven is compromised. I cannot say how many members might be involved with the Purists, but the coordination of yesterday's attack suggests high-level knowledge. Only the three of us here had any knowledge. I do not know which of my coven members is compromised or involved, but at least one of them is."

"You're accusing your own Council," Callimachus observed.

"I am," Camila said, steady despite the gravity of her words. "And I have a request that may seem strange, but I believe it necessary."

"What is it?" Cassie asked.

Camila straightened, her eyes meeting Callimachus's dark gaze. "I ask that you imprison me, along with the entire witch delegation."

"Grandmother!" Cassie exclaimed, shocked. Camila was putting herself in danger, like Alexander had done. The pattern playing out felt obscene, and she didn't want them in harm's way.

Camila raised a hand to silence her. "Hear me out. If members of the High Coven are involved with the Purists, they must be identified and isolated before they can do more harm. By placing all of us in separate cells, without the ability to communicate, you can investigate each of us thoroughly."

"And you volunteer for this?" Callimachus asked, studying her with new respect.

"I do," Camila replied firmly. "I ask only that you not treat me differently from the others. If there is a traitor among us, they must not suspect I've requested this or have any knowledge."

Callimachus considered her proposal. "You understand what you're asking? Such an action could be seen as a declaration of war against the High Coven and the witches. It would render the treaty invalid."

"I understand," Camila said gravely. "But this is already war, a shadow war being waged against your daughters. My granddaughters." Her voice broke slightly on the last words. "I cannot allow any on the High Coven to be harmed without due process, but I will turn a blind eye to their temporary imprisonment if it means protecting my family."

Cassie stared at her grandmother, moved by her willingness to sacrifice her freedom and potentially her standing among the witches. Her grandmother was showing true leadership through her willingness to sacrifice herself. "What about examining the attack site?" she asked. "Wouldn't your magical expertise help identify more of the attackers?"

Camila nodded. "Yes, and I would request permission to do so when it's safe. It is my duty to see to the protection and preservation of the witches, and this includes my family. It does not include traitors that would harm my family or any witch."

"It shall be arranged," Callimachus promised. "Though it will appear to be against your will."

"Good," Camila said, her shoulders straightening with resolve. "The hatred of hybrids and the perceived threat of dilution of the bloodlines has twisted some of the witches. Even though our numbers are dwindling, the hate is too strong, and they might never accept half-vampires, half-witches."

"Their acceptance is not required for my daughters' existence," Callimachus stated flatly.

"No," Camila agreed, "but their cooperation might be necessary for all our survival." She turned to Cassie, her expression softening.

"Child, you and your sister represent something many witches fear: change. But you also represent hope, a future where our declining numbers might be reversed through new bloodlines and children."

Cassie took her grandmother's hands, squeezing them gently. "We'll find Claire," she promised. "And we'll figure out this new world together."

"I know you will," Camila said. "You've always been stubborn that way."

A knock at the door interrupted them. A security officer entered, bowing briefly to Callimachus.

"Your Majesty, Commander Nikolai has an update. It appears he has located an island that he is not able to investigate due to storm activity. He believes he may have a lead to Miss Claire's whereabouts."

Hope flared in Cassie's chest, clogging her throat. She forced it down, afraid to hope. She wanted proof to enable that hope first. It would hurt too much otherwise.

Callimachus nodded sharply. "Thank you. I will follow up in the command center shortly." His voice carried the weight of centuries of command, brooking no argument or delay. The security officer acknowledged with a respectful bow before withdrawing. As the vampire closed the door behind him with a soft click, the room fell into momentary silence, the tension from the news about Claire hanging in the air between the three of them. Cassie watched her father's face carefully, noting how his dark, almost black eyes narrowed slightly in calculation, no doubt already formulating strategies and contingency plans as any seasoned military commander would. The faint lines around his eyes deepened as he turned his attention back to them, his auburn hair catching the light as he moved.

Camila rose, recognizing there were other matters requiring their attention. Cassie got to her feet as well, pulling her grandmother into an embrace. She held the elder witch close for another moment. "Thank you," she murmured against her grandmother's ear. "For everything. I love you."

"I love you also, my dear Cassie. Be careful, child," Camila replied softly. "After you get an update, try to rest and recover this evening to gather your full strength, and then find your sister. She needs you now more than ever." With that, she pivoted and exited through the conference room doorway.

Cassie watched as her grandmother left. She felt a new determination settling into her bones. The world had changed irrevocably in the span of a few days. She had found her father, discovered her true nature, and formed a connection with Alexander that defied explanation. Now, forces were actively trying to destroy her and Claire simply for existing.

But they didn't understand what Cassie Marlow was willing to do for those she loved. They had underestimated the power that flowed through her veins, witch and vampire combined into something new and unprecedented. Most of all, they had underestimated the lengths to which she would go to protect her own.

She got up and followed her father and Alexander through the corridors of the vampire stronghold. As she did so, Cassie made a silent promise to Claire, wherever she was. She would find her. She would bring her home. And anyone who stood in her way would learn exactly what a daughter of Callimachus and Catherine Marlow was capable of when pushed too far. She knew that going down that path would change her. Protecting those she loved might require becoming something more, something darker. The thought weighed heavy on her. She didn't know how much of herself she would lose in the process.

Chapter Twenty-Five

Cassie sat beside her father Callimachus and Alexander in the war room, the electric tension of the upcoming High Coven's intended confinement vibrating through the atmosphere. On screen, Nikolai stood at attention in front of the large display screens on the wall. The vampire's posture was rigid, his face set in grim determination as he delivered his report.

"Every time we attempt to approach the island, a storm materializes," Nikolai explained, pointing to the map that was on display behind him, showing a small landmass off the Washington coast. "Not natural weather patterns, definitely witch-crafted. The energy signature is unmistakable. This is why we believe they are here, and not on the other island we searched, where we found the raft and footsteps. They weren't on that island."

Callimachus leaned forward, his ancient eyes narrowed as he studied the satellite imagery. "And the witch patrols?"

"They've intercepted us twice," Nikolai replied, his jaw tightening. "Ordered us back toward Canadian waters. We've avoided direct confrontation as instructed, but they're becoming more aggressive with each encounter."

Cassie's fingers curled into fists beneath the table. "It's because of the storm keeping you away that you think Claire's on that island?"

Nikolai nodded. He hesitated, glancing at Callimachus before continuing. "There's another detail. We briefly got close enough to observe what seems to be a slight environmental disruption that roughly forms a trail through the dense vegetation before the storm forced our retreat."

He tapped a command into the table's surface, bringing up a series of grainy images. Cassie leaned closer, her breath catching as she recognized what appeared to be a path through the foliage.

"Claire's there," she whispered, hope flaring in her chest. She almost didn't want to say Claire's name aloud, afraid it would tempt fate.

Alexander shifted his body posture forward from where he'd been silently observing. His wounds from the ambush had healed remarkably fast, though Cassie noticed he still moved with careful precision. "Sam wouldn't want to be exposed on the beach if they were being pursued by witch patrols. He'd want them to be inland and hidden."

"Agreed," Callimachus confirmed, satisfaction evident in his tone.

"But why would witches be protecting the island if they're the ones who attacked the yacht?" Cassie asked, her analytical mind working through the puzzle. "Unless they weren't protecting it but were also unable to get close to it."

"Unless different factions are at work," Alexander finished her thought. "The Purists who ambushed us might be the only ones patrolling. It could be them and the witch patrols."

Callimachus nodded slowly. "Alexander and Claire will leave shortly to meet you and work to get close to the island. Pull back to Canadian waters so as not to alert the witch patrols, and wait for further direction."

"Understood. We'll pull back and wait to provide backup as needed," Nikolai muttered.

Cassie rose from her seat, unable to contain her restless energy. "We need to get to that island right away. If Claire's there..."

"We can't simply force our way through," Alexander cautioned. "Those storms are powerful enough to sink even our most reinforced vessels. And a direct confrontation with witch patrols would violate the treaty, potentially triggering open conflict. We also need to be careful not to engage the Purists in open waters."

"I don't care about treaties!" Cassie snapped, frustration boiling over. The laws they needed to observe felt cold, next to the burning need to find Claire. "My sister is out there!"

Callimachus placed a calming hand on her arm. "We all want to find Claire, Cassandra. But Alexander is right, we must proceed strategically and carefully."

Cassie took a deep breath, forcing her emotions back under control. "Sorry. I just, I need to get to her. She's alive, I know it, and she needs me."

"Your connection to your sister might be our greatest asset," Callimachus said thoughtfully. "The witch delegation agreed to a joint search operation. Perhaps we can use that agreement to gain legitimate access to the island."

"The witches won't allow it," Nikolai argued. "They've been blocking our every attempt."

"Those are patrol witches following standard protocols," Alexander pointed out. "With perceived permission from the High Coven representatives, they'd have to at least consider our request. If it comes to that."

"In the meantime," Callimachus turned to Nikolai, "maintain observation from a safe distance. Report any changes in patrol patterns or storm activity."

Callimachus terminated the call and faced Cassie. "Are you prepared to create mayhem?" he inquired with a grin. Cassie smiled and nodded. Her father rose to his feet, and she did the same, trailing after him. The moment had arrived to implement her grandmother's plan.

They took the elevator up a floor and then walked down the hall to where the High Coven witches had congregated. After a brief pause, Alexander and Cassie accompanied him as Callimachus strode into the room, his imposing figure casting a shadow over the three witches gathered around a low table. Cassie followed closely behind, her heart racing with both apprehension and determination. The air crackled with tension as the witches looked up, their expressions ranging from indignation to fear. This wasn't her plan, but she was fully part of it.

"I know of your complicity in the Purist plot," Callimachus began, not mincing words, his voice steady and commanding. "You've intruded upon Vancouver's peace and threatened my daughters."

The witches exchanged glances, their outrage palpable. Miranda leaned forward, fists clenched on the table. "We've done no such thing! You cannot accuse us without evidence!"

"Evidence?" Callimachus raised an eyebrow. "I have ample proof of your involvement with those who seek to harm my family. Your council's negligence has put not just vampires at risk, but all supernatural beings." He gestured to Cassie beside him, her presence drawing attention. "You've endangered my daughter, and harmed vampires."

The witches shifted uncomfortably in their seats, their defiance faltering under the weight of Callimachus's words.

"Whether careless or otherwise, we refuse to be addressed in this fashion. It is intolerable," Miranda declared icily.

"You're forgetting your place," Callimachus said sharply, stepping closer to the table. "Your existence doesn't give you license to conspire against others simply because you disagree with how they choose to live."

The atmosphere thickened as Cassie took a breath, preparing herself for what came next. She'd spent too long living in her mother's shadow; now it was time for her voice to be heard.

"Enough," she said firmly, raising her chin as she locked eyes with each witch in turn. "If you know something about my sister Claire's disappearance, tell us now."

A sharp intake of breath from one of the witches interrupted her. "We don't have anything to do with that!"

"Then you should want to cooperate!" Cassie countered, her frustration bubbling over. "My sister is missing because of Purists, those extremists who think hybrids shouldn't exist! We're all caught up in this together!"

Callimachus watched silently as tension swirled in the air around them like a brewing storm.

"You'll be imprisoned until we uncover more about your involvement," he declared suddenly, cutting through the rising chaos.

The three witches gasped at his words, outrage evident on their faces.

"You can't imprison us!" Giles protested this time. "That will threaten the treaty! You will provoke war!"

"The only war I intend to provoke is against those who would dare threaten my daughters," Callimachus replied coolly. He turned away slightly before looking back at them with piercing eyes that seemed to see right through them. "Until then, you will remain under guard."

"You'll regret this," Camila said through clenched teeth.

Cassie stepped forward slightly but held her tongue. There was little she could say that would make a difference at this moment. She also couldn't say or do anything that would reveal her grandmother's involvement. One wrong word, and everything could unravel.

Callimachus raised a hand dismissively toward them. "Take them away," he commanded to two guards standing at attention near the entrance.

The guards moved quickly and efficiently toward the three High Coven witches, who stood up in protest as they were escorted from the room. Not one of them resorted to spellcraft, apparently grasping the seriousness of their predicament. Employing supernatural powers would only heighten the danger, and considering they were surrounded and outnumbered, such an action would prove reckless.

"This isn't over!" Miranda shouted as they were led out.

Cassie felt a mixture of satisfaction and concern watching them leave. Whatever secrets they held could very well determine Claire's fate. This was necessary, but it didn't feel good. It was happening because of her.

Once they were gone, Cassie turned to her father. "Do you really think they know something? Or are they just using fear tactics?"

"There are always layers beneath such vehemence," Callimachus replied thoughtfully as he approached Cassie's side once more. "Fear makes people lash out without thinking rationally."

"What if neither Giles nor Miranda confesses?" Cassie's voice wavered slightly at this thought.

"Then we will find other means of inquiry," Callimachus assured her firmly but softened his tone ever so slightly when he continued speaking again, offering a mix of reassurance and authority.

"What do we do next?" she asked him quietly yet determinedly.

"I'll prepare for further investigations," Callimachus stated resolutely. "And you and Alexander will prepare to leave to find Claire."

Cassie's heart swelled briefly at hearing those words. Since hearing the update from Nikolai, she couldn't wait to find her sister.

"Ready to finally board the Apollo?" Alexander squeezed Cassie's hand. She nodded. They both left the room together, once again heading toward the harbor to find Claire. She didn't know if she would return with her, or alone. Cassie was afraid of the person she'd be if she came back by herself.

Chapter Twenty-Six

Cassie followed Alexander through the sleek corridors of the *Apollo*, the vessel's gentle vibration beneath her feet a constant reminder that they were moving farther from Vancouver with each passing moment. The ship was larger than the yacht that had brought her north, designed for extended journeys with a full complement of crew.

Alexander paused at a junction where the corridor branched in two directions. "The captain's quarters are this way," he said, gesturing to the left. "I've had a room prepared for you down the other passage. It's comfortable, with a private bathroom attached."

Cassie hesitated, studying his face. In the soft lighting of the ship's interior, his features seemed less severe, though no less striking. Doubt crept in, causing her to second-guess. "You're giving me my own room?"

"I thought you might appreciate some space," he replied carefully. "After everything that's happened."

"I don't want space. Unless you do?" Her stomach dropped. Maybe he didn't mean what he said about forever and her being his mate. Maybe he reconsidered, and she wasn't worth the risk.

"Of course I don't, but I wanted to give you the choice," he said.

A small smile touched her lips. "That's considerate, but..." she took a half-step closer to him, lowering her voice though they were alone in the corridor. "I really don't want space."

Alexander's expression shifted subtly, the controlled mask slipping to reveal something warmer, more vulnerable. "No," he admitted quietly. "I don't either."

Relief washed through her. "Good. Because I'd rather stay with you." She reached for his hand, her fingers intertwining with his. "If that's okay?"

Alexander's response was to tighten his grip on her hand, the gesture speaking volumes. "More than okay."

As they continued down the left corridor, Cassie became aware of the crew they passed, vampires who nodded respectfully but whose curious glances lingered a moment too long. She recognized none of them. Each face was unfamiliar and potentially wary of her hybrid nature.

"The crew," she murmured, "they're all strangers to me."

"They're all under my command," Alexander assured her. "Hand-picked for this mission. Loyal and discreet."

"Do they know what I am?" Cassie tried to ignore the prickling of worry that crept up her spine. Loyal and discreet didn't mean they trusted her. She saw how they looked at her, uncertain of who and what she was. It was the same fear she kept suppressed. If something happened on their journey and she lost control, would they still be loyal and discreet then?

"They know you're the King's daughter and that finding your sister is our priority." His thumb traced a small circle on the back of her hand. "The rest isn't their concern."

She squeezed his hand and repeated to herself, "Not their concern. Right..." Easy for him to say. He knew exactly who he was and what she was capable of. She didn't have that same self-assurance.

The captain's quarters were spacious by shipboard standards, a bedroom connected to a small sitting area, with windows offering a view of the moonlit waters. Alexander closed the door behind them, and the sounds of the ship receded to a distant hum.

"It's not as luxurious as the compound," he said, watching her take in the space.

"It's perfect," Cassie replied, moving to the window. The ocean stretched endlessly before them, dark and mysterious. Somewhere out there was Claire, and with each minute, they were getting closer. The thought both comforted and terrified her.

She turned to find Alexander observing her, his dark eyes intent. "What are you thinking?" she asked.

"That you continue to surprise me," he answered honestly.

Cassie's laugh was soft but genuine. She crossed to him, placing her hands on his chest. "I'm finding I like it when you're near. I like it a lot."

Alexander's arms encircled her waist, drawing her closer. "I do too," he repeated, emphasizing his words with a soft kiss to her forehead.

"Nice," she whispered, resting her head against his shoulder. His solid presence anchored her amid the uncertainty, a constant in the chaos her life had become.

They stood like that for several moments, the gentle rocking of the ship beneath them almost soothing. Finally, Alexander pressed a kiss to her temple.

"You should rest," he said. "The search begins soon."

Cassie nodded, suddenly aware of the fatigue seeping into her bones. The emotional toll of the day's revelations and preparations had drained her more than she'd realized. "Will you stay with me?"

"I need to take care of a few things, then I will be back. It should not take more than a few minutes," he promised, his voice a low rumble she felt more than heard.

Alexander left, closing the door with a soft click. As she crawled onto the bed, she found herself marveling at how quickly Alexander had become essential to her. Just days ago, he'd been a stranger, an intruder in her shop. Now, she couldn't imagine facing what lay ahead without him. She closed her eyes, and before she knew it, Alexander was back, turning the covers down.

She rolled over and snuggled under the blankets. When they were both finally settled beneath the covers, Alexander drew her against him, her back to his chest, his arm a protective weight around her waist. Cassie closed her eyes, focusing on the solid presence behind her rather than the fears that threatened to overwhelm her thoughts.

"We're going to find her," she whispered, as much to reassure herself as anything.

Alexander's arm tightened around her. "We will," he promised. "Now rest."

Cassie didn't want to rest. Not again. She wanted out of her skin, out of her worry, out of the anxiety over the next day, and if she would find her sister or not. She wanted a moment of escape, and rest wouldn't give her that. She wanted an immediate release from all that was pressing in on her. "There are different ways to rest and refresh," she said.

Cassie turned to face Alexander, her eyes luminous in the dim light of the cabin. The gentle rocking of the ship beneath them created a cocoon of intimacy, separating them from the world outside and all its complications. Without hesitation, she pressed her body against his, feeling the cool solidity of his immortal form against her warmth.

"I want you to revitalize me. Can you do that?" she whispered against his lips, her voice husky with desire.

Alexander's response was immediate, his mouth claiming hers in a kiss that started gentle but quickly blazed into something more primal. His hands slid beneath her shirt, fingers tracing the curve of her spine with exquisite care, as if mapping territory he intended to memorize forever.

Cassie broke the kiss, pushing herself up and straddling him in one fluid motion. The newfound strength of her dual nature made her movements more confident, more assertive than she'd ever been before. She looked down at Alexander, his dark eyes widening slightly at her sudden dominance.

"Look who's the captive now," she said, a wicked smile curving her lips as she reached for the hem of her shirt and pulled it over her head in one smooth movement.

The cool air of the cabin kissed her skin, raising goosebumps that Alexander immediately soothed with his hands. His palms slid up her sides, thumbs brushing the undersides of her breasts with tantalizing restraint.

"You're beautiful," he murmured. His eyes never left hers, even with her shirtless body above him.

Cassie leaned down, her auburn hair falling around them like a curtain as she captured his mouth again. This kiss was different. She controlled the pace, the pressure, the depth. Her tongue teased his, demanding rather than requesting entrance.

"Too many clothes," she muttered against his lips, tugging impatiently at his shirt.

Alexander sat up slightly, allowing her to pull the garment off. The movement brought their bodies flush against each other, her soft curves against his hard planes. The contact drew a gasp from Cassie, the sensation of skin against skin sending electricity racing through her veins.

With unexpected boldness, she pushed him back down, her hands splayed across his chest. Her fingernails scraped lightly over his skin, leaving faint trails that disappeared almost instantly due to his vampire healing.

"I like you like this," she said, rocking her hips against him deliberately.

Alexander's hands settled on her waist, his fingers tightening slightly. "Like what?" His voice had dropped to that deeper register that sent shivers down her spine.

"Beneath me. At my mercy." She punctuated each phrase with a roll of her hips, feeling his growing hardness through their remaining clothes.

A low growl rumbled from his chest, the sound more felt than heard. "And what mercy do you plan to show, Cassie Marlow?"

In answer, she reached behind her back and unhooked her bra, letting it fall away. Alexander's eyes darkened further, pupils dilating as he took in the sight of her bare breasts. His hands moved to cup them, thumbs circling her nipples until they hardened into tight peaks.

Cassie arched into his touch, her head falling back as pleasure coursed through her. The position emphasized the long line of her throat, and Alexander couldn't resist leaning up to press his lips to the pulse point that fluttered there.

"I want everything," she whispered, her fingers tangling in his hair. "All of you."

She shifted, moving off him just long enough to shed her remaining clothes. Alexander followed suit, and when she straddled him again, there was nothing between them but heat and desire. She positioned herself above him, feeling his hardness pressing against her entrance.

"Look at me," she commanded softly, needing him in this moment. Needed him to drown out the world, and make it all disappear.

Alexander's eyes locked with hers, dark with need. Cassie held his gaze as she sank down onto him, taking him into her body inch by exquisite inch. The stretch and fullness made her gasp, but she didn't look away, wanting to see every flicker of pleasure cross his face.

When he was fully seated within her, she paused, adjusting to the sensation. Her hands splayed across his chest for balance as she began to move, setting a rhythm that was slow and deliberate at first.

"Cassie," Alexander breathed, his hands gripping her hips, not guiding but following her lead.

She leaned forward, changing the angle as she increased her pace. "Say it again," she demanded, echoing his words from their first time together.

"Cassie," he repeated, his voice rough with desire.

She rode him with growing confidence, her body finding a rhythm that built pleasure with each movement. Her hair fell forward as she lost herself in the sensations coursing through her. She clung to him, letting herself lose control. With him, losing control felt safe, maybe too safe. She didn't think about who she was becoming when his hands were on her, shaping her into someone who felt in control and powerful. She leaned into the illusory power it gave her. Cassie let herself believe it didn't matter who she was in his arms.

Her movements grew more urgent, more demanding as the tension built within her. Alexander met each downward thrust with an upward one of his own, their bodies moving together. Cassie's breath came in short gasps, her skin flushing with the effort and the mounting pleasure.

"Alexander," she moaned. Her muscles began to tighten around him.

In a move that caught her completely off guard, Alexander suddenly sat up, wrapping one arm around her waist while the other hand tangled in her hair. The change in position drove him deeper, hitting a spot inside her that made stars explode behind her eyelids.

"My turn," he growled against her ear, his supernatural strength allowing him to lift and move her with ease.

Before Cassie could protest the shift in control, he had flipped their positions, pinning her beneath him on the bed. Her legs wrapped around his waist instinctively, pulling him deeper as he began to thrust with controlled power.

"Oh, yes," she gasped, her nails digging into his shoulders.

Alexander captured her mouth in a searing kiss, swallowing her moans as he drove into her with increasing intensity. One hand slid between their bodies, finding the sensitive bundle of nerves at her core and circling it with practiced precision.

The dual stimulation was too much. Cassie broke the kiss with a cry, her back arching off the bed as pleasure crashed through her in waves. Alexander continued his relentless pace, drawing out her climax until she was trembling beneath him.

Only when the last aftershocks had rippled through her did he allow himself to follow, his rhythm faltering as his own release overtook him. His forehead pressed against hers, their breaths mingling as they both shuddered, each finding satisfaction.

For several long moments, they remained joined, both reluctant to break the connection. Alexander's weight was a welcome pressure, grounding her when she felt like she might float away on the tide of pleasure flooding her system.

Finally, he rolled to the side, drawing her against his chest. His fingers traced idle patterns on her cooling skin, following the curve of her hip, the dip of her waist, and the line of her collarbone.

"And here I thought I was the one in charge," Cassie murmured, her voice languid with satisfaction.

Alexander chuckled, the sound vibrating through his chest against her ear. "You were. Until I couldn't resist taking control."

She propped herself up on one elbow, looking down at him with mock indignation. "That wasn't the deal. You were the captive."

His expression softened, one hand coming up to cup her cheek. "I find it difficult to resist you in any capacity, Cassie Marlow. That was," he paused, searching for the right word, "intoxicating."

A pleased smile curved her lips. "Good to know." She leaned down to press a gentle kiss to his mouth. "Next time, I might not let you take over so easily."

"Is that a challenge?" His eyebrow arched, amusement dancing in his dark eyes.

"Maybe." She settled back against his chest, her fingers tracing the ancient scar that curved across his ribs. "Or maybe just a promise."

Alexander's arms tightened around her, his lips pressing against her temple. "Either way, I look forward to it."

Cassie closed her eyes, the gentle rocking of the ship and the solid presence of Alexander's body lulling her into a false sense of security, as if the world weren't holding its breath. Although she wanted to fall asleep, she was aware of the darkness pressing against the ship. It was the quiet moment before the world changed again.

Chapter Twenty-Seven

The Apollo cut through the churning waters of the Rosario Strait, its powerful engines pushing against the growing resistance of the sea. Cassie stood on the forward deck, her auburn hair whipping wildly around her face as she stared out at the dark waters ahead. They were approaching Cypress Island, a remote landmass in the San Juan archipelago where the search teams had detected unusual energy signatures that might indicate Claire's presence.

The dawn sky above had darkened ominously in the past few minutes, thick clouds rolling in from the west to blot out the stars. The air felt charged, heavy with moisture and something else, a strange electrical quality that made the fine hairs on Cassie's arms stand on end. It wasn't normal weather. Her witch senses recognized the magical undercurrents rippling through the atmosphere.

"Storm's building fast," Alexander called from behind her, his voice carrying over the strengthening wind. "We need to get you inside."

Cassie gripped the railing tighter, her knuckles whitening. "I can feel something, Alexander. We're getting closer."

Alexander moved to her side, his tall frame shielding her slightly from the worst of the wind. His dark eyes scanned the horizon with the practiced vigilance of centuries at sea. "It's exactly as Nikolai described. This weather isn't natural. Someone's manipulating the elements."

"I know," Cassie replied, her eyes reflecting the occasional flash of lightning in the distance. "It feels like witch magic, but different somehow. More intense."

A massive wave crashed against the bow, sending spray cascading over the deck. The ship pitched violently, forcing both of them to grab the railing for support. Around them, vampire crew members moved with supernatural grace despite the rolling deck, securing equipment and preparing for the roughening seas.

"Cassie." Alexander's voice took on an edge of command. "You need to get below. This is going to get worse before it gets better."

She turned to face him, determination etched into every line of her face. "I'm not hiding while we're this close to finding Claire."

Before Alexander could argue further, another wave struck the vessel, this one powerful enough to send Cassie staggering. Only Alexander's quick reflexes prevented her from falling, his arm shooting out to steady her.

"This isn't about courage," he said, his voice dropping to that deeper register that brooked no argument. "If you're washed overboard, we lose our best chance of finding your sister."

Lightning cracked directly overhead, illuminating the deck in harsh white light. In that brief flash, Cassie saw the genuine concern in Alexander's eyes, not just the protective instinct of a vampire for his charge, but something deeper, more personal. Reflected was the fear of losing her.

"Fine," she conceded, "but I want to stay near enough to sense if Claire is close."

Alexander nodded, guiding her toward the wheelhouse, where two other vampires manned the ship's controls. They moved carefully across the pitching deck, the wind now howling around them with unnatural ferocity. The storm was intensifying at a rate that defied normal weather patterns, the waves growing taller with each passing minute.

They were halfway to the wheelhouse when a massive wave crashed over the starboard side, sweeping across the deck with frightening force. The cold water hit Cassie like a physical blow, momentarily stealing her breath. She felt her feet slip on the suddenly drenched deck, her body lurching dangerously toward the railing.

"Alexander!" she cried out, her fingers scrabbling for purchase on the wet surface.

Alexander lunged for her, his vampire speed allowing him to cross the distance in an instant. His powerful hand closed around her wrist just as another wave broke over the deck. The water surged around their legs, trying to pull them apart, but Alexander's grip remained unbreakable.

"Hold on to me!" he shouted over the roar of the storm, pulling her against his chest.

Two more vampires appeared beside them, moving with the preternatural grace of their kind despite the violently pitching deck. Together, they formed a protective formation around Cassie, creating a living barrier against the worst of the waves as they continued their precarious journey to safety.

When they finally reached the wheelhouse, Alexander practically lifted Cassie through the door, slamming it shut behind them. Inside, the howling of the wind was muffled, though the ship continued to pitch and roll violently.

"Status report," Alexander demanded, his voice instantly shifting to command mode.

"We're holding course, but the storm's intensifying beyond pre-dicted parameters," reported one of the vampires at the controls. "Navigation systems are experiencing interference."

"Magical interference?" Alexander asked sharply.

"Likely," the navigator confirmed. "The energy signature matches witch weather manipulation, but it's unusually powerful."

Cassie pushed wet hair from her face, her mind racing. The storm felt familiar, resonating with something deep inside her. She moved to the windows, peering out at the churning waters and the distant shadow of Cypress Island, barely visible through the sheets of rain.

"It's Claire," she whispered, sudden certainty flooding through her. Her knees became weak with the realization. It definitely felt like Claire, familiar but stronger. Darker. Sharper. The magic of the sister she knew was like a calm pond. This was different. It was a tempest. "She's doing this. I'm sure of it."

Alexander turned to her, his expression skeptical. "Your sister is creating this storm? Not the Purists?"

"Not only creating it," Cassie clarified, her analytical mind piecing together the puzzle. "Enhancing it too. I can feel her energy signature in the magic." She pressed her palm against the cold glass. Blood called to blood, and somewhere out there, she felt the call of her sister. As much as she had a glimmer of hope that it was the Purists, so she could unleash her rage upon them, she wanted to find her sister more. "She's trying to keep something away. Or someone."

Alexander exchanged glances with his crew, then moved to Cassie's side. "You're certain?"

"Absolutely," she nodded. "Claire always had a knack for weather magic, even as a child. She could predict storms days in advance, and summoned rain and fog far too often. But this is more," she gestured to the chaos outside, "this is her witch abilities amplified by vampire strength. Just like I did when I fought against you and the patrol."

Alexander considered this, his tactical mind already adjusting to the new information. "If she's using this much power, she might be in danger, or trying to keep danger away."

Fear clutched at Cassie's heart. "We need to help her. Now."

"We will," Alexander promised, "but we need to navigate this storm first. If Claire is enhancing it, perhaps you can counterbalance it."

Cassie blinked, the idea taking root. "I could try a calming spell. My mother taught me several for walking along the beach during storms."

"Do it," Alexander urged. "Anything that might give us a clearer path to the island."

Cassie moved to the center of the wheelhouse, her feet braced against the rolling deck. She closed her eyes, centering herself as she'd been taught. The dual nature of her power responded immediately. Witch magic and vampire strength combined in a way that felt increasingly natural.

She began to murmur the words she had learned from her mother, her hands weaving complex patterns in the air. The language was old, predating modern witch dialects, passed down through generations of women. As she spoke, she visualized calm waters, gentle winds, and clear skies, not fighting against the storm directly, but offering an alternative pattern for the elements to follow.

The magic built within her, a warm current flowing from her core to her fingertips. She could feel it extending outward, pushing against the chaotic energy of the storm. For a moment, the two forces seemed evenly matched, neither gaining ground.

Then something shifted.

The violent pitching of the ship eased slightly. The howling of the wind diminished from a scream to a moan. Through the windows, Cassie could see the rain thinning, and the waves, while still substantial, were no longer threatening to swamp the deck.

"It's working," one of the navigators reported, surprise evident in his voice.

Cassie maintained her concentration, the spell requiring constant focus to sustain. Sweat beaded on her forehead despite her drenched clothes, the magical exertion taxing her hybrid strength. She knew she couldn't maintain this level of power for long, but hopefully, it would be enough to get them closer to the island.

Suddenly, the energy pattern of the storm changed dramatically. The chaos didn't intensify. Instead, it simply disappeared. The winds died away, the rain stopped as if someone had turned off a faucet, and the clouds parted to reveal a clear blue sky and bright sun.

Cassie's eyes flew open in shock. "That wasn't me," she gasped, dropping her hands. "I was just trying to mute the effects, not stop the storm completely."

Alexander moved to the window, his expression wary. "Someone else intervened."

The sudden calm was more unsettling than the storm had been. The sea surface, which moments ago had been churning with massive waves, now lay almost unnaturally flat, reflecting the sunlight like a mirror. The only sound was the gentle hum of the ship's engines as they cut through the now-placid waters.

"Claire," Cassie whispered, certainty flooding through her. "It has to be."

Alexander turned to his crew. "Maintain course and dock us near Cypress Island, but approach with caution. This could be a trap set by the Purists."

"Or it could be Claire trying to help us reach her," Cassie countered, moving to stand beside him. "I know my sister, Alexander. If she sensed my magic, she would recognize it instantly."

The ship glided forward through the eerily calm waters, the island in front of them. Its forested slopes rose steeply from the water, welcoming in the sunlight. Somewhere on that island, Cassie was increasingly certain, her sister was waiting.

"I felt her respond to my spell," Cassie explained, her eyes fixed on the approaching shoreline. "It was like when we were children and would finish each other's sentences. I'm positive she recognized my magical signature and knew exactly what I was trying to do. But instead of just helping me calm the storm, she completely neutralized it."

"That would require extraordinary power," Alexander observed, his voice thoughtful. "More than most witches possess."

"She's not just a witch anymore," Cassie reminded him. She said it with pride, though the words felt strange. If Claire had been changing like she had, she wondered who her sister had become. How much of her was still her sister, and how was she handling the change? "She's like me. And if her vampire abilities have awakened like mine did, then she's become a powerful weather witch."

"Then she could be capable of manipulating weather on a scale we haven't seen before," Alexander finished the thought. "Especially if she's always had a natural affinity for it."

Cassie nodded, growing admiration for her sister warring with dread. "Claire planned everything, her schedule, her cooking, even minor adjustments to the weather. She always made sure everything was perfectly balanced. If she's using this much power, she must have a good reason."

Alexander studied the island through narrowed eyes, his centuries of tactical experience evident in his assessment. "We'll send a small team ashore first. You'll stay on board until we've secured a perimeter."

"No," Cassie said firmly, turning to face him fully. "I'm going ashore too. Claire will sense me, and if she's scared or defensive, I can help."

Alexander's jaw tightened, clearly not pleased with the idea of putting her at risk. "Cassie."

"This isn't negotiable, Alexander," she interrupted, her eyes flashing with determination. It wasn't bravery that made her go. She didn't know what her sister had become, but she couldn't stomach the thought of not being there for her sister. "She's my sister. If our positions were reversed, you'd do the same."

For a moment, they stood in silent standoff, neither willing to yield. Then, with a barely perceptible sigh, Alexander nodded. "You stay with me at all times. No wandering off, no heroics. We move together at all times."

"Agreed," Cassie said, relief washing through her. She reached for his hand and gave it a quick squeeze. "Thank you."

Alexander's expression softened slightly. "Just promise me you'll be careful. We still don't know what caused that storm or why it disappeared so suddenly."

"I promise," she assured him, though her attention was already returning to the island. Something was pulling her toward that shoreline. Claire was there, she was sure of it. She could feel it deep within her that her sister was there.

As the Apollo came to a stop near the island, Cassie felt a strange sense of déjà vu wash over her. Though she'd never been to this place before, something about it felt oddly familiar, as if she were returning rather than arriving for the first time. Perhaps it was Claire's presence she was sensing, or perhaps something deeper. The Apollo's engines slowed and stopped, the anchor chain rattling as it descended into the depths.

Cassie turned to follow Alexander, her eyes fixed on the small skiff being lowered to the water's edge. The boat hung suspended from the Apollo's side, swaying gently in the eerie calm that had replaced the magical storm. Her body buzzed with anticipation. The pull toward Claire was strong. But would it be Claire she found, or a stranger? Or worse, what if it wasn't Claire and she had led them straight into danger?

"Stay close," Alexander murmured as they approached the rope ladder that would take them down to the skiff. "The sudden calm concerns me more than the storm did."

Cassie nodded, understanding his caution even as impatience burned through her veins. "Claire wouldn't hurt us."

"Perhaps not intentionally," he replied, his eyes scanning the shoreline with centuries of tactical assessment. "But newly awakened powers can be unpredictable."

Alexander descended the ladder first and nimbly moved into the skiff, his movements fluid and controlled. The ladder swayed beneath her feet as she descended, the gentle slap of waves against the ship's hull the only sound in the unnatural quiet. Two more vampires waited above to join them, armed with conventional weapons, a precaution that made Cassie's stomach tighten with apprehension.

When she reached the skiff, Alexander extended his hand, steadying her as she stepped into the small boat. His fingers lingered on hers a moment longer than necessary, the brief contact conveying reassurance she hadn't realized she needed.

"I can feel her," Cassie whispered as she settled onto the wooden bench. "It's like a tugging sensation, right here." She pressed her hand to her sternum, where the connection to her sister pulsed like a second heartbeat.

Alexander nodded once, his expression softening slightly. "Trust that connection. It may guide us better than any tracking equipment."

One of the vampires took position at the outboard motor, starting it with a single pull. The engine hummed to life, surprisingly quiet for its size, another vampire modification, Cassie assumed. The second vampire positioned himself at the bow, scanning the waters ahead with enhanced vision.

As they pulled away from the Apollo's shadow, Cassie watched the island grow larger, its forested slopes rising from the water like the back of a sleeping beast. The shoreline was rocky in some places, sandy in others, with dense forest beginning just beyond the narrow beach.

"There," she said suddenly, pointing to a small cove on the eastern side of the island. "That's the path Nikolai identified. That's where we need to go."

Alexander signaled to the vampire steering, who adjusted their course without question. The skiff cut through the still waters, leaving barely a ripple in its wake. The strange calm extended to the wildlife. No birds called from the trees, and no fish broke the surface. It was as if the entire ecosystem had gone still, holding its breath.

"It's too quiet," the vampire at the bow murmured, his voice pitched for vampire hearing.

Alexander nodded almost imperceptibly, his body tensing in a way that Cassie had come to recognize as combat readiness. His hand moved to rest on the weapon at his hip, though he kept his movements casual and unhurried.

As they approached the cove, Cassie leaned forward, scanning the shoreline for any sign of her sister. The pull in her chest grew stronger, more insistent, confirming they were on the right path. The small boat glided into the protected waters of the cove, where the surface was mirror-smooth, reflecting the trees and sky with perfect clarity.

The skiff's bow scraped gently against the sandy bottom, and the vampire at the motor cut the engine. Silence descended once more, broken only by the soft lapping of tiny waves against the boat's hull.

Alexander stepped out first, the water reaching mid-calf as he pulled the skiff further onto the shore. He turned back to Cassie, extending his hand once more.

"Ready?" he asked quietly.

Cassie took his hand and stepped into the cool water, her eyes already fixed on the tree line ahead. Claire was close, she could feel it with every fiber of her being.

"Cassie!" Her sister's voice rang out, causing her to snap her head toward the source of the sound.

CHAPTER TWENTY-EIGHT

"Claire!" Cassie shouted, her heart leaping as she recognized her sister's voice.

She splashed through the shallow water, breaking free of Alexander's protective grip as she scrambled toward the shoreline. There, emerging from the tree line, was Claire, her dark auburn hair tangled with leaves, her clothes torn and dirty, but unmistakably alive.

Cassie ran across the beach, sand flying beneath her feet. The sisters collided in a desperate embrace, clinging to each other as if afraid the other might disappear. Claire's familiar scent, of herbal tea and old books, was mixed with salt air and pine, but underneath it all was the essence of her sister.

"You're okay," Cassie whispered, pulling back to examine Claire's face. "You're really okay."

Claire's silver-blue eyes, so like Cassie's own, were bright with unshed tears. "I knew you'd find me. I felt you coming." Her gaze shifted to the vampires approaching behind Cassie, and her expression hardened. "Stay back," she warned, raising one hand as the air around them began to crackle with energy and the skies began to darken.

"Claire, no, they're with me," Cassie said quickly, grabbing her sister's wrist. "Alexander helped me find you."

Claire's eyes narrowed suspiciously. "Alexander, the vampire who took you from the shop?"

"Yes, but it's complicated," Cassie said. "A lot has happened. Where's Sam? The vampire who was with you?"

At the mention of Sam, Claire's expression shifted to concern. She gestured toward the trees. "He's back at our camp. He's hurt and he needs blood."

Alexander stepped forward cautiously, keeping a respectful distance. "What happened to Sam?" His voice was calm but carried unmistakable authority.

Claire studied him warily before answering. "We were attacked, and it appeared to be a magical storm. The yacht was damaged, and we barely made it to the life raft. Sam was injured protecting me." She turned back to Cassie. "He got weaker after I tried to help him. My blood did something to him."

Alexander and Cassie exchanged meaningful glances. "Witch blood," Alexander said quietly. "It can be debilitating to vampires."

"Take us to him," Alexander said to Claire. "We can help."

Claire hesitated, then nodded. "This way. But just you two," she added, glancing at the other vampires. "I've been creating storms and shielding us to keep people away. I don't want anyone else near our camp until I know it's safe."

Alexander signaled to his men to remain with the skiff. "Maintain position and alert the Apollo of our status," he ordered before turning back to Claire. "Lead the way."

Claire guided them along a narrow path that wound through the dense forest. As they walked, Cassie kept one hand on her sister's arm, still hardly believing she was real and solid beside her.

"How did you survive the storm?" Cassie asked. "The yacht was badly damaged."

"It was a close call," Claire admitted. "Sam got us to the life raft just before the worst hit. We made it as far as possible in the life raft. Then, we swam to this island, but with Sam in bad shape and bleeding, it wasn't easy." She pushed aside a low-hanging branch. "I've been using weather manipulation to keep anyone from finding us. I didn't know who to trust."

"You created those storms?" Alexander asked, impressed despite himself. "That's remarkable control for someone newly awakened to their abilities."

Claire shot him a guarded look. "I've always had an affinity for weather magic. But after what happened on the yacht, something changed. It's like my power quadrupled overnight."

"Your vampire side has awakened," Cassie explained. "The same thing happened to me. We're hybrids, Claire, half witch, half vampire."

Claire stopped walking, turning to face her sister fully. "So it's true? What Sam told me? Our father is really a bloodsucker?"

"A vampire," Cassie confirmed. "Not just any vampire. He's the King of the Western Canadian Territories. Our father." Cassie grinned.

Claire's eyes widened, her breath catching. "Mom never told us. All those years, I thought he was a night witch. I knew Mom felt sad, and it hurt her to think about it, so I never pressed."

"I know," Cassie said, squeezing her sister's hand. "I was angry at first. But there's so much more to the story. I've met him, Claire. He's been searching for you since you disappeared."

Before Claire could respond, they emerged into a small clearing where a crude shelter had been constructed from branches. Beneath it, lying on a makeshift bed of leaves, was Sam.

The vampire looked alarmingly weak, his normally commanding frame diminished somehow. His skin was ashen, his eyes closed, until they flickered open at their approach. Recognition dawned in his gaze as he spotted Alexander.

"Took you long enough," he rasped, attempting a smile that turned into a grimace.

Alexander knelt beside his comrade, his expression grave as he assessed Sam's condition. "What happened?"

"Witch patrol," Sam managed. "But not a regular patrol. Something else. Potent." He gestured weakly to a gash across his ribs that seemed unnaturally slow to heal. "I was hit by lightning and splinters of wood and silver. It weakened me. Then I tried to feed from Claire when I was too weak to hunt. Bad idea."

"My blood made him worse," Claire explained, kneeling on Sam's other side. "I was trying to help, but after he drank from me, he could barely move. I've been hunting for him, small animals, but it's not enough."

Alexander nodded grimly. "Witch blood acts like a sedative to vampires. For a wounded vampire, it can be particularly debilitating." He turned to Cassie. "He needs vampire blood to recover. The men on the beach should have backup with them." He turned slightly to address Claire.

"My men won't harm Sam," he said. "Would it be alright if they came forward to supply Sam with the blood he requires?"

Claire paused, glancing down at Sam. "Yes, if you can guarantee they're trustworthy."

Alexander assured her they wouldn't cause any trouble, then used his radio to instruct the men on the beach to bring the emergency blood supply. Shortly after, one of the men pushed through the thick vegetation and delivered a small black pouch. Alexander shifted his attention to Sam, raised his head, and placed the pouch against his lips.

For several tense moments, nothing seemed to change. Then, gradually, color began returning to Sam's ashen features. His grip on Alexander's arm strengthened, and his feeding became more vigorous.

When the pouch was drained, Sam reclined, his breathing more regular, his injuries already displaying evidence of enhanced recovery.

"It's working," Claire noted with evident relief.

Sam stirred, pushing himself up to a sitting position with effort. "We need to move," he said. "This island isn't safe. The witches have been patrolling the waters, looking for us."

Claire nodded. "Each time someone Sam didn't recognize came close, I called up a storm to drive them off. We've been here, waiting for someone Sam trusted to find us."

"How did you know to trust us?" Cassie asked.

"I felt you," Claire said simply. "When you started that calming spell, I recognized your magical signature immediately. It was like hearing your voice across the water."

Alexander rose, helping Sam to his feet. The wounded vampire was still unsteady but significantly improved from moments before. "We need to get you both back to the Apollo, then to Vancouver. The King is waiting."

Claire hesitated, uncertainty flickering across her face. "Our father," she said, testing the word. "What is he like?"

Cassie smiled, squeezing her sister's hand. "He's intense. Powerful. Ancient. But he cares about us, Claire. He's been worried sick since you disappeared."

"And Mom? Does she know where we are?"

"Not yet," Cassie admitted. "But Grandmother Camila is working with the vampires now. There's a diplomatic mission underway, witches and vampires working together to find you."

Claire's eyebrows shot up. "Grandmother is working with vampires?"

"A lot of unexpected things have happened," Cassie said with a small smile. "Come on, I'll tell you everything on the way back to the ship."

As they gathered their meager belongings from the campsite, Sam pulled Alexander aside, speaking in low tones that the sisters could still hear thanks to their enhanced senses.

"It wasn't just any witch patrol," Sam murmured. "The magic signature was unusual, robust, and from an older witch. And they specifically targeted the yacht like they knew who was aboard. Someone high up wanted these girls intercepted."

Alexander nodded grimly. "The High Coven claims no knowledge of the attack, but Calim suspects rogue elements within their ranks."

"The girl saved my life," Sam continued, glancing toward Claire. "Multiple times. Her control over weather magic is extraordinary, especially for someone who just discovered her vampire heritage. She's been keeping this section of the island hidden with fog banks and localized storms whenever anyone approached."

"Like her sister," Alexander replied, a hint of pride in his voice as his gaze shifted to Cassie. "They're both remarkable."

The sisters exchanged glances, a silent communication passing between them that needed no words. Whatever lay ahead, they would face it together.

"Ready?" Cassie asked, extending her hand.

Claire took it, squeezing firmly. "Ready."

As they made their way back toward the beach, Claire fell into step beside Cassie, their shoulders occasionally bumping in a familiar, comforting rhythm. The vampires walked ahead, giving them a semblance of privacy.

"So," Claire said quietly, "you and Alexander?"

Heat rushed to Cassie's cheeks. "Is it that obvious?"

Claire smiled, the first genuine smile since their reunion. "The way he looks at you, it's intense. And you keep watching him."

"It's complicated," Cassie admitted.

"I imagine so," Claire replied dryly. "I mean, he did kidnap you."

"He made me a guest of significance," Cassie corrected with a small laugh, echoing Alexander's words.

Claire's expression grew serious. "Are you sure, Cassie? With everything that's happened, and so fast?"

Cassie considered the question, her gaze drifting to Alexander's back as he helped Sam navigate the uneven terrain. "I'm still processing it all. But yes, in a strange way, I am. For the first time in my life, I feel like I understand why I never quite fit in. Why sunlight made me tired, why I craved raw meat." She looked back at her sister. "Don't you feel it too? This sense of finally knowing who you are?"

Claire nodded slowly. "When the storm came, and I felt that power surge through me, it was terrifying but also exhilarating. Like I'd been living with one arm tied behind my back my whole life, and suddenly it was free."

"Exactly," Cassie agreed. "And wait until you meet our father. He's nothing like what Mom described."

"A night witch," Claire recalled their mother's rare references to their father. "That was technically true, I suppose. Vampires are creatures of the night with magical abilities."

"A convenient half-truth," Cassie said. "But I'm starting to understand why she kept it from us. The treaty between vampires and witches is strict, and our very existence violates it."

They reached the edge of the forest, the beach and waiting skiff visible through the trees. Alexander paused, turning back to the sisters.

"Stay alert," he warned. "We're still in witch waters."

Claire nodded, her expression shifting to one of concentration as she extended her senses outward, feeling for any magical disturbances in the area. "It's clear for now," she confirmed. "But I can feel something at the edges of my awareness, like someone searching."

"Then we move quickly," Alexander decided. "The Apollo can outrun most once we're aboard."

As they emerged onto the beach, a surge of relief went through Cassie at the sight of the waiting skiff. Soon they would be aboard the Apollo, heading back to Vancouver, to safety. To their father.

Yet even as they approached the small boat, she couldn't shake the feeling that their troubles were far from over. Claire had been targeted specifically, Sam had said. Someone mighty wanted to intercept them. And that someone was still out there, still searching.

The vampire crew helped Sam into the skiff first, his movements still hampered by his injuries despite Claire's blood. Alexander offered his hand to Claire, who hesitated only briefly before accepting his assistance into the boat.

As Cassie prepared to follow, a strange prickling sensation washed over her skin. She turned, scanning the treeline they'd just left, a sense of unease building in her chest.

"Cassie?" Alexander called, noticing her hesitation. "What is it?"

"I don't know," she admitted, her voice dropping. "Just a feeling."

Claire stiffened in the boat, her head snapping up. "I feel it too," she whispered. "Someone's watching us."

Alexander was at Cassie's side in an instant, his hand going to the weapon at his hip. "Where?"

Before either sister could answer, the unnaturally calm waters around them began to ripple, then churn. The sky, clear moments before, darkened with rapidly forming clouds. Wind whipped across the beach, sending sand swirling around their ankles.

"It's not me," Claire said, her eyes wide with alarm. "I'm not doing this."

"Into the boat, now," Alexander ordered, practically lifting Cassie off her feet and depositing her in the skiff. He pushed them away from shore with one vigorous shove, leaping aboard as the small craft slid into deeper water.

The vampire at the motor pulled the starter cord, but the engine only sputtered and died. He tried again with the same result.

"Magical interference," Sam growled, struggling to sit upright. "Someone's blocking the ignition."

The water around them began to swirl, forming small whirlpools that tugged at the skiff's hull. The wind intensified, howling across the cove with unnatural force.

Claire stood up, bracing herself against the side of the boat. "I can counter it," she said, her voice tight with concentration. "Give me a moment."

As Claire raised her hands, her eyes took on an eerie luminescence that Cassie recognized from her own awakening. The air around Claire's fingertips began to shimmer as she wove counter-spells, pushing back against the magical storm building around them.

For a moment, it seemed to work. The wind died down slightly, and the whirlpools began to dissipate. Then, with shocking suddenness, a massive surge of magical energy slammed into Claire's defenses. She lurched backward, nearly falling overboard before Cassie caught her.

"Too strong," Claire gasped, her face pale with exertion. "Whoever it is, they're incredibly powerful."

Alexander turned to the vampire at the motor. "Row," he commanded. "Get us back to the Apollo. Now."

As the crew grabbed the oars, Alexander positioned himself protectively in front of the sisters, his eyes scanning the shoreline for any sign of their attacker. Sam, still weak but determined, moved to the bow, his own senses straining to identify the threat.

"There," Sam said suddenly, pointing toward a rocky outcropping at the edge of the cove. "Movement."

A figure stood atop the rocks, too distant to identify clearly but unmistakably the source of the magical assault. Robes billowed around them in the unnatural wind, and even from this distance, Cassie could feel the raw power emanating from the solitary form.

"A witch," Alexander confirmed, his voice grim. "High Coven level, by the feel of that magic."

Claire gripped Cassie's hand, her fingers ice-cold despite the exertion of moments before. "They found us," she whispered. "They've been searching all along, but I have been keeping them away from us."

The skiff inched painfully slowly through the churning waters, the crew rowing with vampire strength against both current and magical resistance. The Apollo seemed impossibly far away, though it couldn't have been more than a few hundred yards.

"Can you shield us?" Alexander asked Claire and Cassie. "Just enough to cover our retreat?"

Claire nodded. Though uncertainty flickered across her face, she looked to Cassie, who nodded back at her. "I'll try, but the most I have been able to do was cover me and Sam. Not this many. Maybe between the two of us, we'll be able to do it."

She closed her eyes, and drew in a deep breath. Cassie sensed her sister's power building, the dual nature of witch and vampire combining in a surge of energy that made the air around them crackle. Cassie took a deep breath and drew on her own reserves.

When Claire opened her eyes again, the glow was luminous and striking. Cassie wondered if hers did the same.

Together, they raised their hands, and with the same gesture, sweeping starboard, they appeared to tear the very fabric of reality, casting a spell of protection around the skiff. The magical barrier shimmered into existence just as another wave of hostile energy crashed against them. The impact made the barrier flare brilliantly, but it held.

"Row faster," Alexander urged the crew. "The shield won't last long against that kind of assault."

Opposing magic pressed against Cassie, and she reached out to place a hand of support on her sister's shoulder. She felt Claire trembling with the effort of maintaining the barrier. "Hold on," she murmured. "Just a little longer."

The distant figure raised both arms, and the sky above them darkened further, clouds swirling into an ominous vortex. Lightning cracked across the heavens, striking the water dangerously close to their small craft.

In that moment, Cassie made a decision. Without hesitation, she placed her other hand on Alexander's shoulder and drew upon his strength. The connection between them was strong, and it blazed into something transcendent as their powers merged and flowed through her and to Cassie.

The barrier stabilized, and together, they pushed back against the magical assault, their combined power creating a barrier that even High Coven magic struggled to penetrate.

"It's working," Sam said in disbelief, watching as the lightning struck the wards and dissipated harmlessly. "You're actually doing it."

Alexander's expression was one of awe and pride as he watched the sisters work in perfect synchronicity, even though it was tiring them.

"Get us to the Apollo," he ordered the crew. "Now, while the shield is holding."

The skiff picked up speed as they rowed with renewed determination. Behind them, the figure on the rocks raised their arms higher, summoning even greater power. The very air seemed to bend and distort with the magical forces being unleashed.

"Almost there," Alexander encouraged, his eyes never leaving the sisters. "Hold on."

Cassie could feel Claire weakening beside her, the strain of maintaining such formidable magic taking its toll. Her own reserves were depleting rapidly, the edges of her vision beginning to darken. But the Apollo was close now, its massive hull looming above them like a promise of safety.

With a final surge of effort, the crew brought the skiff alongside the larger vessel. Hands reached down from above, ready to pull them to safety.

"Go," Cassie urged Claire. "I'll hold the wards."

"Not without you," Claire insisted, her voice barely audible over the howling wind.

Alexander made the decision for them, bodily lifting Claire and passing her up to the waiting crew. "Take her," he commanded. "Sam next."

As Sam was hauled aboard, Cassie's strength began to fail her. Without Claire and Alexander's power, the barrier was rapidly thinning, and lightning had begun to penetrate its weakening structure. Alexander turned to her, his dark eyes intense.

"Together," he said simply, wrapping one arm around her waist while maintaining his grip on the skiff with the other.

With vampire strength, he launched them both upward as the shield finally collapsed behind them. They landed on the Apollo's deck just as a bolt of lightning struck where the skiff had been moments before, splintering the small craft into fragments.

"Get us out of here!" Alexander roared to the captain. "Full power!"

The Apollo's engines roared to life, the vessel lurching forward as it began to pull away from the island. On the deck, Cassie sagged into Alexander's arms, her energy completely spent. Claire wasn't in much better shape, leaning heavily against a railing, her face ashen with exhaustion.

"They're still coming," Sam warned, pointing toward the island where the robed figure had vanished from the rocks only to reappear on the beach. They raised their arms once more, and the sea before the Apollo began to churn violently, a massive whirlpool forming directly in their path.

"We can't go through that," the captain called from the wheelhouse. "It'll tear the hull apart!"

Claire straightened, determination overriding her exhaustion. "Cassie," she called. "One more time. Together."

Cassie nodded, pushing herself upright with Alexander's support. The sisters joined hands, standing at the bow of the ship as they faced the magical maelstrom ahead. This time, they didn't try to defend or counter the magic. Instead, they reached for the middle of the vortex itself, seeking to unravel it from within.

Their combined power flowed outward, iridescent energy streaming from their joined hands toward the whirlpool. Where their magic touched the churning waters, tranquility spread like mist settling on bubbling water. The vortex began to slow, then flatten, the unnatural currents returning to their natural state.

On the beach, the robed figure's posture conveyed fury as they realized their magic was being undone. With a final, violent gesture, they sent a massive wave of pure magical force toward the Apollo.

The blast struck the sisters head-on, the impact driving them to their knees. But they held firm, their joined hands never separating as they absorbed and dispersed the energy, turning the destructive blast into harmless light across the water's surface.

The Apollo surged forward, gaining speed as it escaped the island's magical influence. Behind them, the figure on the beach grew smaller, then disappeared entirely as they rounded a headland and entered open water.

Only then did the sisters release each other's hands, both collapsing with exhaustion. Alexander caught Cassie before she hit the deck, while Sam, still weak himself, managed to steady Claire.

"You did it," Alexander said softly, cradling Cassie against his chest. "Both of you. That was extraordinary."

Cassie reached for her sister's hand once more, needing the reassurance of physical contact. "Wait until you meet our father, Claire. I have a feeling you're going to really like him. And our grandmother is there too."

"Yeah?" Claire responded, the exhaustion etched into her face. She looked up at the sky, now clearing as they left the magical disturbance behind. "I never thought I'd be looking forward to going to a vampire stronghold and having our grandmother waiting for us there."

"It's where we belong," Cassie said with quiet certainty. "Where we've always belonged. We just didn't know it." Cassie reached across and squeezed her sister's hand.

CHAPTER TWENTY-NINE

The Apollo's powerful engines churned through the dark waters, carrying them steadily north toward Vancouver. Cassie sat in the ship's medical bay beside Claire, who lay sleeping on one of the narrow beds. Her sister's face was peaceful in sleep, the strain of their magical battle finally easing as exhaustion claimed her. Cassie wanted to sleep too, but she wanted to watch over her sister more.

Cassie gently brushed a strand of auburn hair from Claire's forehead, marveling at her sister. Claire had always been the cautious one, the planner, while Cassie leaped first and thought later. Yet when danger threatened, Claire had shown extraordinary courage and power.

"How is she?" Alexander asked quietly from the doorway.

Cassie looked up, offering him a tired smile. "Sleeping. Dr. Levin says she's just exhausted from the magical exertion and the daytime draw on her vampire side."

Alexander nodded, moving to stand beside her. "And you? You should be resting too."

"I'm fine," Cassie insisted, though the dark circles beneath her eyes betrayed her. "I couldn't sleep. Not until we're safely back in Vancouver, anyway."

Alexander's hand came to rest on her shoulder, a gentle weight that somehow eased the tension coiled within her. "We're well into vampire waters now. No witch patrol would dare follow us this far north."

"It wasn't a regular patrol," Cassie said, voicing the concern that had been gnawing at her since their escape. "That level of power had to be someone from the High Coven or someone with the potential to be."

"I know." Alexander's voice dropped lower. "Sam reported the same. Whoever attacked their vessel and then tracked her to that island was acting with both authority and considerable magical power."

Cassie turned to look at him fully, her eyes troubled. "But Grandmother is on the High Coven. She wouldn't have sanctioned an attack on her own granddaughters."

"Perhaps not all Council members share her perspective," Alexander suggested. "Your existence challenges centuries of established doctrine. Some might view that as a threat enough to warrant extreme measures."

The door opened before Cassie could respond, admitting Sam. The vampire looked considerably improved after additional blood transfusions, though he still moved with the careful precision of someone not fully recovered.

"Nikolai just radioed from the harbor in Vancouver," Sam reported. "The King is awaiting our arrival, and things have changed. Apparently, your grandmother has been quite persuasive in your absence. Miranda was arrogant enough to reveal she had been leaking information to the Purist faction. Your grandmother has been causing quite a stir since then."

"How so?" Cassie asked.

"She's convinced several Council members to support a formal investigation into rogue elements within the High Coven that are involved with the Purists," Sam explained. "The rescue of your sister has become something of a joint operation, at least officially. The attack is still being investigated, and others on the High Council were horrified to hear the details."

Claire stirred on the bed, her eyelids fluttering open. "Cassie?" she murmured, her voice thick with sleep.

"I'm here," Cassie reassured her, squeezing her hand. "How are you feeling?"

Claire pushed herself up on her elbows, blinking as she oriented herself. "Like I've been hit by a truck. A magical out-of-control truck." Her gaze shifted to Sam, and she smiled. When her gaze shifted to Alexander, she stiffened slightly, wariness still evident in her posture despite her exhaustion. "Where are we?"

"Almost to Vancouver," Alexander answered. "Well within vampire territory now."

Claire nodded slowly, processing this information. "And our father? He's really waiting for us?"

"He is," Cassie confirmed. "He's been worried sick about you, Claire. He's the one who organized the search."

Cassie decided not to mention the prior attack she and Alexander had faced. There'd be time for that later. Right now, her sister needed space, and not more to worry about unnecessarily.

"The Vampire King," Claire said, testing the words. "Our father." She shook her head slightly, as if trying to reconcile this new reality. "It still doesn't feel real."

"I know," Cassie agreed. "It's a lot to take in."

Claire's expression turned thoughtful as she studied her sister. "You've changed, Cass. Not just physically, though there's that too. You seem, I don't know, more settled somehow. Like you've finally found where you belong."

The observation caught Cassie off guard. She hadn't considered how she might appear to Claire, who knew her better than anyone. "I guess I have changed," she admitted. "Learning what I am, who we are, it answered questions I've had my whole life."

"And him?" Claire nodded toward Alexander, who had stepped away to confer with Sam by the door. "Is he part of where you belong now too?"

Heat rose to Cassie's cheeks, but she smiled. "That's complicated, but yes."

A knowing smile touched Claire's lips, the first genuine one since their reunion. "It always is complicated with you." Her expression sobered. "Just be careful, okay? Everything's happening so fast."

"I know," Cassie assured her. "But for the first time, it feels like things are falling into place rather than falling apart."

Claire squeezed her hand. "Then I'm happy for you."

The sisters shared a quiet moment, easing some of the tension that had built since their separation. It was a small moment of normalcy amid the chaos their lives had become.

Alexander approached, his expression carefully neutral, though his eyes lingered on Cassie. "We should arrive in Vancouver within minutes. The King has arranged for a secure reception, minimal personnel."

"Will our grandmother be there?" Claire asked.

"Yes," Alexander confirmed. "Councilor Marlow insisted on being present for your arrival."

Claire nodded, visibly relieved. "Good. I have about a thousand questions, and she's always been straight with us."

"Unlike Mom," Cassie couldn't help adding, a hint of lingering resentment in her tone.

"Mom did what she thought was right," Claire said, ever the peace-maker. "We can be angry about it later, when we understand more."

Cassie recognized the wisdom in her sister's words. Claire had always been the more thoughtful one, considering all angles before forming judgments. It was a quality Cassie sometimes envied.

"You should eat something," she told Claire. "Dr. Levin said you need to replenish your energy after that magical exertion."

"I am pretty hungry," Claire admitted. "Though I'm guessing the menu options are limited."

"Actually, the ship is well-stocked for hybrid dietary needs," Alexander quipped. "The King was quite specific about ensuring both raw and liquid options would be available."

Claire's eyebrows rose. "He thought of that? For us?"

"He's been preparing ever since he learned you existed," Alexander said. "The King leaves nothing to chance."

"You'll like our father, Claire," Cassie told her. "Callimachus is intimidating but also awesome."

A complicated emotion flickered across Claire's face. Surprise, wariness, then back to surprise again. "Wait, what? Did you say Calli-machus?"

"Yes," Cassie said, trying to figure out why the name was a surprise to her sister.

"Is he ancient as time itself?" Claire sat up straighter, eager.

"Well, not sure about time itself, but he's definitely ancient," Cassie chuckled.

"Like, ancient, ancient, ancient." Claire's eyes were gleaming.

"Yeah, apparently so," Cassie shrugged.

"So, he genuinely might be THE Callimachus?" Claire asked, ex-pectantly.

"I believe so?" Cassie responded, uncertain about the direction of Claire's questioning.

"I still can't fathom our father is Callimachus. The Callimachus. The Athenian polemarch from the Battle of Marathon," Claire gushed.

"Hold on, what?" Cassie gazed at her sister. "The what from where?"

Claire gave her a look of fond exasperation. "Seriously, Cass? The Battle of Marathon? 490 BCE? One of the most consequential battles in ancient Greek history?"

"History was your thing, not mine," Cassie reminded her. "I kept plants alive while you relived ancient battles and events."

"Our father was the top leader during the Battle of Marathon," Claire explained, her historian's enthusiasm breaking through her exhaustion. "He led the Athenian forces against the Persians, and this is what helped secure a crucial victory. Cassie, it changed the course of Western civilization."

Alexander nodded, a small smile touching his lips. "The King does not often speak of his mortal life, but yes, he was indeed that Callimachus."

"How do you know this?" Cassie asked her sister, amazed once again by Claire's encyclopedic knowledge of history.

"There's a famous passage Herodotus wrote about him," Claire replied, her eyes brightening with scholarly passion. "He was supposedly killed during the battle, pierced by so many Persian spears that his body remained standing upright even in death." She turned to Alexander. "But he wasn't really dead, was he? He was turned."

"Not exactly," Alexander said. "From what I understand, he was mortally wounded but not yet dead when an old vampire found him on the battlefield. The transformation saved him, though the process was different than most turnings."

Claire's expression was rapt with fascination. "Different how?"

"That's a question best asked of the King himself," Alexander replied diplomatically. "He rarely discusses the details of his transformation."

Cassie watched this exchange with growing amusement. Of course, Claire would be more excited about the historical importance of their father than the fact he was a vampire king. Her sister had always been obsessed with ancient history, spending hours poring over texts while Cassie preferred the immediate gratification of growing things.

"I can't believe our father is literally in history books," Cassie said, shaking her head.

"And not just any history books," Claire added eagerly. "Primary sources! Herodotus himself wrote about him!"

Sam cleared his throat from the doorway. "The captain requests Alexander's presence on the bridge. We're approaching the outer marker for Vancouver harbor."

Alexander nodded. "I'll return shortly," he told the sisters before following Sam out.

Once they were alone, Claire turned to Cassie, her expression suddenly serious. "Okay, spill. What's really going on between you and tall, dark, and vampiric?"

Cassie felt heat rise to her cheeks again. "Is it that obvious?"

"To me? Absolutely." Claire grinned. "You practically glow when he's in the room, and he can barely take his eyes off you. So, what happened?"

Cassie hesitated, unsure how to explain the intense connection that had formed between her and Alexander in such a short time. "It's complicated," she began.

"You already said that," Claire pointed out. "Try again."

"Fine," Cassie sighed. "After he kidnapped me, things happened."

"Abducted," Claire corrected with mock seriousness. "The proper term is 'abducted.'"

"After he abducted me," Cassie continued, rolling her eyes, "things changed. At first, I didn't like him and wasn't happy, obviously. But then, I don't know. He protected me. He helped me understand what I am, what we are. And somewhere along the way, well, one thing led to another."

"You fell for him," Claire finished softly.

"I don't know if 'fell' is the right word," Cassie admitted. "It's more like recognizing something that was always meant to be there."

Claire studied her sister's face, her expression thoughtful. "That sounds serious."

"It is," Cassie confirmed. "Vampires don't do casual, Claire. When they commit, it's for eternity."

"And you're okay with that?" Claire asked, genuine concern in her voice. "Eternity is a long time, Cass."

Cassie considered the question carefully. Just days ago, she'd been a witch who believed she'd live perhaps two centuries at most. Now she was a hybrid with an unknown lifespan, possibly as immortal as her vampire father. The concept of eternity had shifted from abstract to potentially personal.

"I think I am," she said finally. "With him, at least. It feels right in a way nothing else ever has."

"Then I'm happy for you." Claire reached out, squeezing her sister's hand. "Confused about pretty much everything else in our lives right now, but happy for you."

Cassie laughed, the sound lightening the mood. "That's fair. I'm still confused too."

"It does, actually." Claire smiled. "At least we're confused together."

The ship's engines changed pitch, the subtle shift indicating they were slowing. Outside the small porthole, the skyline of Vancouver was becoming visible.

"We're almost there," Cassie said softly.

Claire's expression turned anxious. "What's he like? Our father?"

"Intense," Cassie answered honestly. "Powerful. Old in a way that's hard to describe. But also proud. When he realized who I was, who we are, he was genuinely happy, Claire. He wants to know us."

"And the vampire thing doesn't bother you? The blood drinking and all that?"

Cassie shrugged. "We've been craving raw meat and blood-rare steaks our whole lives. Turns out there was a reason for that."

"Good point," Claire conceded. "I guess I've been a little vampiric all along without realizing it." She paused, a new worry crossing her face. "Do you think I'll have to drink actual blood now?"

"It's not bad," Cassie reassured her. "And it's from a cup or cute goblet."

Claire nodded, looking relieved. "Good. Because I draw the line at sucking on people's necks."

The door opened again, and Alexander returned. "We're approaching the harbor," he announced. "The king's personal escort is waiting at the dock."

Cassie rose, offering her hand to Claire. "Ready to meet our father?"

Claire took a deep breath, then accepted Cassie's hand, allowing herself to be pulled to her feet. "As ready as I'll ever be."

Together, the sisters made their way to the deck, where the sights of Vancouver came into clearer view. The Apollo glided smoothly into the harbor, its engines a gentle hum beneath their feet as it approached the private dock where several dark-clad figures waited.

Cassie felt Claire's grip tighten on her hand as the ship drew closer to shore. "It's going to be okay," she whispered. "I promise."

As the vessel was secured to the dock, Cassie spotted two familiar figures standing apart from the security detail. One was unmistakably Callimachus, his powerful frame and regal bearing evident even at a distance. Beside him stood their grandmother, Camila, her silver-streaked red hair catching the light from the dock lamps.

The gangway was lowered, and Alexander gestured for the sisters to precede him. "Your family awaits," he said quietly.

Cassie led the way, Claire following close behind, their hands still linked as they descended to the dock. The cool air carried the scent of salt water and pine, a reminder that they were far from the California coast they'd called home.

As they reached the bottom of the gangway, Camila stepped forward, her arms outstretched. "Claire," she breathed, her voice thick with emotion. "Thank the goddess."

Claire released Cassie's hand and rushed into their grandmother's embrace. "Grandmother," she whispered, clinging to the familiar figure. "I was so scared."

"I know, child," Camila soothed, stroking Claire's hair. "But you're safe now. You're both safe."

Cassie turned to Callimachus, who had remained slightly apart, his timeless eyes fixed on Claire with an intensity that spoke volumes. She moved to his side, touching his arm gently. "Father," she said softly, the word still new on her tongue. "This is Claire."

Callimachus nodded, his expression softening as he watched his younger daughter embrace her grandmother. "She looks like your mother," he observed quietly.

"She does," Cassie agreed. "But she has your determination."

A small smile touched Callimachus's lips. "And your courage, it seems. Creating storms to keep away those who would harm her requires incredible power and will."

Camila finally released Claire, keeping one arm around her shoulders as she turned to face Callimachus. "Your daughter," she said formally.

Claire looked up at the imposing figure of the Vampire King, her eyes wide with a mixture of awe and uncertainty. "You're really him," she whispered. "Callimachus of Athens."

Something like surprise flickered across Callimachus's features. "You know of my mortal life?"

"Of course I do!" Claire exclaimed, her scholarly enthusiasm momentarily overriding her caution. "Herodotus wrote about you! The polemarch who helped defeat the Persians at Marathon!"

A genuine smile spread across Callimachus's face, transforming his stern features. "Few remember those days now," he said, his voice warming. "Fewer still with any accuracy."

"Is it true?" Claire asked eagerly, stepping forward. "Were you really impaled by so many spears that your body remained standing even in death?"

"Claire!" Cassie hissed, mortified by her sister's bluntness.

But Callimachus merely chuckled, the sound rich and unexpected. "Herodotus had a flair for the dramatic," he replied. "But yes, I was grievously wounded. Enough that the Persians believed me dead, which allowed for my transformation to occur in secret."

Claire's eyes lit up with academic fervor. "This is incredible! You're a primary source for one of the most significant battles in ancient history! Do you remember the tactics you used? The troop formations? How many hoplites were actually present? The historical accounts vary so widely and..."

"Claire," Camila interrupted gently, though amusement danced in her eyes. "Perhaps these questions can wait until we're somewhere more private?"

Claire blinked, suddenly remembering where they were. "Oh. Right. Sorry." She blushed, ducking her head.

"No apology needed. It's a trait I find admirable," Callimachus said, his expression warm as he regarded his younger daughter. "Your enthusiasm for history speaks well of your education."

Claire beamed at the compliment, her earlier wariness visibly diminishing. "Thank you. I've always loved ancient history, especially Greek."

"Then we have much to discuss," Callimachus promised. He gestured toward the waiting vehicles. "But first, let us return to more secure surroundings. The night grows late, and you both need rest after your ordeal."

As they moved toward the cars, Cassie fell into step beside Alexander, who had maintained a respectful distance during the family reunion. "That went better than I expected," she murmured.

"Your sister's historical knowledge provided an unexpected connection," Alexander observed. "The King rarely discusses his mortal life, even with those of us who have served him for centuries."

"Leave it to Claire to break the ice by asking if he was really impaled by a bunch of spears," Cassie said with a quiet laugh. "Only my sister would think that's an appropriate first question for our long-lost vampire father."

Alexander's lips curved in a rare smile. "It worked, didn't it?"

"It did," Cassie admitted, watching as Claire continued to pepper Callimachus with historical questions while they walked, her initial fear completely forgotten in her scholarly excitement. "She's going to interrogate him for hours about ancient Greece."

"And he will enjoy every moment," Alexander predicted. "The King values knowledge. Your sister's passion for history will please him greatly."

They reached the SUVs, where Callimachus held the door open for Claire and Camila. Cassie hesitated, glancing at Alexander. "Will you come with us?"

"I need to oversee the debriefing with Sam and secure the Apollo," he replied. "But I'll join you at the compound later."

Cassie nodded, trying not to show her disappointment. "I'll see you then."

Alexander's hand brushed hers briefly, the contact hidden from the others by their bodies. "Rest, Cassie," he murmured. "You've earned it."

"You want me to rest quite a bit," Cassie teased him.

"You've done a lot in a short time to warrant it," Alexander smiled down at her. He leaned down to give her a soft kiss. "I'll see you soon."

After a final quick hug, she joined her family in the waiting car. As they pulled away from the dock, Cassie watched from the back seat as Claire described something to Callimachus, her hands gesturing enthusiastically while their father listened with genuine interest. Beside her, her grandmother observed the interaction with a mixture of wonder and cautious hope.

After a few moments, her grandmother leaned over to tuck a wisp of hair behind Cassie's ear. "We're safe. This car ride back to the compound is being monitored on multiple levels."

Cassie nodded. She knew that she would be kept safe, and so would her sister. For the first time since their ordeal began, Cassie allowed herself to truly believe that everything would work out. Claire had been found, their father welcomed them both, and even the complicated politics between vampires and witches, the hatred and attack by the Purists, seemed momentarily distant. She didn't know what the future held. Not for who she was becoming. Not for the witches or vampires. Not for her and Alexander. But she wanted to find out. Tomorrow might bring new challenges, but for now, most of her family was together.

ACKNOWLEDGEMENTS

To Aisha, Astrid, Amie, Ben, and Heidi,
my first readers and magical companions on this adventure.
Thank you for the gentle feedback, thoughtful insight, helpful edits,
and encouragement.
You all have helped this story grow from a single spark into a new
magical world.

About the Author

Harlow Ann Leroux lives most of the time in the enchanted woodlands of Wisconsin with her husband and son, though her little travel trailer often carries her on new adventures. As a historian, she spends long hours exploring dusty archives, pursuing whispers of the past. Fantasy and romance are her preferred escape routes, gateways to dreaming, wandering, and weaving extraordinary worlds where love and wonder intertwine.